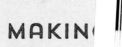

"Sorry for picking your pocket."

"Yeah, sure."

"See you round, Esther."

"Not if I can help it."

Jonah blew her a kiss and then darted back to the road as his dad's car began to crawl away down the street.

Esther unlocked her phone. Everything was gone. All her photos, her contacts, her apps. It had been scrubbed clean, factory reset, and readied for sale on the black market. Only a single contact had been saved. *Jonah Smallwood*, it read, with a red heart emoji next to his name and his phone number below. Her finger hovered over the "Delete" button. You shouldn't keep the phone numbers of rapscallions who robbed you and left you for dead at bus stops, or stood you up on Valentine's Day at the age of eight, even if they looked like Finn from *Star Wars* and dressed like the Fantastic Mr. Fox and smelled like heady cologne.

Esther wasn't entirely sure why she kept his number, but it probably had something to do with the fact that she imagined she would never see Jonah Smallwood again.

It would only be sixteen hours and seven minutes before that assumption proved entirely incorrect.

OTHER BOOKS YOU MAY ENJOY

A SEMI-DEFINITIVE LIST OF WORST NIGHTMARES

KRYSTAL SUTHERLAND

speak

SPEAK
An imprint of Penguin Random House LLC
375 Hudson Street
New York, New York 10014

First published in the United States of America by G. P. Putnam's Sons,
an imprint of Penguin Random House LLC, 2017
Published by Speak, an imprint of Penguin Random House LLC, 2018

LIBRARY OF CONGRESS CATALOGING-IN-PUBLICATION DATA IS AVAILABLE.

Speak ISBN 9780399546600

Printed in the United States of America

1 3 5 7 9 10 8 6 4 2

Design by Jaclyn Reyes and Rae Crawford.
Text set in Laurentian Std, Neutraface, and Trend HM Sans.

This is a work of fiction. Names, characters, places, and incidents either are the product of
the author's imagination or are used fictitiously, and any resemblance to actual persons,
living or dead, businesses, companies, events, or locales is entirely coincidental.

For Chelsea and Shanaye,
and everyone who's ever been afraid:
you are braver than you realize.

A SEMI-DEFINITIVE LIST
OF WORST NIGHTMARES

1

THE BOY
AT THE BUS STOP

ESTHER SOLAR had been waiting outside Lilac Hill Nursing and Rehabilitation Center for half an hour when she received word that the curse had struck again.

Rosemary Solar, her mother, explained over the phone that she would no longer, under any circumstances, be able to pick her daughter up. A cat black as night with demon-yellow slits for eyes had been found sitting atop the hood of the family car—an omen dark enough to prevent her from driving.

Esther was unfazed. The spontaneous development of phobias was not a new phenomenon in the Solar family, and so she made her way to the bus stop four blocks from Lilac Hill, her red cape billowing in the evening breeze and drawing a few stares from strangers along the way.

On the walk, she thought about who normal people would call in a situation such as this. Her father was still interred in the basement he'd confined himself to six years ago, Eugene was AWOL (Esther suspected he'd slipped through another gap in reality—it happened to Eugene from time to time), and her grand-father no longer possessed the fine motor skills required to operate a vehicle (not to mention that he couldn't remember that she was his granddaughter).

Basically, Esther had very few people who could bail her out of a crisis.

The bus stop was empty for a Friday night. Only one other person sat there, a tall black guy dressed like a character from a Wes Anderson movie, complete with lime-green corduroy pants, a suede jacket, and a beret pulled down over his hair. The boy was sobbing quietly, so Esther did what you're supposed to do when a complete stranger is showing too much emotion in your presence—she ignored him completely. She sat next to him and took out her tattered copy of *The Godfather* and tried very hard to concentrate on reading it.

The lights above them hummed like a wasp's nest, flickering on and off. If Esther had kept her eyes down, the next year of her life would've turned out quite differently, but she was a Solar, and Solars had a bad habit of sticking their noses where they didn't belong.

The boy sobbed dramatically. Esther looked up. A bruise was blooming across his cheekbone, plum-dark in the fluorescent light, and blood trickled from a split at his eyebrow. His patterned button up—clearly donated to a thrift store sometime in the mid-1970s—was torn at the collar.

The boy sobbed again, then peeked sideways at her.

Esther generally avoided talking to people if it wasn't completely necessary; she sometimes avoided people even when it *was* completely necessary.

"Hey," she said finally. "You okay?"

"Think I got mugged," he said.

"You *think*?"

"Can't remember." He pointed to the wound at his forehead. "Took my phone and wallet though, so think I got mugged."

And that's when she recognized him. "Jonah? Jonah Smallwood?"

The years had changed him, but he still had the same wide eyes, the same strong jaw, the same intense stare he had even when he was a kid. He had more hair now: a shadow of stubble and a full head of thick black hair that sat up in a kind of pompadour style. Esther thought he resembled Finn from *The Force Awakens*, which was, as far as she was concerned, a very good way to look. He glanced at her, at the Jackson Pollock painting of dark freckles smattered across her face and chest and arms, at the mane of peach red hair that fell past her hips. Trying to place her. "How do you know my name?"

"You don't remember me?"

They'd only been friends for a year, and they'd only been eight at the time, but still. Esther felt a twinge of sadness that he'd apparently forgotten about her—she had certainly not forgotten about him.

"We went to elementary school together," Esther explained. "I was in Mrs. Price's class with you. You asked me to be your valentine."

Jonah had bought her a bag of Sweethearts and crafted a handmade card, on which was a drawing of two fruits and a line that read: *We make the perfect pear.* Inside, he had asked her to meet him at recess.

Esther had waited. Jonah hadn't showed. In fact, she'd never seen him again.

Until now.

"Oh yeah," Jonah said slowly, recognition finally dawning on his face. "I liked you because you protested Dumbledore's death outside the bookstore like a week after the movie came out."

How Esther remembered it: little Esther, seven years old with a bright red bowl cut, picketing the local bookstore with a sign that read, SAVE THE WIZARDS. And then a snippet from the six o'clock news, a reporter kneeling next to her, asking her the question: "You do realize the book was published years ago and the ending can't be changed?" and her blinking dumbly into the camera.

Back to reality: "I hate that there's video evidence of that."

Jonah nodded at her outfit, at the bloodred cape held at her throat by a ribbon and the wicker basket resting at her feet. "Looks like you're still strange. Why are you dressed like Red Riding Hood?"

Esther hadn't had to answer questions about her predisposition for costumes for several years. Strangers on the street always assumed she was on her way to or from a costume party. Her teachers—much to their vexation—could find no fault with her outfits as far as the school's dress code was concerned, and her classmates were used to her coming in dressed as Alice in Wonderland or Bellatrix Lestrange or whatever, and didn't really care what she wore so long as she kept smuggling them cake. (More on this in a moment.)

"I was visiting a grandparent. It seemed appropriate," she said in reply, which appeared to satisfy Jonah, because he nodded like he understood.

"Look, you got any cash on you?"

Esther did have cash on her, in her Little Red Riding Hood picnic basket. She had $55, all of it earmarked for her Get the Hell Out of This Podunk Town fund, which now stood at $2,235 in total.

Back to the previously mentioned cake. You see, in Esther's junior year, East River High had instituted sweeping changes in the cafeteria until only healthy food was available. Gone were the pizzas and chicken nuggets and tots and fries and sloppy joes and nachos that made high school semibearable. The words "Michelle Obama" were now muttered in exasperation every time a new item was added to the menu, like leek and cauliflower soup or steamed broccoli pie. Esther had seen a budding business opportunity and made a box mix of double chocolate fudge brownies. She brought them into school the next day, where she sold each one for five dollars and made a cool profit of fifty bucks. Since then, she'd become the Walter White of junk food; such was the extent of her empire that her customers at school had dubbed her "Cakenberg."

She'd recently expanded her territory to Lilac Hill Nursing and Rehabilitation Center, where the most exciting things on the menu were overcooked hot dog and bland mashed potato. Business was booming.

"*Why?*" she said slowly.

"I need money for a bus fare. You give me cash, and I can use your phone to transfer funds from my bank account directly into yours."

It sounded slippery as all hell, but Jonah was bruised and bleeding and crying, and she still halfway saw him as the sweet young boy who'd once liked her enough to draw her a picture of two pears.

So Esther said: "How much do you need?"

"How much you got? I'll take it all and transfer you that."

"I have fifty-five dollars."

"I'll take fifty-five dollars."

Jonah stood up and came to sit next to her. He was much taller than she thought, and thinner too, like a stalk of corn. She watched as he opened the banking app on her phone, logged in, filled in her account details as she gave them to him, and authorized the transfer.

Funds transfer successful, the app read.

So she leaned down and opened her basket and gave him the fifty-five dollars she'd made at Lilac Hill today.

"Thank you," Jonah said as he shook her hand. "You're all right, Esther." Then he stood, and winked, and was gone. Again.

And that's how, on a warm, damp evening at the end of summer, Jonah Smallwood swindled her out of fifty-five dollars and pickpocketed, in the space of approximately four minutes:

- her grandmother's bracelet, right off her wrist
- her iPhone
- a Fruit Roll-Up from her basket that she'd been saving for the ride home
- her library card (which he later used to rack up $19.99 in replacement fees for defacing a copy of *Romeo and Juliet* with lobster graffiti)
- her copy of *The Godfather*
- her semi-definitive list of worst nightmares
- and her dignity

Esther kept replaying the cringeworthy memory of her Dumbledore protest in her head, and didn't realize she'd been robbed until her bus arrived six minutes and nineteen seconds later, at which point she exclaimed to the driver, "I've been robbed!" To which the driver said, "No riffraff!" and closed the doors in her face.

(Perhaps Jonah didn't steal all of her dignity—the bus driver took what shreds he hadn't managed to scrape away from her bones.)

So you see, the story of how Esther Solar was robbed by Jonah Smallwood is quite straightforward. The story of how she came to love Jonah Smallwood is a little bit more complicated.

2

THE HOUSE OF LIGHT
AND GHOSTS

IT TOOK Esther a total of three hours, thirteen minutes, and thirty-seven seconds to walk to her house, which was on the outskirts of the outskirts of town. The town had expanded in the opposite direction than the developers expected, thus stranding the neighborhood in the middle of nowhere.

On the long walk there, the sky cracked open and heaved water, so that by the time Esther got to her front steps, she was sopping, muddy, and shivering.

The Solar house was glowing, as always, a fluorescent jewel in an otherwise darkened street. A soft breeze licked through the trees that had taken root in the front yard, a forest in the middle of suburbia. Some neighbors had complained about the constant lights a few years back. Rosemary Solar had responded by planting eight oak trees in the lawn, which had grown from saplings to giants that enshrouded the property in the space of about six months. As they grew, she hung their branches with nazars, hundreds of them, the blue, black, and white glass tinkling an eerie song whenever the wind moved. The nazars were to ward off evil, Rosemary said. So far, the only people they had managed to scare away were Girl Scouts, Jehovah's Witnesses, and trick-or-treaters.

Eugene was sitting on the front steps that lead up to the brightly lit porch, looking like he'd time travelled from a Beatles concert, complete with Ringo's haircut and John's fashion sense.

Esther and Eugene were the twins who no one could ever believe were twins. Where his hair was dark, hers was light. Where he was tall, she was short. Where he was lithe, she was buxom. Where her skin was pocked with freckles, his was clear.

"Hey," Esther said.

Eugene looked up. "I *told* Mom you were still alive, but she's already looking up caskets online. Your funeral color scheme is going to be pink and silver, or so I'm told."

"Ugh. I have specifically requested a tasteful black and ivory funeral, like, *a hundred* times."

"She's been watching the emergency death slideshow she made last year, adding new pictures. It still finishes with 'Time of Your Life.'"

"God, so basic. I can't decide what would be more tragic—dying at seventeen, or having the most cliché funeral ever."

"Come on. A pink and silver funeral isn't cliché, just tacky as hell." Eugene had genuine worry in his eyes. "You okay?"

Esther wrung out her long hair; it grew red as blood when wet. "Yeah. I got mugged. Well, not really mugged exactly. Conned. By Jonah Smallwood. Remember the kid who left me hanging on Valentine's Day in elementary school?"

"The one you were desperately in love with?"

"The very same. Turns out he's a rather talented pickpocket. He just stole fifty-five dollars *and* my Fruit Roll-Up."

"Twice scorned. I hope you're planning vengeance."

"Naturally, brother."

Eugene stood and swung his arm over her shoulder and they walked inside together, under the horseshoe nailed above the lintel, the sprigs of dried pennyroyal dangling from the doorframe and the remains of the previous night's salt lines.

The Solar home was a cavernous old Victorian, the kind where even the light had a hazy, faded quality. It was all dark wood paneling and red Persian carpets and walls the distinct pale green color of rot. It was the kind of house where ghosts moved in the walls and neighbors believed the inhabitants might be cursed; for the Solars, both were true.

These are the things people would notice, if strangers were ever allowed inside:

- All of the light switches were kept in the *on* position
  with electrical tape. The Solars loved light, but
  Eugene loved it most of all. For his benefit, the halls
  were decked in string lights, and lamps and candles
  covered every spare surface of furniture and, quite
  often, much of the floor.
- Scorch marks from the Great Panic Fire of 2013
  when the power went out and Eugene bolted
  out of his bedroom into the hall, knocking over

approximately two dozen of the aforementioned candles in the process and setting the drywall alight.

- The steps to the second floor were sealed off by a jumble of discarded furniture, mostly because Peter Solar had been midway through completing upstairs renovations when he had his first stroke and all work had quickly stopped, but partly because Rosemary believed the second floor was genuinely haunted. (Like a ghost was only going to haunt half a house and politely let the residents chill downstairs without any *Paranormal Activity* action. C'mon.)
- There was nothing on the walls, apart from the taped-up light switches and blinds to cover the windows at night. No pictures. No posters. Definitely, definitely no mirrors. *Ever.*
- The rabbits in the kitchen.
- The evil rooster named Fred that followed Rosemary Solar everywhere and was, according to Rosemary anyway, a goblin straight out of Lithuanian folklore.

Green Day was *indeed* playing softly in the living room. Rosemary Solar, in her early forties, sat on the couch in front of the TV, watching the emergency funeral slideshow she'd made several years ago in case either of her children died unexpectedly. Brown hair fell to her shoulders and she tinkled when she moved, her bird-boned wrists and fingers dripping with silver rings and good luck charms. The coins sewn into her clothing—at the hem, at the sleeves, stitched to the inside of every pocket with metallic thread—chimed like raindrops.

These are the things Esther considered the defining aspects of her mother:

- In her younger years, Rosemary had been a champion Roller Derby player called "The She Beast." In Esther's favorite photograph of her, she was in costume on the track and she looked almost identical to Eugene: the same dark hair; the same brown eyes; the same pale skin, unblemished by the freckles that covered Esther. It was uncanny.
- Rosemary had been married once before, when she was eighteen, to a man who left a thin "C" shaped scar hooked through her left eyebrow. The man's name and fate were never mentioned. Esther liked to imagine he had suffered a long and painful demise shortly after Rosemary left him; perhaps he had been eaten by wild dogs or slow boiled in a large vat of oil.
- A horticulturist by trade, Rosemary had the ability to make plants grow with just a touch. Flowers seemed to bloom in her presence and bend toward her as she passed them by. The oak trees in the front lawn had listened to her when she whispered to them and told them to grow. There had always been a hint of magic about her.

This last point was what Esther loved most about Rosemary. She'd felt it ever since she was a child—even as the belief in fairies and Santa and letters from Hogwarts fell away, she still sensed some thrumming croon of power that emanated from her mother.

Esther thought of the magic as a tether. An invisible silver cord that bound their hearts together no matter the distance. It was what brought Rosemary into her bedroom after Esther had nightmares. It was what made the pain of a headache or a toothache or an upset stomach fade away with a palm pressed to her forehead.

Then the curse had come, like it always did. Peter had a stroke and retreated into the basement. Money got tight. Rosemary started gambling and, desperate not to lose, had slowly been consumed by fear of bad luck. The tether that bound mother and daughter had begun to wither and grow brittle and die. Esther didn't love her mother any less, but the magic had started to degrade, and Rosemary had slowly but surely become thoroughly, gruesomely *human*.

And there were few things worse in this world than humans.

Rosemary sprung from the couch and pulled Esther into a strangled embrace, an unimpressed Fred tucked under her arm. The air around her smelled of sage and cedar. Her clothes carried the scent of mugwort and clove. Her breath held a faint hint of pennyroyal. All of these herbs were meant to ward off bad luck. Rosemary Solar smelled like a witch, which was what most people in the neighborhood thought she was, and perhaps how she liked to think of herself too, but Esther knew better.

"I was *so* worried," Rosemary said, pushing her daughter's

damp hair off her face. "Where have you been? Why weren't you answering your phone?"

Esther savored the touch, and the worry, and felt the desire to melt into her mother's arms and let Rosemary comfort her, like she had when she was a kid. But the threadbare analgesic properties of her hands weren't enough to make up for leaving her stranded, *again*, and so she pushed her away.

"Maybe if you'd picked me up like you were supposed to, I wouldn't have been *brutally mugged* on my way home." Jonah's pickpocketing hardly counted as a mugging, but Rosemary didn't need to know that. Sometimes, Esther liked to make her feel guilty.

"You were mugged?"

"*Brutally mugged.* You should have picked me up."

Rosemary looked pained. "I saw a *black cat*."

Not for the first time, Esther felt the sting of the strange push-pull sensation that had defined their relationship for the past few years. The pull that drew her in, made her want to cradle Rosemary's cheek in her hand and assure her that everything would be okay. And at the same time, the push, this dark thing that leaked acid into her gut, because it wasn't fair. It wasn't fair that this is what her mother had become. It wasn't fair that all the Solars were cursed to live in such ridiculous fear.

"Go tell your father that you're safe," Rosemary said eventually.

Esther went to the dumbwaiter in the kitchen and found the pen and pad that lived there and wrote a note that read: I'm safe—please disregard any previous correspondence to the contrary. I miss you. Love, Esther. Then she rolled the note up and put it in the dumbwaiter and tugged the pulleys that would take the tiny elevator into the basement. Once upon a time, it might've been used to transport wood bound for the boiler; now it was used only for communication.

"Hello Esther," echoed Peter Solar's voice up the shaft a minute later. "I'm glad to hear you're no longer missing."

"Hi Dad," she called back. "What are you watching this week?"

"I'm on to *Mork & Mindy*. Never saw it when it was first on air. Funny stuff."

"That's nice."

"Love you, dear."

"Love you, too." Esther closed the dumbwaiter door and headed to her bedroom, the hundreds of candles in the hall hissing as drops of water flicked from her hair and clothes. The room looked somewhat like those fallout shelters in postapocalyptic movies where they store all the art from the Louvre and the Rijksmuseum and the Smithsonian, trying to save what they can of humanity. Most of the furniture once belonged to her grandparents: the black metal bed frame, the teak writing desk, the carved chest her grandfather brought from somewhere in Asia, the Persian carpets that covered most of the wooden floor. Everything she could salvage from their quaint little home. Unlike the rest of the house, which was bare and sparse apart from the taped-on light switches and lamps and candles, the walls of her room were covered in framed paintings and Indian tapestries and hammered-in bookshelves, the red wallpaper beneath barely visible anymore.

And costumes. Costumes everywhere. Costumes bursting from the armoire. Costumes in various stages of development hanging from the ceiling. Costumes pinned to three vintage dress forms; giant hoopskirts and shimmering black dresses and river-green strips of leather so soft they felt like melted chocolate in your hands. Peacock feathers and strands of pearls and brass pocket watches all showing different times. A Singer sewing machine—her late grandmother's—draped with swaths of velvet and silk ready to be cut into patterns. A dozen masks slung over every bedpost. A whole chest of drawers devoted to makeup—pots of gold glitter and turquoise eye shadow and bone white face paint and liquid latex and lipstick so red it burned to look at.

Eugene usually refused to go in there because all the clutter made the room look darker than it really was, but also because the light switch wasn't taped permanently on and could theoretically be switched off by a vengeful spirit at any time, if they were so inclined. (Vengeful spirits were of great concern to Eugene. They were something he thought about often. Very often.)

Esther put down her basket and started taking off her wet cape before she noticed a wraith standing by a heavily laden coat-rack in the far corner of the room. Hephzibah Hadid was half hidden by a cluster of scarves, wide-eyed, looking like a ghost who'd been seen by accident.

"Christ, Heph," Esther said, clutching at her chest. "We talked about this. You can't just silently lurk in here."

Hephzibah gave her an apologetic look and stepped out of the corner.

For the first three years of their friendship, Esther had been legitimately convinced that Hephzibah was her imaginary friend. To be fair, she didn't speak to anyone, and the teachers never called on her *because* she didn't speak to anyone, and she just kind of floated around Esther and followed her everywhere, which Esther didn't mind because she was a deeply unattractive child with few other friends.

Everything about Hephzibah was lanky and thin—lanky, thin hair; lanky, thin limbs; and she had that whole ashy haired, pale-eyed Bar Refaeli thing going on.

Before Esther even got her cape off, Hephzibah grabbed her and hugged her roughly—a rare sign of affection—before going back to stand in the corner and giving her a "What happened?" look. In the decade that they'd known each other, they'd gotten pretty good at nonverbal communication. Esther knew that Heph *could* speak—she'd overheard her talking to her parents once—but Hephzibah had busted her eavesdropping and hadn't talked to her for a month afterward. Or hadn't *not* talked to her, rather. Whatever.

"I got robbed by Jonah Smallwood. Remember that kid from Mrs. Price's class who bamboozled me into having a crush on him and then disappeared?"

Hephzibah gave her a filthy look that she interpreted as, "Yes I remember." Then she signed, "Did he bamboozle you again?"

"Yes, he did. Swindled me out of fifty-five dollars and stole my grandmother's bracelet and my phone and a Fruit Roll-Up." Hephzibah looked incensed. "Yes, I know, the Fruit Roll-Up was a real low blow. I, too, am incensed."

"We're still going to the party, right?" she signed. As good as they were at communicating as children, it became clear, as teenagers, that they might need a slightly more complex system than miming things out, so Hephzibah's parents had paid for the three of them—Heph, Eugene, and Esther—to learn ASL.

Esther didn't still want to go to the party. She hadn't wanted to attend in the first place. Parties meant people, and people meant eyes, and eyes meant scrutiny, boring into her skin like judgmental little weevils, and being judged meant hyperventilating in public, which only lead to *more* judgment. But Heph crossed her arms and jerked her head in the direction of the front door, a gesture Esther interpreted as, "This is a nonnegotiable friendship request."

"Ugh, fine. Let me get ready."

Hephzibah smiled. "We should probably take Eugene," she signed.

"True. If Mom goes out . . . There's no way we can leave him here on his own."

Not only could Eugene not stand to be in the dark, he also couldn't stand to be alone in the house at nighttime. Things came for you, when you were alone—or so he said.

So Esther went to fetch her brother.

Eugene's bedroom was the antithesis of hers: bare walls and

no furniture apart from his single bed situated in the center of the room, right underneath the ceiling light. Eugene lay on his thin mattress, reading, surrounded by a dozen lamps and thrice as many candles, like he was at his own funeral. Which, in a way, he was. Eugene faded every night when the sun went down and was replaced by a hollow creature who moved quietly through the house, trying to soak up every particle of illumination so that his very skin burned bright enough to ward off the dark.

"Eugene," she said, "do you want to go to a party?"

He looked up from his book. "Where?"

"Out at the old nickel refinery. There'll be bonfires."

Fire, as far as Eugene was concerned, was the only trustworthy source of illumination, and he worshiped it more than any caveman. He never left the house without his flashlight, spare batteries, a lighter, matches, kindling, an oil-soaked rag, rubbing sticks, a bow drill, flint, and several flame starters. He'd been able to build a small fire from scratch since he was eight, courtesy of the Boy Scouts. Eugene would be a great addition to any apocalypse survival team, if it weren't for the pesky fact he couldn't be outside without a light from dusk until dawn.

Eugene nodded and closed his book. "I'll go with you to the party."

Esther changed into a costume of Wednesday Addams, and then they went, the three strangest teenagers in town: a ghost who couldn't speak, a boy who hated the dark, and a girl who dressed as someone else everywhere she went.

THE NICKEL REFINERY came into view an hour later, a castle of metal and rust, its insides coal-bright from the bonfire burning in its belly, shadows flickering across its glassless windows as teenagers danced around the flames like moths.

"Well, let's go weird the place up," Esther said as they walked toward the warehouse.

Artists held exhibitions out at the refinery sometimes, and avant-garde film screenings, and hipster couples went there for their wedding photo shoots, but mostly it was used by Banksy wannabes and high schoolers getting drunk on the weekends. A temporary chain-link fence had been set up across the entrance to the warehouse, like that would be enough to keep out a horde of rabid teenagers looking to party on the last weekend of summer break. Already the corner had been clipped with fence cutters and pried open. They were foxes sneaking into the chicken coop: they would always find a way.

Music spilled out from portable speakers. Laughter and chatter were amplified by the echoing vastness of the warehouse. About fifteen feet from the fence, Esther hit the force field. Heph and Eugene took five steps apiece before they realized she was no longer walking next to them. The two paused and looked back at her.

"You guys go ahead," Esther said. "I'm gonna get some air here for a few minutes."

Heph and Eugene looked at each other but didn't say anything. Hephzibah didn't talk so that wasn't such a big surprise, but

Eugene didn't say anything either, because that would make him a gigantic goddamn hypocrite.

"Down your liquid courage and come find us," he said eventually. Then he hooked his arm through Heph's and they went inside.

"Okay, social anxiety," Esther said to herself, opening one of the warm bottles of red wine she'd commandeered from her mother's collection. "Time to drown."

She took three gulps. The aftertaste was of something exotic and rotten, but she didn't care, because alcohol was not consumed by teenagers because of its palatable qualities. It was consumed because it was a useful tool to make you cooler and funnier and less of a socially awkward mess.

The worst part was that anxiety didn't just affect the way you thought, or the way you talked, or the way you were around others. It affected the way your heart beat. The way you breathed. What you ate. How you slept. Anxiety felt like a grapnel anchor had been pickaxed into your back, one prong in each lung, one through the heart, one through the spine, the weight curving your posture forward, dragging you down to the murky depths of the sea floor. The good news was that you kind of got used to it after a while. Got used to the gasping, brink-of-heart-attack feeling that followed you everywhere. All you had to do was grab one of the prongs that stuck out from the bottom of your sternum, give it a little shake, and say, "Listen, asshole. We're not dying. We have shit to do."

Esther tried that. She took a few deep breaths, tried to expand her lungs against the crushing tightness of her rib cage, which didn't help much because anxiety was a bitch. So she drank some more wine and waited for the alcohol to go to battle with her demons, because she was a totally sane and healthy seventeen-year-old girl.

THE BOY AT THE BONFIRE

ESTHER WALKED back and forth along the mouth of the warehouse, balancing on a rusted beam fallen from the roof, occasionally glancing at the shadows cast long across the concrete by the flickering light of the bonfire. She thought about going into the party. She perhaps even *wanted* to go in. She stepped away from the beam and pulled open the hole in the fence and stood there, trying to force herself through. *Find Eugene. Find Hephzibah. You'll be fine. You'll be okay.*

But then a group of juniors stumbled drunkenly toward her and she let the fence close and scuttled away into the darkness like a startled raccoon. She couldn't field questions about why she was out there because she had no good answer. How to explain to strangers that there was a force field around them, an invisible barrier that buzzed around people she didn't know, that pushed her back?

So Esther climbed a set of rotting, taped off stairs that led to the second floor of the warehouse, wended her way through the labyrinthine halls, and dusted off a patch of floor to sit on. She took a long swig of wine and looked around now that her eyes had adjusted to the low light. Firelight punched through the holes in the floor. Eugene wouldn't be able to survive for long in the room, both because the light was minimal and wavering and because others—presumably teenagers—had been there before, and they'd splattered red paint all over the walls like blood. The words *GET OUT GET OUT GET OUT* were repeated over and over again in finger-painted smears. Eugene would've had a panic attack and/or spontaneously combusted.

Esther was ever so *fractionally* braver, and perhaps slightly intoxicated, so she lay on her front next to one of the larger holes overlooking the party and drew patterns in the dust and watched a line of small black bugs crawl down her forearm to perch on her fingertips as she drank. She didn't mind it there, on the peripheries, where she could watch from on high. Eugene was by the fire, also drinking a stolen bottle of Rosemary's wine. Esther watched her brother for a little while, trying to understand how he fit into the strange social puzzle she couldn't quite wrap her head around.

Eugene had an easy, mysterious popularity that baffled him as much as it did Esther. He should've been a prime target for teenage assholes: he was thin and kind of effeminate, he dressed like a weirdo, and he was deeply interested in things like demonology and religion and philosophy. He was smart, quiet, thoughtful, and gentle, and—perhaps above all—his name was Eugene. High school should've been a waking nightmare for him, but it wasn't.

Daisy Eisen was trying desperately to flirt with him, completely oblivious to the fact that his gaze kept darting away from her to land on a statuesque black guy telling a story to a group of people on the other side of the flames. Esther watched him for a little while, watched his animated movements, the way he climbed up on an anvil to make sure everyone could see him, watched the way he took a drink in each hand and snatched sips as he told his wild tale. He moved like a shadow play, like an actor on stage in a century past. She could see why Eugene was mesmerized.

And then he turned around.

And, for the second time that day, she recognized him.

There, glowing in the warm light of the bonfire, was Jonah Smallwood. Even from here she could tell that the bruise that had been swelling across his cheek that afternoon was gone, that the split at his eyebrow had healed, which meant that he was either a) a Highlander, or b) a pretty decent makeup artist, both of which seemed equally implausible.

Esther wasn't usually prone to violent outbursts, but for a half second she considered busting her wine bottle against a wall and getting stabby with Jonah's lower intestines. Then she remembered that blood was number forty on her semi-definitive list, so she gagged a little bit and then decided to punch him instead. She abandoned the bottle, slipped down the stairs, passed through the chain link fence, and strode toward the fire, her rage temporarily dislodging the anxiety anchor from her chest and giving her extraordinary courage.

Jonah didn't immediately recognize her because she was dressed as Wednesday Addams, which was the desired effect of the costumes. Confusion. Disorientation. Camouflage from predators.

When she was about three feet away from him, it clicked. Jonah put her face together with the memory "girl I robbed at the bus stop and left for dead" and said, "Oh shit!" He stumbled off the anvil and dropped one of his drinks and made to bolt, but it was too late. Esther was already there. She grabbed him by the shirtfront and swung. She'd never punched anyone before, not really, not with the intention of genuinely hurting them. Her blow landed two inches to the north of her intended target (left eye) and kind of glanced gently off the left side of his forehead before sailing like a soft breeze over the top of his hair.

"You hit me," Jonah said, like he was wholly bewildered by this fact, "in the hairline."

"You stole my money! And my *Roll-Up*!"

"It was *delicious*." He enunciated every syllable in a way that made Esther's eye twitch like a cartoon villain's.

And that's when the sirens came.

"Oh shit! Run!" Even though she'd just punched him very poorly in the left side of his head, Jonah dropped his remaining drink and grabbed her hand and pulled her after him toward the back of the warehouse. Esther's first thought was for Eugene, who couldn't run, who couldn't leave the light of the bonfire, but the cops were already on them, shouting, the beams of their flashlights darting all around. There was the sound of barking police dogs and the delighted squeals of teenagers who knew the nickel refinery like their own homes, knew the secrets of the place, the hidden crevasses and the labyrinthine catwalks and the holes rusted in boilers, just large enough for someone to crawl through and hide. They knew that they were fast enough to get away and so they howled and laughed and then went silent as the refinery swallowed them whole, one by one. And then there was Esther and Jonah, breathing heavily but quietly, knowing that even though they were running, they'd been seen and that escape was questionable.

Her second thought was that she shouldn't be running at all. She should stop and turn and wait for the cops and identify Jonah Smallwood as the petty criminal who'd swindled her out of fifty-five dollars and a much anticipated Fruit Roll-Up hours before. But she didn't. She ran and she ran and she ran and Jonah never let her go. Then they were outside at the edge of a copse of trees, wading—and then tumbling—through the undergrowth. She landed on top of him, her right knee between his thighs, her chest against his chest, her hand still in his hand.

A flashlight beam swept over her head. A dog snarled. Jonah pulled her down by the crucifix (an important feature of any Wednesday Addams costume), so close that her nose was pressed against the skin of his neck and she had no choice but to breathe in the scent of him again and again. Not his shampoo or laundry powder or cologne (or—let's be honest here, he was a teenage boy after all—his cheap Axe Body Spray), but *him*, that smell you smell when you walk into someone's bedroom or get into their car and it doesn't smell bad or good—it's just *them*. The essence of them. Normally you needed to know a person for years before you knew the way they really smelled. Needed to parse away the perfume and the sweat and the shampoo and the detergent. But there he was, laid bare before her.

The cops were getting closer. Jonah pressed his finger to her lips, pulled her closer to him, tried to make their two bodies smaller than they were, which was difficult, because he was tall and she was wide and her blood was pulsing so brightly and loudly through her veins that it should have been like a beacon in the dark. As she breathed him in, a curious thing began to happen—the grapnel anchor lodged in her back loosened slightly, letting her lungs expand to their fullest. When you have anxiety, you don't really get to have deep breaths. Your ribs are too small to let your shriveled lungs expand beyond half their size.

Yet for a few calm seconds in the dark, Esther wasn't worried about velociraptors or cougars or an unprovoked alien invasion, which were her usual go-to concerns when falling asleep at night. She wasn't even particularly worried about getting arrested, because Jonah didn't seem to be all that alarmed.

Then a flashlight beam landed full on their faces, her nose still in Jonah's neck, his finger still at her mouth.

Jonah's lips parted into a magnificent smile. "Evening officer," he said pleasantly, like this was the least compromising position law enforcement had ever busted him in. "What seems to be the problem?"

"You're trespassing on private property," said the cop, who was still nothing but a deep voice and a bright hovering light in the dark.

"Oh dear. We were just out for a spot of nighttime bird

watching. The rare Common Barn Owl was said to have been seen around—hey, ow, hey, okay man, okay, Jesus," Jonah said as the cop wrenched him out from under her by his collar. More police appeared, and Esther, too, was hauled to her feet by a burly female (possible ex–MMA cage fighter) and steered back toward the flashing lights at the front of the warehouse.

Eugene, as it turns out, hadn't tried to run from the police, so no one had paid any attention to him. He was standing next to one of the cop cars, reveling in the red and blue lights, his hands in his pockets like he was waiting to meet someone at Starbucks and not waiting to be arrested.

Hide, Esther mouthed to him. Eugene looked around and shrugged and then walked back to the fire, where he'd remain until dawn, unable to leave its circle of light until the sun rose. The police didn't notice him. It worried her when others couldn't see him. Sometimes, when the light was right, when he turned his body at the right angle, she could swear Eugene was transparent. You know those weird memories you have from childhood, the ones you can't explain, those half-remembered dreamscapes of impossible things? A book flying off a shelf by itself; a breath taken underwater; a black lump of shadow at the end of the hall with teeth and claws and acid white eyes. Esther's were all of Eugene. When they were younger, when he was very sad or very scared, he would flicker. Like he was being projected into reality but wasn't really part of it, like he could turn himself off at will.

A boy made of lightning bugs.

As a poor man's Ronda Rousey pushed her head into the cop

car, Esther saw her brother vanish, just for a moment, into thin air. Then Jonah was shoved into the back seat on the other side of her. And that was how, the same night he robbed her, Jonah Smallwood accompanied Esther Solar during her first arrest.

As it turns out, they weren't really under arrest, which they should've guessed from the lack of handcuffs and Miranda rights. The cops drove them back into town and took them to the station and walked them into separate holding cells, which they referred to as "custody suites." Jonah's cell was empty, while Esther's held a very thin woman in a red wig who was picking at scabs on her arm. She introduced herself as Mary, mother of God.

Esther tried to explain to Ronda that a great injustice had been done to her, and that Jonah should be charged with theft and she should be set free, but Ronda ignored her and said, "One phone call."

Esther didn't have her phone (obviously) and couldn't remember any of her relatives' numbers, except for her grandfather's, which wasn't very helpful. So she called Hephzibah's cell.

Esther: "Hephzibah, I've been apprehended by law enforcement. I need you to tell my mom to bail me out."

Hephzibah: [SILENCE]

Esther: "I assume the fact you just answered your phone means you got away when the cops raided the place."

Hephzibah: [SILENCE]

Esther: "I know Mom will be at the casino until, like, sunrise, but you need to tell her where I am, okay?"

Hephzibah: [SILENCE]

Esther: "Also, I left Eugene alone at the refinery. Can you please go rescue him?"

Hephzibah: [SILENCE]

Esther: "I'm gonna go back to being a hardened criminal now."

Hephzibah: [SILENCE]

Esther: "Okay, good talk."

The cop led her back to her cell, at which point she proceeded to lie facedown on the ground so she didn't have to talk to Jonah, who was sitting cross-legged on the far side of his cage, watching her.

"I wouldn't lie there if I were you," Jonah said.

To which she replied: "Can I live?"

To which he replied: "Think about all the piss and vomit and blood that's been on that floor. You know they don't pay these cops enough to clean it."

"He's right, you know," croaked Jesus's mom. "I peed in here just last week."

"It does smell a lot like urine." Esther sat up and mirrored Jonah's stance, her back pressed against the bars. Jonah was led out for his phone call, which—judging by the amount of yelling and swearing he did—went much less smoothly than hers.

"You know, I've been thinking about you ever since I robbed you this afternoon," he said when he sat down again. The cop at the desk closest to the cells peered up over his glasses and raised his eyebrows. "It's a metaphor for, uh, sex stuff," Jonah explained quickly. The cop narrowed his eyes but looked back down at his phone.

"About how you want forgiveness for your heinous crime?" Esther said.

"Nah, about your weird family, the ones you did a presentation on back in elementary school."

"Oh." Esther had specifically enrolled at East River High School because no one from her third grade class (bar Hephzibah) was going there, and thus no one would remember her third grade report about the Solar family curse.

"Yeah, how are they weird again? They're all lactose intolerant or something?"

"It's definitely that. They cannot handle milk."

"Nah, that isn't it. Phobias, right? They all have a great fear. Scared of spiders and heights and all that. Cursed by Death himself. And whatever you're afraid of, that's what kills you one day."

"How do you even remember that?"

"I paid a lot of attention to you when I was eight. Like, *a lot.*"

Esther blushed, and then filled Jonah in on the two rules of the curse, which were these:

- The curse could befall a Solar at any stage of their life at any time without warning, like a dormant disease in the blood, waiting to strike. Reginald, her grandfather, had not become terrified of water until he was in his thirties, when Death told him that he would one day drown. Eugene's fear of the dark, on the other hand, had developed when he was a child.

    – Whatever you feared would consume your life until
       it eventually killed you.

"So what about you?" Jonah asked. "What are you scared of?"

"Nothing."

"You can't be the special snowflake, letting the rest of the cursed family down. You wanna bring shame to your bloodline?"

"It's not funny."

"Yeah, I remember your report. Your cousin's scared of bees. Your uncle's scared of germs. Your granddad's scared of water. Your dad was a veterinarian, and he didn't know his great fear yet."

"Dad knows his fear now. He has agoraphobia. He hasn't left the basement in six years."

"Well, there you go. You must be afraid of something."

"Not that I know of."

"Sure you are. You just gotta figure out what."

"That's really inspirational."

"Thank you."

They didn't speak again until Jonah's dad, Holland, arrived to bail him out (well, to pick him up, technically, because he wasn't under arrest). Holland kind of looked like Jonah if everything about Jonah was bigger and puffier. Bigger, puffier shoulders, bigger, puffier belly, bigger, puffier hair.

"Hey Dad. Can we give Esther a ride home?" asked Jonah as budget Ronda Rousey freed him from his cage. Holland looked Esther up and down with mean eyes and then turned to leave, which apparently meant "Yes," because Jonah said, "C'mon."

Holland's car was a squash-colored '80s station wagon with caramel leather seats that were so badly cracked they left scratches on Esther's legs. She did not mention this as she gave directions to her house. When they slowed in front of the old Victorian, Jonah said, "Jesus Horatio Christ!" Her home, as always, was seeping light, casting the long shadows of oak trees across the street. The nazars were whispering in the breeze, singing softly, ominously, of the terrible fate that would befall anyone who wished the Solars harm and dared to stray too close. Esther scrambled out before the car had stopped. This was why she never invited friends from school over.

"Esther, wait!" called Jonah. She didn't wait, but he was faster than she was, so he caught her among the trees. "Hey, I have something for you. I sold the bracelet already and the money's gone, but you can have this back." He dug in his pocket and handed Esther her cell phone.

"Gee, thanks."

"Sorry for picking your pocket."

"Yeah, sure."

"See you round, Esther."

"Not if I can help it."

Jonah blew her a kiss and then darted back to the road as his dad's car began to crawl away down the street.

Esther unlocked her phone. Everything was gone. All her photos, her contacts, her apps. It had been scrubbed clean, factory reset, and readied for sale on the black market. Only a single contact had been saved. *Jonah Smallwood*, it read, with a red heart emoji next to his name and his phone number below. Her finger hovered over the "Delete" button. You shouldn't keep the phone numbers of rapscallions who robbed you and left you for dead at bus stops, or stood you up on Valentine's Day at the age of eight, even if they looked like Finn from *Star Wars* and dressed like the Fantastic Mr. Fox and smelled like heady cologne.

Esther wasn't entirely sure why she kept his number, but it probably had something to do with the fact that she imagined she would never see Jonah Smallwood again.

It would only be sixteen hours and seven minutes before that assumption proved entirely incorrect.

4

STRING LIGHTS
AND SERIAL KILLERS

HOME WAS, as she knew it would be, bright but abandoned. Esther went to the kitchen and searched the drawers for the book where Rosemary scribbled down all their phone numbers in case of an emergency. Rabbits, small and gray and twitchy, hopped at her feet, hoping to be fed. Like most everything Rosemary brought into the house—the chamomile tea she washed her hands in before she went to play the slots, the sage leaves she carried in her wallet, the coins she sewed into her clothing, the horseshoe, that goddamn evil goblin rooster—the rabbits were for good luck. Most people just carried around a single rabbit's foot, but why buy a single foot, her mother reasoned, when you could buy a whole rabbit and get four times the amount of luck without spilling any blood?

Esther called Rosemary on the landline, but she didn't answer, so she checked all the downstairs rooms, but her mother wasn't in any of them. Rosemary thought the house was haunted, but really, the only ghosts inside these walls were her parents.

(That still didn't mean Esther was going to go snooping around upstairs—that's how horror movies started.) She tried Eugene and Heph on their cells, but they both went straight to voicemail.

What she did next was a testament to how much she loved her stupid brother: She located her long-abandoned bike in the garage, pumped up the tires, pimped the thing out with half a dozen bike headlights scavenged from Eugene's bedroom, and then wrapped a string of lights around her chest and torso, just for good measure. Have you ever seen a horror movie where someone gets murdered with a string of madly flashing lights wrapped around them? Of course not. No one wants to murder ridiculous people. It gets the cops asking too many questions. Plus, no one was going to forget if they saw Wednesday Addams wrapped in string lights. Murderers want, like, drifters and prostitutes. Fade-into-the-background type people that no one will remember seeing and no one will miss.

Nobody would forget seeing *her*.

Outside, the early morning was dark and quiet. Esther slowly peddled past the 7-Eleven, because it was about the only thing still open and therefore the only place that her "last known sighting" would occur if someone *did* decide to murder her. She thought about this too much. Like, what if Jonah Smallwood was the last person to see her alive (apart from her killer, obviously). What would the cops make of the grainy 7-Eleven CCTV footage that showed her riding past with a loop of string lights around her chest? Would they simply conclude she'd gone bat-shit crazy and cycled off a cliff somewhere? Probably. Her mutilated corpse wouldn't be discovered for months. Years maybe.

"Get it together, Esther," she muttered.

The bright lights of the 7-Eleven faded and then she was riding on gloomy back streets, and then no streets at all, making her way toward the industrial part of town where no one but serial killers and drunk teenagers went anymore.

"Fuck you, Eugene," she chanted as she bowed her head and rode as fast as she could, her heart hammering in her chest. "Fuck you, Eugene. Seriously, Eugene, fuck you."

When she finally made it to the refinery, the light inside was dead. No more coal-bright flames, no more whooping teens, no more long shadows dancing in the windows. Esther ditched her bike and climbed through the chain link fence, the lights around her chest barely puncturing the heavy dark. Two figures huddled close to what was left of the bonfire, now no more than a pit of slow-burning embers. Hephzibah had her arm around Eugene's shoulders and was whispering in his ear, singing maybe, to keep him calm as the firelight died. Around them, Eugene had set up a safety circle of flashlights all pointing in their direction, an island of bright light in the shadows. A stranger stumbling upon them might have mistaken them for spirits: the ashen girl with the ashen hair in the ashen dress, softly singing tunes about love and death, and the boy, dressed like a faded memory, shaking in the ghost light.

Eugene had tried therapy a few times when he was younger, when the family had money for that kind of thing, before Rosemary had started feeding all their spare cash into the slots. But the vehemence with which he believed his delusions—the consistency of them, the depth of the detail he used to describe the monsters he saw in the dark—well, it crept under the skin of each therapist he saw. The things he spoke of filled their heads with half-remembered horrors they'd seen or heard or felt as young children, things they'd spent a lifetime convincing themselves weren't real, things most people successfully stopped noticing after they reached a certain age. And here was a boy of no more than eleven, twelve, thirteen, who had them half convinced that these impossible memories were true.

No one slept in the dark after sessions with Eugene Solar.

Hephzibah spotted Esther hovering at the entrance to the warehouse and smiled brightly and waved, but she wouldn't speak or sing again, not with Esther so close. She used to get upset that Heph could whisper to Eugene but not to her. That he knew what her voice sounded like, really *knew*, and she didn't. It took Esther a couple of years to work out that Hephzibah was in love with him. That whatever magic had once burned brightly in their mother had lived on in Eugene, and his enchantment over her had done what no therapist could: get her to talk.

"Thanks for coming back for him, kid," Esther said to Heph.

"Anytime," she signed.

Esther sat on the other side of Eugene and put her arm around him too, so that he was wedged safely between them, so that—as always—the demons would eat them first. They stayed there pressed tight against each other until dawn, Heph and Esther holding hands behind Eugene's back, Eugene's fingers curled around a sprig of yarrow plucked from Rosemary's garden, trying and failing to find courage in the strong, sweet scent of the devil's nettle. When the sky finally lightened, he rose and went out into the gray sunlight and breathed it in and in and in, angry at himself and exhausted and above all shocked, as always, to have survived another long night in the dark.

"Come on you beautiful weirdo," Esther said, standing on her tiptoes to rest her chin on his shoulder. Even though they looked different and felt different and disagreed on most things, she'd never be able to think of Eugene as anything less than the second half of her soul. "Let's get you home."

5

DEATH AND

HORSE-SIZED LOBSTERS

WHEN THE twins finally arrived back at the house, Rosemary didn't ask them where they'd been all night, because Rosemary wasn't there. Their father, Peter, heard their footfalls and called up the stairs, but they didn't answer him. Esther sent him a note down the dumbwaiter. Most kids would get in trouble for ignoring their parents, but it wasn't like Peter was going to come out of the basement anytime soon to discipline them.

A few years ago, Eugene had devised a series of trials to try and draw Peter out of his burrow and proceeded to spend the next week:

- Setting the fire alarms off and pretending to choke on smoke at the top of the basement stairs.
- Cooking several dozen slices of bacon and leaving the plate at the top of the basement stairs.
- Dropping stink bombs down the basement stairs.

Alas, Gollum remained in his cave, and the Solar children no longer feared parental retribution from either side.

What they lost in Peter Solar: a man who loved hiking and poetry and taking his children to the zoo, where he explained to them, in detail, each conservation project being undertaken. A man who took them to yard sales and bought them binoculars and went on weeklong birdwatching expeditions. A man who taught them how to play chess and read to them at bedtime and sat beside their beds and stroked their hair when they were sick.

Peter Solar. Their father. That's who they lost.

Eugene took a blanket into the backyard and rested in what little sunlight filtered through the oak trees, his sleep fitful. The creatures that came for him in his dreams hated sunlight, he said, so whenever he *did* sleep—which wasn't often—it was usually in the sun. Esther napped in her bed, slipping in and out of that heavy, sluggish haze that comes with sleeping during the day, the kind that made you think that Jonah Smallwood (red love heart) had sent you a message asking what navarrofobia was.

JONAH SMALLWOOD ♥:

What's navarrofobia?

Esther sat bolt upright. Jonah Smallwood had, and was reading, her semi-definitive list of worst nightmares.

Before she replied, she went into her contacts and deleted the stupid heart from next to his name.

ESTHER:

Fear of cornfields. Bring me that list back *immediately*. Do not even glance at it again.

JONAH:

You really afraid of all these things? Some of these are pretty stupid. Who the hell is scared of moths?

ESTHER:

DO. NOT. EVEN. GLANCE.

JONAH:

Fine, fine. I'll drop it by tonight.

ESTHER:

Put it in the mailbox and then delete my phone number and then get abducted by aliens and never return to this planet.

JONAH:

I glanced. Couldn't help it.

To which Esther sent five rows of angry emojis before going back to sleep.

ROSEMARY WOKE THEM UP in the afternoon and took them to visit their grandfather, Reginald Solar, at Lilac Hill, a building that looked like it may have once been a prison, but now smelled faintly of cheese and strongly of death. If Tim Burton and Wes Anderson had a love child, and that love child grew up to be an architect/interior designer that focused solely on constructing/ decorating sad nursing homes, then Lilac Hill Nursing and Rehabilitation Center would be that kid's magnum opus. Glossy, olive green floors, orange pleather chairs, and wallpaper with tiny pink lobsters all over it, despite the fact that a) the town was an hour's drive from the seaside, and b) most of the residents couldn't take a lobster in a one-on-one fight to the death.

Reginald Solar, in his prime, could've kicked the crap out of a horse-sized lobster, but that was before the dementia snuck up on him in his sleep. (He maintained that it never would've been able to sink its claws into him if he'd been awake.)

They walked through the too-bright halls toward Reg's room, Eugene quietly sliding from window to window in case there was a sudden power outage. In his hand, as there always was in untrustworthy buildings (i.e., buildings that didn't have the light switches taped in the *on* position, and a generator, *and* a backup generator), was a flashlight, the same industrial black and yellow flashlight Peter used to take with him on house calls when he still left the house.

The hall was lined with shucked shells in the shape of people, all of them hunched over in wheelchairs and looking fuzzy somehow, like spiders had already started spinning webs in their hair.

"I could rule this place with a small lobster army," Esther muttered to herself. "Thirty, forty lobsters, tops, and I could be queen." The more she thought about them—their beady eyes, their abundant legs, the way they moved, how much their claws would hurt—the more uncomfortable she started to feel. If Jonah hadn't stolen her semi-definitive list of worst nightmares, she might have added lobsters to the roster, just in case.

Then there he was, Reginald Solar, once a hardened homicide detective, now the owner of a nonoperational brain inside a paper-skinned body. Esther was always shocked by how much worse her grandfather looked every time she saw him. Like he was a clay statue left outside, and every time it rained, more and more of him washed away, leaving deep grooves all over his body and a puddle of everything he used to be at his feet. He wore a red cap—the last one her grandma had knitted for him before she died—and was sitting in his wheelchair in front of a chessboard, playing (and losing) a game with no one.

"Hey Pop," said Eugene, sliding into the empty chair across from Reg.

Reg didn't say anything, didn't acknowledge their presence, just stared and stared at the chessboard until he made the only move he could make: the one that would lead him straight into checkmate. "You always win, you old bastard," he mumbled to Eugene. Reginald was, technically, still alive, though his soul had died several years earlier, leaving behind a thin cadaver to be dragged slowly and messily toward the grave.

"Tell us about the curse," Eugene said as he reset the chessboard. Despite everything else that had roared out of his head like a landslide, Reg could still describe the handful of times he'd personally met Death with perfect clarity, so that was the only question Eugene ever asked.

"The first time I met the Man Who Would Be Death . . ." he

began, his speech slurred, his voice rasped, his eyes far away. The story was a mechanical thing now, no longer recalled with flair and passion as it once was, though the nurses said it was a miracle he could remember anything at all. "The first time I met him," he said again, trying to form his lips and tongue around words his brain no longer recognized, "was in Vietnam."

Reg spent the afternoon slowly recounting the story with as much detail as he always had—the humidity of the jungles, the bright colors of wartime Saigon, the sweetness of the Vietnamese hot chocolate, and the Man Who Would Be Death, a younger man with a pockmarked face, as war weary as the rest of them. Eugene rested in a chair by the window, his thin eyelids closed against the sun. Esther was on the floor, her head on a pillow, her body wrapped in a cloak of falcon feathers because today she was the Valkyrie Freyja, Norse goddess of death.

These are the things she remembered about her grandfather as he spoke:

- The way the rest of the world had seen him as a hard-assed homicide detective, but she'd only ever known him as Poppy, the man who grew gardens of orchids and let her pick the flowers even when no one else was allowed to.
- The way the only animals he'd ever liked were birds, until Florence Solar rescued a puppy (that Reg very much didn't want to keep). The way the puppy would follow him around the greenhouse as

he tended to his orchids, and the way he pretended
to hate that the dog was obsessed with him. The
way the dog remained nameless, and the way he
only referred to it as "Go Away," yet let it nap on his
knees when he watched TV and sleep at the foot of
his bed every night.
– The way he laughed. The way he'd tip his head back
when he found something particularly funny. The
way he'd wipe his right eye with his index finger as
the laugh subsided, whether he'd been crying happy
tears or not.

The memory of the laugh was perhaps what made Esther
most sad. She had no recordings of the sound, and once Reg was
gone, it would survive only as a snippet in her imperfect memory,
where it could be distorted or forgotten altogether. As a tear
slipped from her right eye, she used her index finger to wipe it
away, and replayed the fragment of her grandfather's laugh again,
already unsure how true it was.

When the story was done she stood and stretched and
pressed her lips to Reg's waxen forehead, and he asked her if she
was an angel or a demon come to reap his soul, and that was when
they left him.

6

THE CURSE
AND THE REAPER

IN THE evening the sun began its ominous sink into the mountains, a ball of red-hot nickel drowning in the sky, and the Solar household prepared for another night in the trenches. Another battle against the ever-encroaching dark. A procedure that had been going on every night for six years.

Eugene was lighting candles like a maniac, slipping through the halls of the house armed with matches and his favorite novelty lighter, a dragon that shot flames out of its ass. It was a long process. Every now and then he looked out a window and said "Fuck. Fuck me. Fucking sunset" or something to that effect and went back to madly clicking the smiling dragon's tongue until it shat blue fire from its bowels. Occasionally he asked Esther what time it was and she checked her phone and said "five thirty-two" or "quarter to six." And each time she gave him a number, no matter what number it was, Eugene swore and started moving faster, lighting candles without even touching them, all the illumination he'd saved up in his skin jumping from his fingertips to the wicks. Not many people could light a candle with sheer willpower alone, but Eugene Solar could. Eventually the whole house was humming with electricity and glowing with firelight and the air smelled of burnt wick and melting wax.

Esther's role to play in this psychotic ritual was security; she closed all the windows, drew the curtains, sprinkled salt lines across doorways, and ensured the front door was securely locked. She was about to complete this last task, her hand hovering inches from the dead bolt, when there came a series of bangs from the other side of the door, which was alarming. Everyone in the neighborhood knew not to come to their house (no one ever answered), which meant that the person banging was almost certainly a violent home invader. Esther was midway through weighing her options—call the police, grab a knife from the kitchen, barricade herself in the basement with her father—when the violent home invader called out.

"Esther! Esther, open up!" said a familiar voice.

Jonah Smallwood was on her front doorstep, sobbing. She knelt by the mail slot.

"I'm *not* falling for that again," she said. "Steal my Fruit Roll-Up once, shame on you. Steal my Fruit Roll-Up twice—"

"Open the damn door!" Jonah said.

"Put the list in the mail slot and—"

Jonah banged the door again. "Come *on*, it's an emergency!"

What a person with anxiety hears: *I am here to murder you and your family.* Esther looked behind her, but Rosemary and Eugene had disappeared, swallowed by the house after the first knock. They wouldn't reemerge from their hiding places until the coast was clear.

So—knowing the risk was only to herself, and feeling *fairly* certain Jonah wasn't the murdering type—she took a breath and opened the door.

"I hit it with my moped!" Jonah said, rushing inside. Cupped in his hands, he held what she first mistook for a wet ushanka, one of those furry Russian hats, but was, in actual fact, a very limp kitten. Out in the front yard, Jonah's cream-colored moped was toppled in some tree roots, its tires still spinning.

The kitten was clearly not breathing.

"I think it's dead," she said, closing her hands gently over Jonah's.

"It's not dead!" He pulled the kitten away from her and pressed it to his chest.

"What do you want me to do?"

"Your dad's a vet, isn't he?"

"Jonah, he hasn't . . . He hasn't left the basement for six years. I don't think he's seen a stranger in all that time."

Jonah Smallwood, to his credit, didn't seem to find this half as weird as most people who knew about Peter Solar's condition. "Where's the basement at?" he asked, so she led him to the orange door her father walked through on a cold Tuesday morning six years ago and never walked out of again. They descended the stairs together, the feathers of her cloak lifting eddies of dust from the wood. Even down there, the lights were taped on with electrical tape for when Eugene had still visited their father.

The basement that was now Peter Solar's whole life looked like what you'd expect if someone hadn't left it for six years. The walls had been hung with yards and yards of red fabric so that the space kind of had an opium den vibe. The only furniture consisted of what had already been down there the day he decided he couldn't ever leave. A ping-pong table, a couch that had been fashionable in the '80s, four mismatched bar stools, and a black-and-white TV, all surrounded by the usual basement clutter—a ladder, three lamps, a stack of board games, bags of old clothes earmarked for Goodwill years ago, golf clubs, a guitar, two fake Christmas trees (both decorated and lit up, all year round—Peter loved Christmas), Reginald's record player, and dozens of precariously balanced towers of books and newspapers.

Six years ago, Esther thought this was cool. She looked at his basement and saw the Room of Requirement from Harry Potter and believed her dad was an eccentric wizard worthy of a position at Hogwarts. Now she could smell the anemic scent of human skin that hadn't seen sunlight for half a dozen years, see the layer of fine grease settled over the tomb that had become his life.

Peter Solar had come down here one afternoon when Esther was eleven to hook up the second generator that Eugene had requested. Perhaps he was deep in mourning for his brother, Uncle Harold, who had recently succumbed to his fear of germs, or perhaps the horror of suffering a stroke had driven him into the comfort of the dark, or perhaps it was simply his time to fall victim to the curse. Whatever the case, what happened was this:

At the foot of the stairs, he had a panic attack and found

himself unable to climb any farther than the second step. That afternoon, Peter quit his job, hired a plumber to get the basement toilet operational, ordered enough canned food to see him through two apocalypses, and vowed never to come to the surface again.

The vow, so far, had remained unbroken.

Peter was sitting on the couch in a tartan bathrobe and slippers, sipping home-distilled spirits and listening to Christmas carols. Before his interment, he'd always been impeccably groomed, his hair slicked back and his handlebar moustache curled. For the first year or so, he'd been careful to maintain his appearance. Then people stopped visiting. His coworkers first, and then his best friends, and then even his sister. They wrote him off as a lost cause pretty early on. It took Esther and Eugene and Rosemary at least two years more, but eventually they all stopped visiting too. It was too painful to watch his slow-motion transformation into a grotesque.

Peter Solar was a wild man now. His hair was matted and tangled. His beard was disheveled and streaked with gray. Once trim, he was now huge; not fat, exactly, just broad and massive. He looked like something out of a legend, Esther thought. A Viking after a long and lonely journey at sea, weathered by salt and sun.

The left side of his face sagged and had begun to petrify, and his left hand curled into his body. Another stroke, the doctors thought, this one worse than the last. It was three months before anyone knew. Peter could feel that something was wrong but was so afraid he'd have to leave the basement he never dared to ask for help. Three months. Two strokes. It was hard to be down there, knowing that. As much as Esther loved him, every time she saw him now (which wasn't frequently), it reminded her of the man she used to know. The man she couldn't save.

Months had passed since she last dared look upon the ruined remains of her father.

"Dad—" she said, and he turned, the light glistening off the petrified side of his face. Peter had her eyes. Or rather, she had his; eyes with thunderstorms in them. Eyes that broke her heart.

Jonah was already weaving through the stacks of junk toward him.

"I hit it with my moped!" Jonah said, pressing the damp kitten into the wild man's chest.

A long time had passed since Peter's last interaction with a stranger. Even more time had gone by since he'd practiced medicine. Esther tried to remember when she'd last seen her father treat an animal. The twins had been ten or maybe eleven, and he'd taken them on a bike ride to the playground near their house. On the way home, Esther had found a bird in the gutter, injured and left for dead after being hit by a car.

The sparrow was in a bad way, and in retrospect, Peter probably knew from the beginning that it would die, but he couldn't bear to tell his daughter that. Instead he scooped the bird up and carried it home, and they stayed up all night together, just the two of them, feeding it and keeping it warm and comfortable. Esther had named the sparrow Lucky. It died in the morning, its little heart unable to keep beating, and Peter held his daughter on his knee while she cried into his shoulder.

Not long after, he went into the basement, and everything changed.

Esther wondered if he would freak out and have a panic attack at this sudden and unexpected invasion of his safe space, but he didn't. She stood back and watched them from the shadows, watched as Peter put down his potent gin and looked from her to Jonah to the kitten in his hands and ordered Jonah (slowly, speech slightly slurred from the strokes) to fetch his med kit from beneath a stack of newspapers and bring it to him. She watched as he found the source of the bleeding and stopped it, watched as he reinflated a collapsed lung, watched as he gave the kitten painkillers and stitched a wound and set a broken leg and said—though he couldn't be one hundred percent sure, but he was pretty sure—that it had no other mortal injuries, just a bad concussion that might lead to permanent brain damage. It would be touch and go for a few days, but that it might just make it. All this he did one-handed, with Jonah assisting when Peter couldn't do something himself.

"Put your hand here, very gently," Peter said. Jonah put his palm over the kitten's thin ribs. His hand moved up and down, up and down in time with its rapid breaths. It mewled groggily at his touch.

"Looks like a stray," Peter said as he handed the bundled up kitten to Jonah with his good hand, who took and held it as if the animal was glass. "Her fur's matted and she's malnourished and she has an eye infection. Esther," he said, turning to his daughter, "we should still have some cat milk substitute upstairs in the garage. Think you can bring it down?"

Esther's first instinct was to say, "What makes you think you know anything about the world upstairs?" But this was the first time he'd showed interest in something beyond the orange door that led to the basement in more than half a decade. So she said, "Sure," and left Jonah, now rocking the concussed cat like a baby, sitting next to her father on the '80s couch.

Over the next hour, Peter taught Jonah how to feed the kitten now-expired milk supplement, how to clean her infected eyes, how to treat her fleas and unmat her fur and make sure she stayed warm, make sure she stayed breathing.

Esther watched Jonah warily in this space. Her father had lost everything. To lose even more to a pickpocket would be unforgivable. So she kept her eyes on his long fingers to make sure they didn't dip into the pockets of her father's bathrobe, or wander too close to the gold watch strapped around his wrist, but Jonah seemed wholly uninterested in anything except the cat. Eventually, she found herself relaxing in his presence. She felt strangely . . . calm.

"Can you take her home?" Peter asked Jonah.

"Nah. Probably not the best idea," he said as he stroked her nose. "Not such a nice place right now."

"I'm sure Esther wouldn't mind helping you out by looking after her here."

And that was how she got stuck with the responsibility of caring for Jonah's stupid cat, who he named Fleayoncé Knowles.

Naturally.

BEFORE THEY LEFT THE BASEMENT, Peter put his good hand on Esther's shoulder. "It was nice to see you," he said. For a moment, Peter looked like he was thinking about hugging his daughter, but he hesitated and raised his glass of gin to her instead.

"It was nice to see you, too," she said, forcing a smile. In her head she was chanting *I'm sorry, I'm sorry, I'm sorry* even though she didn't quite know what she was sorry for. For not visiting more often? For thinking, on the days when she most missed the man he used to be, how much easier it would be to explain his absence if he was simply dead? "Do you want to come up for dinner?"

It was Peter's turn to fake a smile. "Maybe next time."

Esther so badly wanted to save her father, to bring him back from the half death that had become his life. Every time he reminded her that he couldn't be saved, Esther's heart broke a little more.

"DO YOU WANT TO STAY FOR FOOD?" she asked Jonah once they were upstairs because she didn't know how else to make him feel better about possibly brain-damaging a kitten, which was not something you really wanted on your conscience. So the day after he robbed her at the bus stop and they had been apprehended by law enforcement together, Jonah made the acquaintance of her family and joined them at the table, where she had to push aside two lamps and a dozen candles and scrape off several years of built up wax to make room for his plate. He said nothing about her basement-dwelling father, nothing about the taped-on lights, nothing about how Eugene let his palm hover for slightly too long over a candle flame, barely reacting as his skin began to burn and blister. What he was *not* doing a good job of was *not* staring at the cock perched on Rosemary's shoulder.

On the list of strange things in her household, Fred, the big black rooster with plumes of fiery feathers sticking out of his butt, was admittedly on the stranger end. Rosemary had purchased him from their Lithuanian dry-cleaning lady for one thousand dollars three years ago, and Fred had been terrorizing the house ever since. Why does someone pay one thousand dollars for a rooster? Because, according to the woman who sold him, Fred the rooster was not, in fact, a rooster at all: Fred the rooster was an Aitvaras, a supernatural goblin capable of bringing good luck to those who lived with him.

Fred had, so far, not done much except be a rooster, but that didn't stop Rosemary from vehemently believing he'd bring "wealth and grain" into the home if she treated him well and that he would spontaneously combust into a spark when he died.

Jonah chewed slowly, staring at Fred. Fred stared back, cocking his head from side to side, because that's what roosters do.

"So, Jonah," said Rosemary, making the kind of small talk that gets injected into your veins when you procreate or something. "What do you do in your spare time?"

"Effects makeup, mostly," Jonah said around his mouthful of slightly burned store-bought lasagna, Rosemary's specialty. "You know, like gunshot wounds and gashes across the forehead and bruises and stuff." Jonah looked at Esther apologetically. She narrowed her eyes at him and pressed her tongue into the back of her teeth. That little *shit*. The swollen cheek and split in his eyebrow at the bus stop had been fake after all.

"What a handy skill to have," Esther said slowly.

Jonah winked. "Comes in useful from time to time."

"Is that what you want to do when you grow up?" Rosemary asked.

"Mom, he's not seven."

"Sorry, when you graduate?"

"Yeah, I wanna work in movies I guess. I try and practice as much as I can using YouTube tutorials. I'm learning how to make prosthetics at the moment, like the fake noses from *The Lord of the Rings*. My dad hates it, says I'll never make any money, but I'm saving up for film school anyway, kind of without him knowing."

"Oh, Esther bakes to save for college. Do you have a job?"

"Um . . . It's more of an *entrepreneurial* endeavor."

Esther couldn't hold her tongue. "What he means to say is, he pickpockets helpless people at bus stops."

Jonah looked sheepish, but shrugged. "I mean, at least you know your stolen goods are going to a charitable cause."

At that moment, Fred decided to be his diabolical self and swoop down from Rosemary's shoulder to have a major freakout in the middle of the table (probably because Fleayoncé was asleep on Jonah's lap and therefore getting more attention than he was). Candles and lamps went flying. Their plates ended up broken on the floor, their half-eaten meals strewn all over the table and the wood and the walls. Fred squawked and flapped his wings, his evil work done, and then waddled off to the kitchen to terrorize the rabbits.

Once he was gone, Rosemary hovered her hands over the spilled wax and scattered lasagna, her eyes closed. "Something big is coming," she said ominously. "This is a bad omen."

"A bad omen for my stomach," added Eugene as he knelt to scoop his dinner off the floor.

"I think you better go," Esther said to Jonah.

Unsurprisingly, he did not protest.

OUTSIDE, THE NIGHT was warm and heavy with humidity. Crickets chirped in the oak trees. The nazars sang quietly.

"Do you ever hate your family?" Esther asked.

Jonah chuckled. "All the damn time. I think you can love people and still disapprove of stuff they do. Your family . . . they're weird but they love you."

"I know."

"So what's this about?" he said, taking out the semi-definitive list of worst nightmares he'd stolen from her at the bus stop. It was six years old, worn thin at the folds, the writing that detailed her fears going from barely legible chicken scratch (*3. Cockroaches*) to the slightly more legible entry she'd made in green ink the day before Jonah had stolen the list from her (*49. Moths and/also Mothmen*). Over the years, she'd taped on extra pieces of paper and bits of colored card so she had enough room to keep track of all the things that seemed scary enough that they could one day become a great fear. There were photographs and small diagrams and printed Wikipedia definitions and maps of streets/towns/countries/oceans to be avoided at all costs.

"Fears can't become full-blown phobias if you avoid them, and phobias can't kill you if you don't have them," she explained, taking the fragile document back from him. The list was a roadmap of the last six years of her life: darkness appeared at number two, around the same time Eugene developed his phobia of the night. Heights was number twenty-nine, after the first time they had been to New York and she had a panic attack at the top of the Empire State Building. Fear by fear, Esther had constructed a list of everything the curse could use to get to her, every weakness it could exploit to make its way into her bloodstream. She couldn't live like Eugene, or her father, or her mother, or her aunt, or her uncle (when he was alive), or her cousins, or her grandfather.

Three Solars had already been claimed by the curse:

1. Uncle Harold, Peter's brother, had been afraid
    of germs, and had died from the common cold.
    Eugene said this was a self-fulfilling prophecy,
    brought about by two decades of Harold taking
    unnecessary antibiotics, vacuum sealing his house
    so no outside air could get in, and wearing surgical
    masks wherever he went. So fragile was his immune
    system from lack of exposure to infection that a mild
    virus was eventually enough to do him in.

2. Martin Solar, Esther's cousin, had been afraid of bees. When he was fourteen, he'd disturbed a beehive while at summer camp and subsequently stumbled into a ravine as he tried to escape their stings. Eugene maintained that it was the ravine that had killed him, not the bees.

3. Reg's dog, Go Away, had been afraid of cats—which is exactly what had been chasing him when he darted out onto the road in front of a pickup truck.

Yes, the Solars died from their fears. Esther couldn't let herself get so deeply, bone-shakingly afraid of something that it took over her whole life and, eventually, led to her death. So every time she felt a twinge of fear in her gut at the thought of something, she put it on the list and avoided the item forevermore thereafter. If you didn't dwell on the anxiety, didn't indulge it, it couldn't get to you.

"I'm trying to outsmart the curse," she said. "I'm trying to hide from Death."

"You don't really believe that voodoo shit."

"Do I believe my grandfather genuinely met Death a handful of times and thus somehow cursed our family for eternity?" She wanted to say no, but Jonah Smallwood, with his coin-wide eyes and unfairly full lips, was hard to lie to. "I do. I believe. Eugene thinks it's just a silly tale, and that the Solars are predisposed to mental illness, but . . . Reg Solar is a compelling storyteller."

"So your grandpa says Death is a real person?"

"Yeah. They were, I don't know, like friends I guess. They met in Vietnam. Ran into each other a few times since then."

"So try and find him. Talk to him. Get him to lift the curse."

"You want me to go *looking* for Death?"

"Sure. If you really believe Death is just some dude walking around, some guy that actually *knew* your grandpa, then you can find him and talk to him."

"That makes a large amount of sense."

"Why's the top space empty?" The ink in number one had run from an old coffee stain, and the numeral was half eaten away by moths (hence their appearance at forty-nine on the list, furry *bastards*), but there was no fear recorded there.

"One great fear," she explained. "That's what you get cursed with. One great fear to rule your life and then take it. My granddad's afraid of water. My dad of leaving the house. Eugene of darkness. My aunt of snakes. My mom of bad luck. If I leave that slot empty, and put everything else below it . . ."

"Nothing can touch you?"

"Exactly. The list keeps me alive. I'm not more afraid of any one of these things than another. They act like a dam. A kind of levy to keep the big bad fear away."

"Have you forgotten about Katrina? Levies break."

"Thank you, Dr. Phil."

Jonah went down the porch stairs and walked through the trees toward his moped. Esther followed him. "Where did you go?" she asked him. "When you disappeared?"

Jonah shrugged. "I changed schools. Kids do that."

"Everything got so bad after you left. People got mean again, without you there."

"What are you talking about?"

"Do you remember how we met?"

"We were in the same class. Mrs. Price."

"No one ever talked to me or Heph. Before you, kids used to tell me how ugly I was. Red hair, thousands of freckles. I was always going to be bullied. And Hephzibah was an even easier target. Kids used to trip and hit her, just to try and get her to speak. No one would sit near us; they said my freckles and her muteness were diseases and they didn't want to catch them."

"Kids are assholes."

"Then one day at recess you sat down with us. You didn't say anything, you just ate your food and glared at every person who walked past, daring them to harass us. Within a week, you were one of my best friends."

"I remember that. We were the freaks. We had to stick together."

"Then you were gone. And Heph and I went back to being freaks on our own. We needed you, and you disappeared."

"I don't know what to say, Esther." Jonah ran his hands through his hair. "I'm sorry I wasn't there, but it wasn't my choice. I was eight. It wasn't my job to protect you."

Esther thought about her family as she watched him go. Eugene would die of the darkness. Her father would die in the basement. Her grandfather would drown. And one of these days, Rosemary Solar would cut herself on a broken mirror, or trip over a black cat, or walk under a ladder, only to have a great weight come crashing down on her moments later.

One great fear to rule your life. One great fear to take it. There was no escaping her fate, and no way to save the members of her family from theirs; this Esther's grandfather had told her since she was a child.

Unless . . . *Unless* . . .

"Where would you start?" she asked Jonah hurriedly as he lifted his moped off a knot of tree roots. "If you were looking for Death? If you wanted to find him so you could ask him a favor, where would you start?"

Jonah paused to think, then answered her question with another question. "What are you doing tomorrow?"

She thought about lying. It would be so easy to say, "Oh, I'm moving to Nepal for senior year to learn the ways of the Sherpa," and let Jonah forget that she existed. But she remembered, in that moment, the way he smelled at the warehouse last night, the truth of it, and how sad he'd looked when he thought Fleayoncé was dead in his arms, and—even though he'd robbed her and left her abandoned to walk home for three hours by herself in the rain— she didn't want to say good-bye to him. Not again. Not quite yet.

So she said, "Looking for Death."

And he said, "Sounds good."

"How?"

"You know that saying, 'You should do something every day that scares you'?"

"Yeah."

"That's how we find Death, I think. Everyone's afraid of dying, right? Maybe that's what attracts Death. Maybe that's what brings him to you. *Fear*. So that's what we do: we find him, we talk to him, we get him to lift the curse."

"No more great fears?"

"No more great fears. You in?"

Esther weighed her options. On the one hand was certain death, for herself and everyone she loved. For six years, she'd avoided everything that had sent even a twinge of fear up her spine in an attempt to save her own life. As long as you avoided the curse, it couldn't kill you, so charging headlong into the grip of fear seemed to border on insane.

But there was a chance, however small, that she could save everyone. Save Eugene from the dark. Save her mother from bad luck. Save her father from the basement. Save her grandfather from drowning—and that was a chance worth taking.

A small spark of what she would later recognize as bravery pinged up her spine as she nodded and said, "Yes."

Esther noticed, even though a breeze hummed through the trees, the nazars had gone silent, as though they approved of Jonah Smallwood's presence at the house. When he was gone, she added *lobsters* to her list, in fiftieth place, then went inside and checked eight times that all the doors were locked before going to bed.

7

1/50:

LOBSTERS

THE NEXT morning, Esther woke early and dressed in her grand-mother's egg-yolk-yellow 1960s stewardess uniform and waited for Jonah to arrive. Then she paced around the house for half an hour and decided to message him saying that she was sick, because maybe tempting Death wasn't such a great idea after all.

ESTHER:

I have contracted the measles.
Please don't come over.

Jonah didn't write back, so she assumed she was off the hook and wouldn't ever have to see him again, which left her both relieved and a tiny bit . . . sad? It was the last Sunday before school started up again after summer break, and she had a lot of baking to do if she was ever going to escape the gravitational pull of the black hole that was her hometown, but a small part of her had been curious about him. A small part of her felt calm when he was around. A small part of her missed him when he wasn't there.

Not ten minutes later there came the distinct sound of a moped parking outside her house. She dashed out onto the porch.

"You ever dress like a normal person?" was the first thing Jonah said when he saw her.

Esther regarded his clothes. "You do realize you look like you've been thrift shopping with Macklemore, right?" Then she remembered that she was *severely infected* and forced a cough. "I told you, I have the measles."

"You don't have the measles."

"I am *very ill* with the measles."

"You *do not* have the measles."

Esther threw her hands up in the air. "Fine! This is a stupid idea. I don't want to do it."

"That isn't an excuse I'm willing to accept."

"What *is* an excuse you're willing to accept?"

"That you urgently have to reupholster a couch."

"That's a weird excuse."

"Yeah, but it's not one you can use right now, so I'm sticking with it. Besides, you think I'm just gonna run out on my baby like that? Where's my little Fleayoncé? Tell her Daddy's here."

"Ugh. Fine. Come in. She's in the living room."

Esther believed that what Peter diagnosed as a concussion was probably going to be something more permanent. Already Fleayoncé's tongue lolled out of her mouth and her head was tilted, so that when she walked (which she hadn't quite yet mastered with the cast), she moved diagonally, as if her head was weighted on one side with sand. Jonah didn't seem to notice. They sat in the living room together and he fed the cat her kitten milk replacement with a syringe, drip by drip.

While he was feeding Fleayoncé, he looked around, taking in the bare walls, the clumps of candles and clusters of lamps in every corner of the room, the mound of cast-off furniture blocking the stairs, the sprigs of dried herbs hanging over every window and doorframe, the rabbit that had escaped the confines of the kitchen and was now gnawing at the foot of a sofa.

"Guessing you guys don't have many houseguests, huh?" he said.

"Oh no, we have parties here all the time. People just keep bringing lamps as gifts. It's becoming a real problem."

"Let me look at your list," he said, so she did. Jonah unfolded it gently and scanned, making comments like "hmmm" and "okay" and "not sure what that is, but sure." And finally, "Hell, I might have to sit that one out. That is actually some scary shit!"

"We'll work backwards," he said, and then he was handing the list back to Esther, who still didn't really understand what was going on.

Jonah set Fleayoncé down in her bed and handed Esther a helmet.

They drove for a while—or puttered, if you want to get technical—and ended up on the outskirts of the outskirts of the outskirts of town. The day was warm, the last of summer still clinging to everything. There wasn't much out there but fields of long sun-bleached grass swaying as if they were underwater. Jonah stopped in front of a sign that read: PRIVATE PROPERTY. TRESPASSERS WILL BE PROSECUTED.

"Where are we going?" Esther said as she (quite ungracefully) dismounted the moped and followed him past the sign into the brush beyond. At that moment, her brain decided to remind her that the Zodiac Killer had never been caught and—even though Jonah was *slightly* too young to have murdered eight people in the 1960s—to an anxious person, logic didn't matter. She fished her house keys out of her bag and held them in the webs of her fingers in case he tried to strangle her. They walked for ten minutes, and then fifteen minutes, treading a path that left scrapes on her legs and snagged long tendrils of red hair out from under her cap so that by the time they stopped she looked like a flight attendant who'd survived a plane crash.

And then, from close by, came the sound of water lapping at a shore. The shrubbery fell away and a clear water lake opened up before them. No one else was there. Sunlight sank through the mid-morning mist on the water and gave everything an amber glow. The white stone beach was littered with debris from the lake: seaweed, shells, bits of green glass rubbed smooth from the waves. The wind whistled. The water lapped. It was lovely, in a horror movie opening kind of way.

"You're not going to murder me, are you?" she asked, but Jonah was already getting organized (hopefully not to murder her). He took a GoPro out of his pocket and strapped it to his head.

"Where did you get that, I wonder?" she said.

69

"I *found* it," Jonah said.

"Yeah, found it in someone else's backpack."

"That's prejudiced."

"It's a comment based purely on past observation and personal experience."

"C'mon," he said, and then he was taking off his clothes, all of his clothes, down to his boxers, which Esther was *not* about to do, because a) stretch marks and cellulite and all that boring body image stuff, and b) she hadn't been aware that partial nudity was going to be required today, and thus had not worn her Very Nice Underwear, which she kept especially for Potential Sexual Encounters, the current tally of which stood at zero. Not that this constituted a Potential Sexual Encounter in any way, shape or form.

Esther smoothed down the front of her dress. "I will remain clothed, thank you."

To which Jonah replied, "Suit yourself. Ha. Get it? Suit yourself?" Then he ran back up the beach and foraged around in the grass and dragged out a rowboat painted pale blue and white, as pretty as a fondant cake. "You can float out in this," he said when he reached her again, breathless, his brown eyes wide with excitement. Esther found it ridiculous that someone with such a strong jaw and stubble could somehow look so young and vulnerable.

"How did you even know that was there?" she asked him.

"My mom used to bring us here when we were kids."

And that was how, on a warm late-summer morning two

days after he robbed her, Esther Solar rowed out into a lake with Jonah Smallwood while dressed as a flight attendant.

The boat had room enough for two, but Jonah swam by the side of it instead, and they went out, out, out until the mist swallowed the land and it was just them, two solitary humans in the bright abyss. The water was deep but clear, and Jonah dived every now and then, the GoPro still strapped to his head as he darted into schools of silver fish, his body a long shadow in the depths. The bottom was carpeted with swaying sea grass, the kind that was generally populated by great white sharks (unlikely in a lake, Esther knew—but she feared them even in swimming pools) and those freaky merpeople from Harry Potter. Esther was very happy to be in the boat.

Far out from the shore was a small karst island of white rocks that jutted out of the water like a single shark tooth. They moored the boat and Jonah sat in the shallows, looking down to the rocky lakebed. Esther looked too and saw dozens of hard-shelled bodies in dull green and vein blue. Crawfish.

Freshwater lobsters. The last fear added to her list. Jonah was going to set a crustacean on her.

She slapped her hands so hard over her eyes that her skin stung. "Don't you even *dare* think about bringing one of those things near me."

"Lobsters are mermaids to scorpions," Jonah said. She heard him slide into the water. "Why are you even scared of them?"

"One, they have claws. Two, they give you food poisoning.

Three, they look like the face huggers from *Alien*. Four, they have beady eyes. Five, that sound they make when you cook them."

"What sound?"

Esther made the hissing sound lobsters make when they're being cooked.

Jonah shook his head (or at least she imagined he shook his head; she still had her hands over her eyes). "You get yourself dunked in boiling water, see how you sound."

The boat rocked a little. Esther peeked between her fingers. A lobster had been placed on the seat across from her, its black beady eyes locked on hers. *I will kill everyone you love*, it rasped in lobster-tongue. Its antennae twitched. Esther stood up quickly. Lost her balance. Fell backward into the water. The lobster, she imagined, was pleased. She came up gasping, shocked at the cold of the water, at the depth of it, at the sudden panic that there might be freshwater sharks in the lake, or a school of piranha, or one of those flesh-eating parasites that crawls up your urethra when you pee and, like, lays eggs in your kidneys or whatever.

"Esther?" growled a quiet voice.

The lobster, was her first irrational thought. *It knows my name.* And then: *For the love of God, do not pee.*

She scrabbled to find her footing on the rocks and pushed a sopping curtain of hair out of her eyes. The rocks were too slippery to stand on, so she grabbed hold of the side of the boat and hauled herself up. Two lobsters were being held like puppets on the other edge of the boat.

And then Jonah's voice, with a terrible English accent reminiscent of the Impressive Clergyman from *The Princess Bride*:

"Two lobsters, both alike in dignity,
In this fair lake, where we lay our scene,
From ancient grudge break to new mutiny,
Where civil blood makes civil claws unclean."

"*What* are you doing?" she said. Esther could see almost nothing of Jonah, just his long dark fingers as he made the lobsters dance, made them kiss, made them dramatically commit suicide (i.e., plop back into the water), all over aquatically altered lines from *Romeo and Juliet*.

"Lobster Shakespeare," Jonah said. "Obviously."

"O happy claw," said Lobster Juliet in her shrill, offensively feminine voice. Lobster Romeo had already been dropped back into the water, where he'd quickly scuttled to the rocks, no doubt eager to spread his incredible tale of survival to the others. "This is thy sheath. There rust and let me die." Jonah mimed Lobster Juliet stabbing herself in the chest with her own claw, and then she, too, gasped and collapsed backward into the water and sank down, down, down to the white sandy bottom.

Jonah dragged himself up and hooked his arms over the side of the boat, mirroring Esther's pose, his grin mischievous.

"You're not funny," she said.

"Then why are you smiling?" he asked.

He had, she had to admit, a very good point.

After seeing them stripped of their dignity and resigned to their fate, the lobsters didn't seem quite so face-hugger-y. The two spent the next hour in the water, Esther still fully clothed, shoes and all. They dove down to see how long they could hold their breaths, how many lobsters they could catch by hand, how many they could carpet the bottom of the boat with. They climbed to the top of the rocky outcrop and cannonballed into the water and let themselves sink to the bottom, all the air pulled ragged from their lungs, and then they waited underwater for Death, but he didn't show.

In the end, the rowboat was alive with black beady eyes and wobbling antennae. Esther and Jonah were breathless, lungs aching, but alive. When the mist cleared, they floated on their backs in the last of the warm summer sunlight, and Death still didn't come looking for them, and it didn't escape Esther that Jonah was, in fact, not unfortunate looking, which she found more annoying than she should, mostly because you weren't supposed to have "that guy is actually mildly to moderately attractive" thoughts about people who'd both abandoned and swindled you.

They emptied most of their catch back into the water—all but an unlucky two. When Esther and Jonah grew hungry, they rowed to shore, where she lit a small fire on the beach. (Eugene, naturally, had passed on his fire-starting knowledge to her.) Jonah disappeared and reappeared ten minutes later with a pot, two plates, cutlery, candles, a picnic blanket, a loaf of bread, and a not-unimpressive selection of condiments, lobster sauce included.

"I found a lake house," he said as explanation.

"And it was . . . *deserted*?" she said hopefully.

"Yes. I definitely did not break and enter."

"*Jonah.*"

"What? We're only borrowing, I promise. Everything goes back after this. They won't even know. Besides, the doors weren't even locked. People who don't lock their doors are too rich to care if anything gets stolen."

"Yeah, or—hear me out here—they live on a large tract of private land and don't expect anyone to trespass."

They debated for a while about whether lobsters could feel pain and whether it was humane to plop them in boiling water or if they should sever their heads first or something. No conclusion could be reached on a nice way to kill the crustaceans, so they released them back into the water. The lobsters scuttled into the depths as fast as their little legs could carry them.

Esther and Jonah decided to eat the loaf of bread with the lobster sauce in lieu of eating the actual lobsters.

"We could do this, you know," Jonah said between mouthfuls. "Every Sunday for the next year. Fifty fears. Fifty weeks. Fifty videos." He tapped his GoPro. "What do you think?"

"Why are you filming exactly?"

Jonah lifted one shoulder in a casual half shrug. "Maybe I can use the footage to apply for film school scholarships one day. Then my dad would have to let me go."

"I better not see *any* of that footage on the internet. Ever. Promise me."

Jonah put his hand over his heart.

Esther thought about the offer he was making: a chance to have someone by her side as she worked her way through the list. A chance, however slim, to live a life without fear. But the challenge was harder than Jonah made it out to be. The curse was real to her, a weight she carried every day. The thing that would kill her was possibly on the list somewhere. Avoiding it meant a long life. Facing it meant fear, and ruin, and eventual death. Just because lobsters hadn't turned out to be her great fear didn't mean that snakes or heights or needles wouldn't be, and then, once she *knew*, once it *had* her, it would consume her from the inside out. "Fear has ruined the lives of all the people I love," she said finally. "I don't want to be like them. I don't think I want to find out what my great fear is. It's better to live in fear than to not live at all."

"What if you're not afraid of anything?"

"You're the one that said everyone's afraid of something."

"Yeah, but what if your great fear is of, like, Halley's Comet or something, and you spend your whole life avoiding all of this good stuff for no reason. Seems like a waste."

Esther had never thought of it like that before, and she had to agree, he had a point. Still, the risk was too great. "I can't," she said to him. "I just can't."

Jonah didn't cross *50. Lobsters* off the list now that it had been conquered. Instead he tore it off and shoved the little bit of paper in his mouth and chewed it up and swallowed it. "You'll be swayed. Once you see the footage, you'll be so swayed."

Death didn't come for them on the beach, or when they were riding Jonah's moped home, or later, when they didn't get food poisoning from the expired lobster sauce.

How Esther imagined it in her head: Death was busy most of that day with a car bomb in Damascus and a particularly stubborn widow who refused to shuffle off her mortal coil. Dark robes fell like tar over a skeleton as he moved silently down the hallway of a palliative care ward of a hospital. Eight foot tall, scythe in one hand, crow atop his shoulder, his darkness swelled until it filled the hall from floor to ceiling, but the nurses and visitors walking past him noticed nothing.

In her hospital bed, a white-haired woman, little more than animated dust now, woke with a start and stared wide-eyed at something she could feel more than she could see. She stretched and reached and grasped for the call button but it was no use. It was time. The Reaper was at the end of her bed, his cloak swirling around him like he was underwater even though there was no breeze. The woman raised her hand toward Death. She reached out to him, embracing him, ready for the pain to be—ah, no, wait, actually . . . she flipped him the bird.

The Grim Reaper spent the night by the woman's bedside, tapping his skeleton fingers on the metal railing of her bed, occasionally checking his watch, then tapping his fingers some more. The only reading material was a trashy magazine with the Kardashians on the cover. Death sighed and picked it up and started flipping through the pages.

It was going to be a long night.

THE NEXT MORNING, Esther was pulled from sleep by the sound of someone knocking on the front door (the doorbell had been disabled many years ago, around the same time the WELCOME mat was removed)—a noise capable of sending a chill of terror down the spines of all the inhabitants of her home. All of the morning sounds that had permeated the atmosphere seconds ago—the birdsong, the sizzle of butter frying in a pan, Eugene humming—went silent, as though the house itself had stopped breathing. It was a defensive tactic, like an animal hunted in the forest would use. Remain still. Remain silent. Wait for the threat to pass. Such a strategy was normally employed by people trying to avoid getting sucked into conversations with religious door-knockers or political canvassers.

Esther, too, had become part of this collective silence. She remained still in her bed, unbreathing, until the intruder's footsteps went down the stairs and across the oak-strewn lawn. Then came the distant sound of a moped starting, muffled by trees and the glass of her bedroom window. The house woke up again. Eugene scuttled down the hall. Fred crowed. Rosemary turned the stove back on. Esther imagined her mother crawling out from where she liked to hide, squirrelled away in the crawl space under the sink that she'd cleared out after watching *Panic Room* for the first time.

Someone opened the front door. This was followed by Eugene yelling: "Esther! Delivery!"

Esther got out of bed and went to find her brother in the kitchen. In his hand was a box wrapped in newspaper. On it was a quote written in thick black marker:

"Everything you want is on the other side of fear."
—Jack Canfield

"It's from Jonah," she said. She went back to her room and grabbed her phone. She already suspected what she'd find inside the box.

ESTHER:

I'm not watching the video.

JONAH:

Why not?

ESTHER:

Because I shall not be swayed.

JONAH:

You'll be swayed. Oh girl, you'll be so swayed.

Esther didn't watch the video. She would not be swayed.

THE LOCKER BANDIT

THAT MORNING, Esther brewed her coffee with Red Bull instead of water. "I wish to enter the fourth dimension," she explained to Eugene. He screwed up his face as she sipped her chemical concoction while sitting cross-legged on the kitchen floor. Laid out on a picnic blanket before her was the swag she intended to smuggle and sell that week, everything she had baked the night before: a dozen double chocolate fudge brownies, peppermint shortbread, two dozen cookies, two dozen Rice Krispies Treats, and one entire caramel tart. She wrapped each piece individually and stuffed everything she could carry into her backpack.

Late last year, an inexplicable spike in adolescent obesity (despite the changes in the cafeteria) had led to rumors among the faculty that Cakenberg was dealing sugary treats to the student population. Esther couldn't afford to get caught; getting caught would mean suspension, and suspension would mean the end of her little business. In the last year, she'd made a decent profit—not enough, yet, to get her to college, get her out, but a couple thousand dollars, enough for an emergency fund.

When the batch was ready to be smuggled, she went upstairs and dressed as Eleanor Roosevelt. Three strands of pearls at her neck, hair pinned off her face in curls, legs encased in sheer hose, sensible brown shoes fit for wartime. Esther liked to dress as powerful women—it made her feel powerful in turn, like stepping into their skin. One needed to feel formidable on the first day of school. Who better to go into battle than Eleanor Roosevelt? (Well, Genghis Khan, maybe, but the goal was to survive the day with dignity, not rape and murder the entire student population and take over their lockers through sheer brute force to ensure that all subsequent generations of seniors shared her DNA. Eleanor seemed the safer option.)

On the ride to school, Eugene seemed quieter than usual, which meant that Eugene wasn't speaking at all. Whenever they stopped at traffic lights, he would press his thumb deep into the raw burn on his palm, though he never flinched with pain. Sometimes he slipped into a shadow that was inside his own head, where not even the brightest light could reach. Esther didn't know how to help him, so she simply put her hand on his forearm as he drove and hoped that would be enough to communicate how much she loved him.

They picked Heph up on the way to school, and she drifted down to the car from her house, tall and gangly and ghostlike as ever.

"How did your adventure with Jonah go?" she signed.

"I no longer fear lobsters," Esther said.

Hephzibah's eyes widened. "It worked? That's fantastic!"

"Don't get too excited. I'm not doing it again."

"Why not?"

"Because it's too dangerous, tempting fate like that."

Hephzibah gave a disapproving glance, but Esther looked away from her before she could sign something too sensible and/or inspirational about facing her fears.

As Eugene turned the familiar corners that would take them closer and closer to the school grounds, Esther began to sweat. It always happened like this. Every school day. First the sweating, then the fidgeting, then the hammering heart and the hand that closed around her throat and choked her words before they could get out of her mouth. Esther pictured herself as she knew her classmates saw her: ugly and imperfect and too weird to be allowed. Red hair, unbrushed, falling in wild tendrils past her hips because the length of it made her feel safe and she was too scared to get it cut. Skin flushed with freckles, not the cute smattering on the cheeks that some people had, but dots so thick and dark they made her look diseased. Hand-sewn clothes, the stitches as flawed and lacking as she was.

To try and calm herself, Esther unfolded and read the note Rosemary had written for her. The same one she wrote at the beginning of every school year.

To Whom It May Concern:

*Please excuse Esther from participating in any
and all class discussions, presentations, and sports
activities. Please do not call on her or single her
out in class, read her work in front of other
students, or go out of your way to acknowledge
her existence in general.*

*Warm regards,
Rosemary Solar*

Esther held the note tightly and took a deep breath. One more year of people staring. One more year of people laughing. One more year of desperately trying to disappear.

When she got to school, she went to her locker before first period to store her baked goods so she wouldn't have to walk around all day smelling like a vanilla-scented criminal.

"You sneaky son of a bitch," she muttered when she opened it.

There, sitting solitary in the middle of her securely padlocked locker, was a single raspberry Fruit Roll-Up.

9

THE TERRIBLE SECRET
OF DAVID BLAINE

THE REST of the week went like this: On Tuesday, Esther put a second padlock on her locker in addition to the first, a combination one this time, something that Jonah couldn't pick. In the afternoon, she discovered three more Fruit Roll-Ups in her locker, along with her grandmother's stolen bracelet. The locks didn't appear to have been tampered with.

On Wednesday: her library card, a copy of *Romeo and Juliet* from said library (which now had two lobsters in Elizabethan clothing on the front cover instead of people), and seven Fruit Roll-Ups.

On Thursday: Eugene helped Esther seal her locker with industrial strength magnets and a new padlock. By this point in time, the legend of Jonah Smallwood, apparent master thief, had spread throughout the school, and a small group of people huddled outside her locker after last period waiting to see if he'd been able to break in today. Esther hated being observed by them, until she realized they weren't watching *her*—they were there for the magic show. Inside her locker—a dozen Fruit Roll-Ups and fifty-five dollars in an envelope.

"That guy is *good*," said Daisy Eisen.

"I'm getting a David Blaine vibe here," Eugene said seriously. The twins firmly believed that Blaine was capable of performing genuine magic.

"It's possible," Esther conceded with a grin.

On Friday: Thank God she'd shifted her entire haul of illegal baked goods, because now even some of the faculty had come to watch the unlocking of her locker. She'd duct-taped it shut that morning to prevent tampering. The locker still looked untouched, but when she sliced open the tape with a pair of nail scissors borrowed from her English teacher, a small avalanche of Fruit Roll-Ups spilled onto the floor. The crowd cheered. There, wedged in between her biology and math textbooks, was the unopened box that he'd delivered to her house on Monday morning.

"I'm fairly sure this constitutes harassment," she said as she prized out the newspaper-wrapped box with the stupid inspirational quote written on it.

"Only if you're not enjoying it," signed Hephzibah.

"God, Hephzibah, you're so wise." Because she *was* enjoying it. Seeing Jonah's handiwork was like having her own personal magic show every day.

Esther put the box into her bag and drove home with Eugene and Heph, wondering if Jonah Smallwood was sprinkled with some kind of enchanted dust as a child.

ONCE she was in her room, she messaged him.

ESTHER:

Did you break into my house?

JONAH:

No! Your mom got the box from your room. I didn't go snooping or anything.

ESTHER:

How'd you know I hadn't opened it yet and had just decided to never see you again?

JONAH:

'Cause if you had, you would've already sent me a message that said: "I'll see you on Sunday."

ESTHER:

So cocky.

JONAH:

Open the box.

ESTHER:

This had better not be Gwyneth Paltrow's severed head.

Esther unwrapped the newspaper. Inside was a box, inside of which was a thumb drive.

ESTHER:

Are you trying to infect my laptop with a virus?

JONAH:

My dastardly plan has been foiled.

ESTHER:

I can almost promise you this won't sway me.

JONAH:

Key word: almost. Now watch the damn clip, woman.

So she did. She plugged the thumb drive into her laptop and when the media player opened, she hit play.

The clip was short—two minutes and thirty-seven seconds to be precise—but it was beautiful. Where Jonah acquired the necessary cinematography skills to make GoPro footage look like a movie trailer she wasn't entirely sure, but he had, and it did. The background was muted and misty, but Esther was bright. She shone like the sun, caked in butter. Her hair was spun sugar. Her eyes were blue candies. He'd edited the footage to create a short story. Like they were intrepid teen explorers, plunging out into the unknown to face their fears.

Jonah filmed Esther mostly in moments when she hadn't realized she was being filmed. When she'd floated in the water alongside the boat, her hair fanned out around her like a mermaid, looking particularly odd because she was fully clothed and fully shoed, a lobster resting in each of her palms. The goddess of crustaceans, our lady of hard exoskeletons. And then the last shot: her, on her front porch, her hair a damp twist of red sorbet, freckles bright across her cheeks, grinning into the camera.

"What are we, Esther Solar?" came Jonah's voice from offscreen.

"Fear eaters," she said. Except it wasn't her who said it, or at least not how she remembered herself saying the words. She remembered being weirded out by Jonah's paper eating, but this Esther . . . this Esther on-screen was part wolf, her breath hot and her eyes wide with fire. She'd never seen herself this way before. Sometimes, when she looked in the mirror, she faded at the edges. Not like Eugene, not like how he flickered in and out of existence. Her edges were soft, and her color was dim, and sometimes little particles of her dusted off and bled out into the air. But not in the video. In the video she was whole and solid and the saturation had been turned way up so that the freckles on her skin looked like a flurry of fall leaves.

1/50 said the final frame.

"Every Sunday for the next year," Jonah had said at the lake. "Fifty fears. Fifty weeks. Fifty videos. Fifty chances to meet Death personally and ask him to break the curse."

Esther picked up her phone and sent him a message that was only five words long.

I'll see you on Sunday.

10

THE FORTY-NINTH fear on Esther Solar's semi-definitive list of worst nightmares was moths, thanks to the repeated watching of *The Mothman Prophecies* and *The Silence of the Lambs*, and one particularly traumatic run-in with a common house moth when she was in middle school. (The insect flew into her mouth.)

Esther sat on her front porch in the rain, elbows resting on her knees, dressed as Jacqueline Kennedy Onassis. Her semi-definitive list of worst nightmares was folded open next to her. *49. Moths and/also Mothmen* was circled.

Jonah pulled up on his moped and ran through the rain with his hands over his head. Esther was relieved to see that he had not, in fact, dressed as the Mothman, which was much appreciated.

"Damn, Jackie O," he said when he saw her. "Not enough people can pull off white gloves these days." Then he sat next to her, not so close that he was touching her, but close enough that she could feel the warmth radiating off him as his skin dried his damp clothes. He smelled intensely of himself and was, like her, dressed for another decade, with orange corduroy pants and a pale blue silk shirt with ruffles, his hair a thicket atop his head.

"Pretty sure I told you I was reupholstering a couch today," she said, tapping her phone. Esther had sent the message when she woke up that morning in a panic that she would have to see him again. It seemed worth a shot. After he hadn't replied, she'd resigned herself to the fact that Jonah Smallwood was a parasite who could not easily be shaken off, and had come to sit on the porch to wait for him in an ever-increasing state of dismay.

"Which is why I brought this," he said, unzipping his back-pack and spinning a staple gun around his fingers.

"Are you ever going to let me skip a fear?"

"Nope."

"What excuse can I try next week?"

"You have to graffiti public property."

"That's not fair. You know I won't do that."

Jonah grinned. "Yeah, that's the point."

Cut to: A shot of Jonah and Esther from behind, now inside her house, kneeling in front of a ratty sofa. He turned to her, in profile, and said, "Did you really go out and buy a couch to reup-holster just so you wouldn't have to face your fear of moths?"

Esther turned to him. Their faces were very close together. "I found it on the street and dragged it two blocks to my house, but yes."

"That's nasty. This couch is definitely some kind of crime scene."

"Which is why we have to reupholster it," she said, holding up the empty staple gun and clicking it twice.

Three and a half hours later, Jonah, Eugene, and Esther were sitting on the reupholstered couch. It was hideous, a lumpy, yellow, floral monstrosity. They were not very good upholsterers. Or perhaps they were excellent upholsterers, but the couch was simply beyond redemption.

Either way, the situation wasn't good, couch-wise. Fleayoncé didn't seem to mind too much, though. She sat on Jonah's shoulder, purring like an idling lawnmower while he played absentmindedly with her ears. A long tentacle of drool hung from one side of her mouth.

They were watching *The Mothman Prophecies* and passing a bowl of popcorn among them.

"Where did this hideous couch come from?" Eugene asked between mouthfuls of popcorn. Esther and Jonah both shrugged without looking away from the screen. It was up to the part where that one dude, Gordon, gets a prophecy from his sink that ninety-nine will die. Jonah paused the movie.

"You want me to believe you're scared of some talking sink?" he said.

"That sink, with the help of moths, predicted the murder of ninety-nine people," Esther said.

"Psychic sinks are not to be trifled with," Eugene added.

"Punk ass sink needs to sit down and reevaluate its life choices. C'mon. Enough procrastinating. Let's go find some moths."

"Are you sure you don't want to watch *The Silence of the Lambs* first?" Esther asked hopefully.

"Nah."

"Fine. But if my sink starts making prophecies, you'll be the first to hear about it."

"Eugene, man, do you wanna come with?" Jonah said.

"Where are you going?"

Jonah whispered something in his ear. Eugene shivered. "God. No."

That's how she knew it was going to be bad.

THEY ARRIVED at the butterfly sanctuary midafternoon. It was a great glass structure, like a greenhouse only larger, and so packed with plants it looked like part of the set from *Jurassic World*. There was an admission fee, but Jonah said, "Yeah, I didn't think so." Instead they found a side door, and much to the protest of Esther's wildly beating heart, snuck in without paying.

"Let the record state that I am deeply dismayed at this blatant disregard for the rules," she said, but Jonah shushed her as he strapped the GoPro to his forehead.

"Would you shut up for two seconds and look at where you are?"

So she did shut up. And she did look at where she was.

Arching over them was a tall glass ceiling, hundreds and hundreds of shards held up by a white frame. There was a gazebo, a pond, a small bridge crossing over a stream, an unsettlingly large moth sculpture, thickets of ferns and flowers, and a grassy area where children were playing. And there were butterflies *every-where*. Mostly orange ones—monarchs, she vaguely remembered them being called from elementary school—that were so abundant they made the trees appear as if fall was already here.

Jonah did his typical Jonah schtick; he led her around the sanctuary and narrated every species of butterfly they saw in a not unreasonable impersonation of David Attenborough, and Esther laughed.

Until they got to the moths.

The moths, antisocial assholes that they were, had their own small section at the back of the sanctuary, for two reasons:

1. Moths were evil and therefore probably plotting the downfall of all the more attractive butterflies, and thus needed to be kept contained like any villain worth their salt.

2. Nobody went to a butterfly sanctuary to see moths, and the moths knew it, which had only contributed to their general evilness.

It was a vicious cycle, really. The hate only led to more hate, but she couldn't help it. Moths were nasty.

They ventured into moth territory and already she was drawing deeper breaths, because no insect had a right to be that *chunky*. They were huge and hairy and had these powerful-looking legs and furry antennas. There were all different species of all different sizes. There were even some of the death's-head moths, the ones with the little skulls on their backs, which was sufficient enough evidence for her that moths were portents of doom and shouldn't be messed with.

Esther did her best to move as little as possible. Jonah, on the other hand, was fascinated.

A furry white moth flitted over to land on his hand, this beast of a thing with black button eyes. Jonah stroked it. Straight up ran his finger down its back, like it was a miniature puppy. "Kinda looks like a Pokémon," he said, holding it at eye level to inspect it closer. "Bring me the eagles," he whispered. "Show me the meaning of haste!" Then he threw it up into the air and it flittered away to go and do moth pastimes. Like crawling into the mouths of corpses and terrorizing small towns.

"Tolkien knew a lot of stuff, but he knew nothing about the dark souls of moths. No way a moth would've helped Gandalf," Esther said. "Least believable part of Middle-earth."

"Your turn," Jonah said, pointing to the largest moth in the enclosure, a brown monstrosity with wing patterns that would have made a nice wall hanging for Urban Outfitters.

"I am *not* touching that thing."

"That's what she said."

"Gross."

"C'mon, they aren't skittish. Not like it's gonna get up in your face or anything. It's the butterflies you gotta watch out for."

"I'll do it on one condition."

"Okay."

"Tell me how you got into my locker every day."

"A magician never reveals his secrets."

"Good thing you're a pickpocket and not a magician then."

Jonah smiled as the big moth crawled onto his hand, flapped its big wings a few times, and then settled there. "Hephzibah gave me the combos to the locks and helped me with the tape."

"That *weasel*. And the magnets?"

"Eugene makes a good double agent."

"I'm surrounded by traitors."

Jonah held out the moth to her. "They both think you facing your fears is a really good idea."

"Hypocrites!" she shouted. Then she put one hand over her mouth to: a) stop herself from vomiting, b) stop herself from hyperventilating, and c) stop herself from screaming. "Oh my god," she said through her fingers. "It's so big."

"That's *also* what she said."

"Shut up or I'll punch you again."

"Please, spare me the pain." Like with the last moth, Jonah ran his finger down this one's back. As she looked into its big beady eyes, Esther supposed that the insect didn't really seem *that* evil.

"Poor moths got the real short end of the stick," Jonah said. "Everyone's always talking about butterflies and their effect. What about moths? What happens if they flap *their* wings? All moths get is some Richard Gere movie."

He held the insect out to Esther again, and she let it amble onto her hand; to its credit, it didn't do anything for the next few minutes except chill there. When she finally admitted that okay, maybe moths weren't *that* bad, maybe they were kind of cute, Jonah coaxed it back onto his fingers and set it back on a tree branch.

"Split?" said Jonah.

"The torture's over already?" she asked. "Hell yeah."

As they headed toward the exit in the main butterfly area, a kid tripped and slammed into the base of a tree, which sent the monarchs up in a storm of orange. The whole greenhouse seemed to take to the air, as if gravity had been momentarily suspended. All the adults in the general vicinity ran to the aid of the screaming (and therefore clearly alive) child, as Esther and Jonah turned in slow circles, staring up through the growing firestorm. She put her hand up into the burst, so bright and frantic that she wondered if it would burn her. They moved like slow birds, churning upward toward the sun as a single creature. One butterfly landed on her outstretched fingers, and then another, and then another, before they too were swept up in the tornado.

A few minutes passed before all the butterflies were settled enough to land, once again bringing premature fall to the greenery.

"*That,*" she said, "was insane."

"Hey! Hey, you two! You need to come to the front office and pay your admission fee!"

"Oh shit, run," Jonah said, already bounding toward the exit.

Esther was not a runner. She was more of a shot put kind of girl. Still, in times of absolute need, she was able to improvise, and since going to jail for the second time in as many weeks didn't seem worth it for an illicit visit to a butterfly farm, she followed Jonah. He threw open the side door and they plunged out into the bucketing rain and ran and ran and ran. There was far too much running associated with this boy as far as she was concerned, but Jonah was loving it, sprinting through the rain and clicking his heels as they made their great escape. Esther did the best she could to keep her cleavage from detaching by holding her hands to her chest.

They came to a stop under a tree and waited to see if the butterfly guy had followed them, but who was gonna chase two teenage hoodlums through the rain for minimum wage? And for that matter, how many people were so desperate to look at butterflies that they broke into the butterfly sanctuary? Couldn't be many.

Esther peeled off her white gloves. Her pillbox hat was missing, lost somewhere along the getaway. Her Jackie O costume was soaked.

"Why is it I always end up wet when you're around?" she said as she wrung out her gloves. Jonah collapsed to the damp grass, flat on his face, unable to breathe from laughing so hard before Esther realized what she'd said. "Oh God. Oh God," she muttered as she walked quickly back into the rain, her cheeks tight and burning.

Through gasped breaths, Jonah yelled, "Wait, wait!" She didn't wait, but he caught her anyway and buried his head into her shoulder and was still laughing, the bastard.

"Sorry I get you wet all the time," he said.

"It's not funny!" She yanked her shoulder away from him. "You're not funny!"

"It's a *little* funny."

"I'm going home."

"You gonna walk all the way there in the rain? 'Cause I'm not game to get my moped back until they're closed."

"That's what I did the night you *mugged* me."

"*Pickpocketed*, Esther. I *pickpocketed* you. Don't say mugged. You make me sound like a thug. Pickpocketing requires finesse."

"Whatever. I'm calling my mom. Maybe she can give us both a lift." Esther knew that Rosemary wouldn't answer, not if she was at the slots, but she rang her three times anyway. "I can't get a hold of her."

"You can come to my house if you want. 'Til the storm finishes. It's not far from here. We can walk."

"Yeah?"

"It's just . . . It's not *nice*."

"Neither is my house."

"Yeah, but this is different."

"It's up to you."

Jonah rubbed the side of his neck. Esther thought, for a moment, that he would say no. But then he looked up from the sidewalk, his uncertainty replaced by a grin. A grin that she noticed, for the first time, had a layer of sadness behind it. "Let's get you out of those wet clothes," he said, rubbing the material of her sleeve between his fingers. "Maybe you should bring spares from now on. You know, if you're always going to end up wet around me."

"Are you ever going to let me live that down?"

"Don't think so, Solar. Don't think so at all."

11

SHAKESPEARE, STARS, AND AN AQUATIC OPTIMUS PRIME

"NOT FAR from here," as it turned out, was an overstatement. Jonah's house wasn't much closer to the center of town than Esther's, but the subdivision was newer. His street was nice, but his house looked more sad and disheveled than the rest, like one of the starters you move into at the beginning of *The Sims* when you've got no money, six children, and no other choice.

They didn't go inside. They ran through the rain to the backyard. The lawn backed onto unkempt wilderness; the grass was taller than Esther's head.

Jonah let her in the door to the screened-in back porch.

"Well, this is my kingdom," he said, taking off his wet jacket.

Esther took off her dripping jacket and wrung out her hair and tried to find something safe to start a conversation with. She didn't stare at the fist-sized hole punched through the plasterboard, or how one of the screens had been boarded up with cardboard and duct tape. Her eye was taken and held by the walls and ceiling. Every square inch of available space was painted. The ceiling was a sea scene in swirling green and bright coral, *Starry Night* if it were an ocean. In the eddies were mermaids and fish and sharks and, strangely, Optimus Prime with a tail. Jonah saw her staring at it.

"It's not as bad as it looks. We just try to hang out here and stay out of Holland's way," he said as he pulled blankets down from the top of a bookshelf. "My sister Remy likes pictures, so I paint her what she wants. Sometimes that means giving Transformers gills."

There were the stories from Esther's own childhood, mixed with the tales of a kid who'd either a) grown up too fast, or b) had impeccable taste in entertainment, depending on your perspective on what's appropriate for elementary schoolers. There was a picture of Vincent Vega holding a gun to Oscar the Grouch's head, Ryuk from *Death Note* hovering in one corner, and Deadpool singing Christmas carols with Justin Bieber.

Even patches of the floor had been painted so that it appeared the walls were waterfalls.

And behind her, painted on the door that led into the rest of the house, was the Grim Reaper from Esther's head: darkly robed, dripping tar, scythe resting gently in his long-boned hands. But— like every other story on the walls—this one had been changed, hybridized, made ridiculous. Death wore a flower crown of orange and purple blooms, and around his neck was strung a plaque that read: BALL SO HARD MUHFUCKAS WANNA FIND ME. Two small figures danced at his feet, tying his toe bones up in a web of twine:

a small, peach-haired girl and a small, dark-skinned boy. Both tricksters. Both unafraid of Death.

"Oh yeah. The newest edition," Jonah said, and his voice was strange, almost like he was . . . sheepish? Since when was Jonah Smallwood *sheepish*? He cleared his throat. "I, uh . . . I kind of painted that one for you."

Esther had already guessed this, because although the Reaper took up the whole door, it was the girl—no larger than a forearm—who shone with the most detail. The outline of her body was spun gold, and even the numerous freckles that dotted her skin glistened in the light.

Esther was pretty sure most teenage girls had fantasied about the idea of some guy painting a goddamn *mural* with them in it, but this was dangerous territory. Murals were a well-known gateway drug to feelings, and she couldn't have any of that. Losing him the first time had sucked, and had taught her a valuable life lesson: If you didn't let people get close to you, they couldn't hurt you when they left. So that's what she'd done, and what she intended to continue doing now.

You couldn't tell people that when they'd painted you into a mural, though. You couldn't immediately throw the gesture back in their face and be all like, "Sorry, but I'm far too emotionally damaged for my likeness to be included in murals." So she said, as he draped a blanket around her shuddering shoulders, "It's beautiful." Because it was.

Outside, the sun was setting, its dull orange beams leaking

through the screens of the porch, casting their long shadows on the wall so that they were taller than the Reaper. For a moment they were very close together, her chest almost pressed to his, both larger than Death, and she supposed it would be very easy to kiss him, and she thought he very much wanted her to, but she didn't. Mural notwithstanding.

When the sun set, they turned on the lights and lay on the floor together, staring up at the ceiling. Jonah pointed out all the little hidden Easter eggs around the room that she'd missed the first time around. He had been working on the painting for years, he told her, changing parts of it every few weeks. There were constellations up there, hidden in the tumbling waves, one for his sister and his mother and himself. Jonah pointed them out. Virgo. Scorpio. Cancer. He couldn't always be there to read to Remy or help her with her homework, so he did the next best thing—he gave her the stars.

"Tell me about them," Esther said, so he did, smiling to himself as he talked. His mom, Kim, had died in a car accident nine years ago. Esther, who'd only met her a handful of times as a child, remembered her as a short yet commanding woman whose laugh was so ridiculous and infectious it would leave anyone in the room smiling. Jonah said she liked to wear coral: coral clothes, coral shoes, coral lipstick. She liked the way the color popped against her black skin, said it made her feel like a sunrise.

Remy, now nine, was her mother all over: fiercely intelligent, a little rebellious, halfway obsessed with Shakespeare. She was independent during the day but at night she demanded to be within hand-holding distance of Jonah at all times.

"Why you wear costumes everywhere, Jackie O?" he said when he'd finished.

Esther didn't want to tell Jonah the truth. That the costumes were, in part, because of him. After he left elementary school, left her to the cruelty of their classmates, she couldn't bear it anymore. Couldn't bear the name-calling, and the unkind laughter, and the way eyes left hot tracks on her body as they moved across her skin. People were going to tease her no matter how she dressed, so one morning not long after Jonah disappeared, Esther decided to dress as someone else entirely: a witch.

Kids were still mean, but somehow, when she was in costume, it hurt less. The words were meant for whatever character she was outfitted as, not Esther herself; eyes and words slid over her, a weapon glancing off armor.

And then later, when the curse had befallen her brother and mother and father, Esther *kept* wearing the costumes as a way to hide from fear. Death was looking for Esther Solar; as long as she never dressed as herself, she hoped he'd always have trouble finding her.

Esther wouldn't tell Jonah this though, of course, so she gave him the only explanation that made sense to her: "I guess I don't like people . . . looking at *me*."

"Got a funny way of showing it." He ran his fingers over the pearls at her neck. "You stand out in a crowd. People look at you everywhere you go."

"Yeah, but they don't see *me* when they look at the costumes. They see a historical figure or a cartoon character or whatever."

"I see you."

Esther laughed. "No, you don't."

"Yeah I do."

"Then you see way too much."

"You wanna see what I see?"

"What are you gonna do, draw me like one of your Optimus Primes?"

"Why not?" he said, and then he stood and disappeared through the Death door into the dark house. "Close your eyes," he said a few minutes later. There were footfalls, a door closing, the sound of something heavy scraping against the wooden floor. "Okay, open."

Esther opened her eyes. Jonah had set up an easel in the corner of the room and draped it with a sheet so that she couldn't see the size or shape of the canvas.

"How long will it take?" she said. "Can I move?"

"I'm thinking it'll take a while, so yeah, you can move."

A little girl wandered out of the house then—Remy, she assumed—and came to sit on Jonah's lap while he painted. She looked so much like him: warm black skin, dark hair, full lips, wide brown eyes that made her kind of appear like she'd been drawn for a Disney movie. Remy giggled as she looked from the canvas to Esther. Jonah put his finger to his lips—not shushing her, but asking her to share the secret—and she grinned widely and slipped out of his fingers and went into the backyard to play. Esther co-cooned the blanket around herself and sat in a chair by one of the screens and leaned on the sill and watched Jonah's sister, as quiet as she'd ever heard a child play.

She wondered how he'd paint her. As Eleanor Roosevelt? As a '60s flight attendant? As Little Red Riding Hood? Optimus Prime with gills? And then she started to worry. What if the version he painted was not how she thought of herself at all? Worse yet, what if he painted her *exactly* as she thought of herself, all freckled and awkward and anxious about everything? In truth, she wanted to see what Jonah saw, because she didn't know anymore. She didn't know what was left under the costumes she wore every day.

It was a short session, only twenty minutes, because the front door slammed and a light turned on in the belly of the house and the sound of heavy footsteps came from the hall, which made Jonah jump and say, "You should probably leave."

"Can I see it?" Esther asked as he dumped all of his paints and brushes in a corner and covered them with a sheet.

"It's not finished yet."

"When will it be done?"

"When you're ready to see it."

"You're so cryptic."

The storm had long passed and their clothes were almost dry, so she shrugged off the blanket and snuck out the back door with him. Remy watched them go. Esther waved good-bye. Remy didn't wave back.

"Wait for me at the end of the street," Jonah said when he let her out the side gate.

Esther wandered in the warm, damp evening, her jacket slung over her shoulder, and watched as the clouds peeled back in strips to reveal the stars. Then she stood under a streetlamp, walking in slow circles around the perimeter of light. Occasionally she let her fingertips drift out into the darkness, to see if she could feel what Eugene felt in the shadows.

They weren't empty, he said. There were things that moved in the dark that only he could see. Only he could hear. Terrible, thin creatures that lurked in the dim corners of his bedroom, waiting for him to fall asleep. And right at the moment he couldn't keep his eyes open anymore, that's when they came for him. Sometimes he saw them, watching him. Sometimes he felt them resting heavily on the end of his bed, even when the lights were on. Crawling up his body. Sitting on his chest and draping their long black hair over his face.

Eugene said it was sleep paralysis. A trick of the mind. Esther knew it was the curse.

A dog barked down the street. Esther snatched her hand back, afraid that something would clamp down on her fingers and drag her into the abyss.

"Scared the dark will bite you?" Jonah said from behind her, and she jumped.

"Don't do that." She looked back at his house. "Why are we sneaking around like the von Trapp family fleeing Austria?"

"Give me the list."

She did. Jonah tore off *49. Moths*, struck a match, and set the little piece of paper alight in his hands.

"Not gonna eat it this time?"

"It occurred to me after I ate it that that paper was super old and probably nasty as hell. If I die of Ebola or something, I'm coming back to haunt you."

"I don't think you can get Ebola from eating paper." *49. Moths* burned, flickered, turned to ashes in a couple of seconds. Esther felt herself being released from her fear of moths. They both watched the particles drift into the night sky, and she thought, for the first time, that this might actually work. "So, when do I get to see the footage from today?"

"In about forty-eight weeks."

"What?"

"That's the deal. You don't get to see the rest of my genius filmmaking skills until the end. I need some kind of bargaining chip to keep you coming back every Sunday, Solar."

"Why are you even doing this? I mean, what do you get out of it?"

Jonah seemed to think very carefully about his answer. "You've seen my house. I know what it's like to live in fear. I can't help my sister, not yet, but I can help you."

That was just about the best reason Esther could think of.

They walked back to the now-closed butterfly farm and Jonah drove her home in the muggy nighttime.

"See you on Sunday," he said when he parked in front of her house, which was bright as ever on the dark street.

"Sorry. I'm busy this Sunday. I have to urgently deface public property."

Jonah grinned. "I'll believe that when I see it."

Esther went inside, and even though every light was taped on, and even though Peter was a pasty basement dweller, and even though Rosemary was at the casino and wouldn't be back for hours, and even though Eugene said there were demons waiting in the dark for all of them, and even though Fred the rooster was in the kitchen pecking at ants and screeching at the rabbits because he was terrified of them, and even though the upstairs was blocked with shopping carts and furniture and there was potentially a vengeful ghost up there, she felt safe. She didn't fear the slam of front doors or the sound of heavy boots, and despite how weird her family was, she'd never really stopped to appreciate that before.

That night, she only checked that all the doors were locked five times before she went to bed.

12

THE STORAGE KING

HEPHZIBAH HADID, as previously mentioned, had been Esther's best friend since elementary school. How does a selective mute make and maintain a friendship? Well for starters, she picked the weirdest kid in class with a severely overactive imagination. At six years old, Esther Solar had only three things on her mind:

1. Building a giant castle fort from sand and filling the basement of said fort with money printing machines, thus beginning her ascent to Emperor of the World.

2. In the event that the fort couldn't be built, she was happy to settle for a small, candlelit pit under her grandparent's house. She drew up plans and even started digging it herself. Apparently she was easily appeased.

3. Becoming a Jedi.

Esther didn't have a very firm grasp on reality, so accepting that Heph was her imaginary friend wasn't outside the realm of possibility for her at the time. By the time she found out Heph was, in fact, a real human being, she'd grown too attached to her to be mad that they'd accidentally become friends.

So how does a kid become a selective mute? Esther had looked it up on Wikipedia, and found out that selective mutism was a social anxiety disorder. Now, you might be thinking, "Well, Hephzibah obviously had a traumatic childhood, that's why she doesn't speak at school." Alas, you're wrong. Kids with selective mutism aren't more likely to have suffered trauma than kids without it, and they're almost always self-confident in other situations (i.e., at home). Besides, Heph's parents were pretty awesome, even if they did float around the house like tall, airy ghosts, just like her. The most traumatic experiences they'd inflicted on their child were naming her Hephzibah (which, admittedly, was probably pretty traumatic) and letting her dress herself (again, quite traumatic). But apart from that they were solid folk and Heph was normal and happy.

After she discovered other people could also see Hephzibah, Esther invited her over to her house in the afternoons after school, and since they couldn't really communicate, they played lots of computer games and watched movies. Esther had to credit Heph with sparking her obsessive love of costumes. This was back in the late '00s, so people still bought these archaic shiny disc things called "DVDs." If there's one thing the rise and rise of Netflix had negatively impacted, it was the abundance of DVD extras, including but not limited to director and actor commentaries and interviews with costume designers.

It was Heph who bumped the remote twenty minutes into a planned 653-minute *Lord of the Rings* extended edition marathon and switched the audio over to the commentary by Peter Jackson, Fran Walsh, and Philippa Boyens by accident, but the two were hooked. Almost eleven hours later, they emerged from a haze of orcs and a sugar high into the early morning sunlight and Esther knew she wanted to work in costume design.

By the time they were in high school, Heph had lost interest in movies and instead became fixated on Generation IV molten salt nuclear reactors (she was *definitely* going to be a supervillain) and becoming a physicist, so it was fair to say that their interests hit a fork in the road. The good thing about having a mute best friend was that she didn't try and talk to Esther too much about uranium tetrafluoride, and Esther didn't bug her about the latest outrageous costuming mistake in a period drama, so really, it was a perfect match.

So it was Heph who Esther messaged the Monday afternoon after 3/50 (which had been bridges, or more specifically *jumping off bridges*—Esther had ended up wet *yet again*) to come help her and Eugene clean out her grandpa's storage space he'd rented when he moved into Lilac Hill. Esther wasn't entirely sure what possessed someone with Lewy body dementia to rent a storage space for all their worldly possessions—the hope for a sudden and unexpected discovery of a cure, perhaps?—but that's what Reginald had done, and now the prepaid rent had run out, and it had fallen to his grandchildren to sort through everything he saved from his life and decide what to keep and what to throw away, which was too depressing a task to consider doing without Hephzibah, and—she decided at the last minute—Jonah Smallwood.

STORAGE KING'S UNITS were housed inside a massive warehouse that had a *Matrix* kind of vibe. Each corridor was a bland copy of the one before it, a never-ending cycle of déjà vu. Reg's rented space was so deep within the warehouse that Esther started to wonder if they'd ever be able to find their way out of the maze, but then there it was, the small blue roller door behind which he'd locked all the things he loved most from his life.

"This better not be like *Silence of the Lambs*," Esther said. "I don't think I can handle finding out that Pop's a serial killer."

"Not to mention a lotion-loving cross-dresser," Eugene added.

"It's the twenty-first century," signed Heph. "Your grandpa can be a cross-dresser if he wants."

"True that," Esther said. "Well, here goes."

Esther turned the key in the lock and rolled up the door, which was no easy task, because the Storage King, though a benevolent ruler, apparently didn't believe in oiling the rails. Inside, the space was completely black. Eugene recoiled, slinking backwards down the corridor lest some unnamed horror leap from the dark to snatch him up. Esther fumbled around for a light switch and eventually found it and flicked it on, illuminating the small space, which was—apart from a little wooden box sitting on its side in the corner of the room—completely empty.

"Eugene, it's okay," she said, kneeling to pick up the box.

"What the hell?" Eugene said. Esther checked the key, but yes, it was the right one, they were at the right storage unit, the same one Reginald rented and squeezed all of his most cherished possessions into before he checked himself into his nursing home.

It had been a hard month, boiling down the contents of her grandparents' home to the space of a 5 x 5 room. A prefuneral, of sorts, which was even more depressing than a postfuneral, because the soon-to-be-dead person was there, hovering over you, and you were expected to keep your shit together for their sake. Regardless, everyone cried a lot as they helped him sift through seven-odd decades worth of memories, deciding what was worth keeping and what wasn't. Pretty damn tragic. They took a lot of stuff to their house, all the sentimental things they couldn't get rid of, like photos and jewelry and knickknacks collected on vacations to far off destinations. Most of these things now resided in Esther's bedroom. But cataloguing someone else's life while they were sitting three feet away and being like, "Now, Pop, I know you love this old transistor radio and have listened to it every day for the last thirty years but we don't really have a place for it in our house so it's gonna have to go to Goodwill," was *the worst*.

For starters, you felt like a carrion bird, swooping in and snatching up the best bits. Esther wanted (and got) her grandmother's bracelet. Eugene wanted (and got) Reg's coin collection.

Their cousins were there smuggling pocket watches and old books and all of Florence Solar's crystal champagne glasses. Uncle Harold (then still living) was into the liquor cabinet. Peter (then uninterred in the basement) had only one request: his father's reading glasses, which he couldn't have until the very end, because Reginald still needed them, or at least hoped he'd still be able to use them even though Esther hadn't seen him read anything for at least three years.

Most of the furniture was sold to pay for Lilac Hill. All the cutlery and crockery that her grandma had loved was given to Goodwill, as were the suits Reginald wouldn't wear anymore. The armchair he loved to sit in to read his terrible detective novels. The katana he brought back from Japan. All of it had to go, and so all of it went.

Day by day, room by room, they stripped back the house he'd lived in, raised a family in, watched his wife die in, until there was nothing left but pockets of old air bound up by walls. They stripped the wallpaper, tore up the carpet, replaced the light fittings, modernized the bathrooms, and then, when the house was bleached of everything that had made it his home, they sold the place to an investor from Greece, whose only stipulation regarding the property was that the orchid greenhouse in the backyard remain untouched and filled with flowers. The profits were split between Peter and his siblings, Auntie Kate and (the then still living) Uncle Harold, and Reginald checked himself into Lilac Hill to wait for the Reaper to come for him, which, he seemed to think, wouldn't actually happen.

Esther went to speak to the clerk at the front of the warehouse, this burly dude with a goatee and trucker's cap.

"Uh . . . we just went to clear our grandpa's storage space but there's nothing in there," she said, sliding him the key.

"Let me check our system," the guy said. He clicked and typed. "Okay, so someone came and cleared out the space this morning. We left you about a dozen messages, but no one ever got back to us—eventually the other key holder came in."

"There *was* no other key holder," said Eugene.

The guy rechecked his computer screen. "Sorry, but it looks like there was. Another key holder, registered at the same time your grandpa first opened the storage unit."

"Who has the key?" Esther asked. "Auntie Kate maybe?"

"I don't have a name or any contact details, only that there was one and only that they cleared everything out today."

"So what, this random person can just come in whenever they want and steal all our granddad's stuff?" Eugene said.

"They didn't *steal* anything, kid. They had a key. Your grandfather obviously doesn't mind them being here."

"What did they look like?"

"Lot of people come through here for a lot of reasons. You seen *Breaking Bad*? I try not to pay too much attention to our clientele. Plausible deniability."

"Maybe this will help you remember," Eugene said, sliding him a ten dollar bill.

The clerk sighed and pocketed the cash. "I *honestly* don't remember. My memory of him is kind of . . . fuzzy. Little dude in a black coat. Bad scars on his face. Bit of a weirdo, but that's not saying much in a place like this."

Esther and Eugene looked at each other. They rarely had twin telepathy, but right now, she was pretty sure they were thinking the same thing. "Thanks," she said. "You can close the account now. Everything's gone."

Outside, the four of them crossed the road and bought rocket pops from the convenience store. Then they sat on a patch of grass by the sidewalk, a tree shading them from the sun, the locked box in the center of them all.

"You heard what he said," Esther said to Eugene. "Scars on his face. It *has* to be him."

Eugene ran his fingertips over the box. "Anyone can have scars. It's not like it's the hallmark of the Grim Reaper or anything. Now, if the counter guy said he'd had a cloak and scythe and skeleton fingers, I'd be more likely to believe it was him."

"Wait, you think because the dude had a scarred-up face, he was Death?" said Jonah. Heph nodded vigorously, having heard the story almost as many times as the twins had. "Did I miss something?"

"It's an old family legend Pop used to tell us when we were kids," Eugene said. "Esther has an overactive imagination. Reg never meant for us to actually *believe* it."

Esther shrugged. "Sometimes people tell true stories as though they're fake because it lends them verisimilitude."

Eugene rolled his eyes.

"What's this?" she said. "The boy who believes in demons doesn't believe in Death?"

"I believe in what I can *see*."

Jonah made short work of the locked box. Esther didn't see how he did it exactly, but the lock bloomed open beneath his fingertips after only a handful of seconds. Inside they found a small notebook full of newspaper clippings, mostly about a series of unsolved murders and missing children: the Bowen sisters (murdered), the Kittredge siblings (four of them, all missing), a little girl named Isla Appelbaum (murdered), two boys—school friends, both only seven—still missing five weeks after they were last seen walking home from school together in 1996, and Alana Shepard (murdered). The titles said things like *Harvestman Suspected in Appelbaum Disappearance* and *No Leads in Second Confirmed Harvestman Murder*. Dozens and dozens of clippings about these cases and some more from surrounding states. And then the last clipping on the last page, a short piece with hardly any detail, about a man who'd drowned in his bathtub.

"Maybe your granddaddy was a serial killer after all," Jonah said as he flipped through the pages. "Jesus. This is some nasty shit to scrapbook."

"He was a homicide detective," Eugene explained. He flipped back to the page about the Bowen sisters. "This was his case. Never caught the guy who did it. It kind of messed him up, actually."

Jonah read the article about the two small girls who were abducted not far from where they currently sat. The so-called

Harvestman's first suspected killings. "Ugh," he said, gagging. "Humans are the worst."

"The last one," said Esther, "Alana Shepard, was confirmed to have been killed by the same guy."

"Christ."

"Yeah. Not something you get over quickly. Reg had nothing to do with their deaths, obviously, but . . . he blamed himself for the murders. Especially Alana Shepard. Him and Death got into a fistfight about it, apparently."

"What? Your granddad . . . ?"

"Punched Death square in the mouth," Eugene said. "So he says."

"Badass. How does a guy go about making the acquaintance of the Grim Reaper anyway?" Jonah said. "Might be handy to know, considering that's what we're trying to do."

"I'm sure it's not an exact science, but it helps if you go someplace where you know Death is going to be," Esther said. "In Saigon during a war, for example. If you're going to meet the Reaper anywhere, that's a good place to start."

"In fair Vietnam, where we lay our scene?" Jonah asked.

"Exactly."

For the first time, Esther told Jonah what she knew about the Man Who Would Be Death.

13

THE MAN WHO WOULD BE DEATH

THE STORY of how the Solar family each came to be cursed with a great fear began in Saigon in 1972.

It was a warm tropical evening on the fragrant streets of the city, everyone in a slow-moving haze from the leftover heat of the day and years-long exhaustion that follows war without end. Everywhere, the French past of the town was laid bare. the little bistros frequented by diplomats and their families, the white columns of the neoclassical post office and the bare breasted marble statues of the opera house, the tree-lined streets, and the brightly colored colonial terraces, stuck together like little squares of candy melted by the sun.

Signs of war were all over, but Saigon had escaped the worst of it; the city was shabby, dilapidated, but still a thing of grandeur, the streets alive and bustling with activity. Small Vietnamese women sat in doorways, chopping meat on tree stumps wedged between their knees. Then, as now, mopeds clotted the roads, honking and grunting and swarming around each other, a chaotic avalanche cascading down every major avenue and flooding every tiny lane alike. Old men, faces leathered by the sun, fixed up-turned bicycles or invited Americans into their restaurants or smoked while leaning against the hoods of their white and royal blue taxis, waiting for a fare.

A whole city, swaying and uneasy, the anxious population going about their evening tasks, unsure when the war was going to end, not knowing, yet, that the Northerners would take and hold the city in a matter of a couple of years.

It was in a smoky, nameless haunt frequented by soldiers that Reginald Solar first laid eyes on young Jack Horowitz, who was not yet Death, but would soon become him. Esther's grandfa-ther had just that day arrived in Saigon to take the place of a fellow lieutenant who'd lost his life the week before. The fallen man's pla-toon members were among those drinking in the bar that night, though they didn't know that their new commanding officer was among them.

The Man Who Would Be Death sat not far from them, by himself. They knew him as Private Jack Horowitz, eighteen years old, born in the South, raised on a farm, and the weirdest son of a bitch any of them had ever met.

"He's a fucking warlock, I'm telling you," said Private Hanson, the only one of these soldiers Esther's grandfather ever mentioned by name.

"He's a *vampire*," said another. "Needs a stake through the heart."

None of them would say what they really, truly believed

about strange Jack Horowitz: that he was Death incarnate. Maybe not the Grim Reaper himself, but a cousin at the very least, an ill omen sent to shadow them through the jungles, act as a beacon for the Horsemen to come trampling after their mortal souls. The soldiers were not unaccustomed to the presence of death, as one can imagine. In 1972, the war was very close to its end for US troops, and all those who remained in Vietnam had grown intimate with the Reaper. They knew the sound of him, the smell of him, the burnt flesh taste of him that lingered on the tongue. Sometimes he was loud, the screaming that accompanied sheared-off limbs or shrapnel tearing through skin and muscle to bury itself deep in bone. Sometimes he was quiet: an infected wound, a poisoned water source, the last gurgling gasp of tired lungs exhaling at the witching hour when everyone but the nearly dead was sleeping.

Yes, they were very intimate with death, which made them certain to their bones that young Jack Horowitz was some kind of henchman. They had three reasons for this belief:

1. Before his arrival, they weren't doing too badly, not compared to the rest of the platoons stationed around them. They lost men, sure, but their losses were far below average. Then Horowitz arrived and they started being sucked into the jungle.

2. Horowitz himself had been shot a total of eight times. Eight times, and each time, without screaming, without flinching, without breaking a sweat, he dug his combat knife into the flesh of his arm or

his gut or his leg, cut out the bullet, and patched himself up. Didn't wait for the gunfire to stop either. Just sat himself down in the cross fire, the occasional bullet dinging off his helmet, dug around in his wounds for a bit, mended the rent flesh, and was off again, darting through the jungle like a weasel.

Now, most soldiers this would kill, or at the very least land them in an evacuation hospital with a one-way ticket back to the US. Every time Horowitz got shot, the platoon was relieved. Surely *this time* the wound would be bad enough to ship him home.

It never was. Horowitz never came back from medical with more than a couple of stitches: the bullets never seemed to leave more than a graze on him. The one time that they were *sure* he was dead—when two rounds sank into his chest—both bullets hadn't managed to make it more than an eighth of an inch into his skin. Something about the angle of the shots glancing off his sternum, even though the soldier closest to him *swore* he saw the shots tear Horowitz's chest apart.

3. The way Horowitz breathed at night. Most of the men in the platoon hadn't slept—really *slept*—in months. They lay awake at night in their cots, listening to the quiet rattle of Horowitz's breathing, and since it sounded so much like death, they found themselves unable to concentrate on anything else, and listened to the sucking wheeze—in and out, in and out, in and out—of his desperate lungs.

AT THE BAR THAT NIGHT, also sitting by himself, was Lieutenant Reginald Solar, already a seasoned war veteran at the age of thirty-five. Like his granddaughter, he had red-tinged hair, a face that burned quickly in sunlight, and barely a square inch of skin that wasn't spattered with freckles of a dozen different tones. Unlike his granddaughter, he had large ears and a large nose that would only grow larger as he aged, but he was, at that time, quite unconventionally handsome, and looked tack-sharp in his officer's uniform, as the portraits of him from that time attest.

Lieutenant Reginald Solar was called the Milkman behind his back by the men he commanded, because even when the luxury of alcohol was available, Reg preferred milk. Cow's milk, goat's milk, coconut milk—whatever he could get his hands on. The son of a violent alcoholic, spirits had only passed his lips once, when he was eighteen and curious to see how a liquid could turn a gentle man into a monster. Much to his surprise, being drunk didn't make him angry, just sad, but he decided to steer clear of it all the same.

During the war, the only thing he missed as much as his wife was strawberry milkshakes, though he didn't mind the cinnamon hot chocolate the Vietnamese made with sweetened condensed milk, which was what he sipped on then, the first night he met the Man Who Would Be Death.

There were whispered superstitions that the platoon was cursed, but Reg was neither a godly man nor one to believe folly (he had seen too much war for the former and been an officer too long to allow the latter), so he accepted the transfer without hesitation.

What he overheard as he sipped his hot chocolate: "I've seen flowers and plants wilt as he walks past them. I'm telling you, he's a warlock, and a bullet magnet, and bad *fucking* luck. We should do something about him ourselves if Charlie can't get the job done."

"I don't think he *can* die. What if we stick him with a knife and he just patches himself up like he does out in the jungle and then goes to the brass?"

Reginald looked over his shoulder at the man whom they were talking about. Jack Horowitz was drinking—to Reg Solar's great surprise—warm milk. Horowitz didn't look much like a vampire, or any other kind of supernatural creature at all. He was young, hardly a day over eighteen, with deep-pitted acne scars all over his cheeks and chin, like the skin of his face had been eaten away by termites. Apart from the scars, he was unremarkable; no one who met him could later recall the color of his eyes, or his hair, or what his voice sounded like. The only things that could be agreed upon were that he was a) short and slight, b) very unattractive, and c) unsettlingly calm.

Over the course of the evening, the concern that Horowitz wasn't dying grew so great, and the plots against him so elaborate, that Reginald eventually had to pull the young private aside and speak with him personally.

"Private Horowitz," he said when he followed him out of the bar. Reginald was not a man who was easily scared, but the way Horowitz moved without making a sound, the way his footfalls made no noise, well—it was strange, to say the least.

"Lieutenant Solar."

Reginald motioned to a pair of stools on the roadside, left there earlier in the night by men in sedge hats with rolled cigarettes burning between their fingers. "Please, take a seat." Horowitz took a seat. The chair made no sound as it scraped across the ground. "How are your wounds treating you? I hear you recently took a round to the shoulder."

"Oh, I barely notice it. It was only a graze."

"Do you mind if I see it?"

"Triage advised me to keep it covered to prevent infection."

"I'm sure, I'm sure. Still. If you wouldn't mind."

"Yes, sir."

Horowitz stood, shrugged off his jacket and peeled back the dressing taped to his left shoulder. Beneath it was a bullet graze, about the length of a finger. The wound, no more than a few days old, was fresh pink and smooth. A scar.

"You heal quickly," said Reginald.

"Like I said, it was a graze."

"Do you know why I asked to speak with you?"

"Because the other men think I'm a warlock and are planning to murder me in my sleep."

Reg was taken aback by both his honesty and deadpan delivery. "You heard them? They aren't really planning to murder you."

"Oh, I assure you they are. There's no cause for alarm though. Their attempt will fail."

There was a beat of silence. "Are you?"

"Am I what?"

"A . . . warlock?"

Horowitz smiled. "You don't strike me as a superstitious man, Lieutenant Solar."

"I'm not. Yet you still haven't answered my question."

"I'm not a warlock."

"You seem to have a lot of close calls with bullets. Took two in the chest not long back, I heard."

"What can I say. I've been perpetually lucky."

"Luck tends to unnerve the luckless, especially in the middle of a war."

"Are you suggesting I should try not to be lucky?"

"Perhaps you should be a little luckier and not get shot at all."

Horowitz laughed. "I shall keep that in mind for the future."

"One last thing. The men, I overheard them say . . . but I'm sure this can't be true . . . They say they've never seen you so much as point your weapon, let alone pull the trigger?"

"Oh, it's true. I've not killed anyone. It wouldn't be fair if I discharged my weapon."

"Excuse me?"

"You see, Lieutenant, I never miss. If I were to shoot into the jungle, even if I don't aim, my bullet would find its way into the chest of some poor Vietnamese man."

"That's the point. That's what we want from you."

"No, Lieutenant. It would be wholly unfair for me to fight in this war. I am an impartial party."

"Why the hell did you come to Vietnam if you're an impartial party?"

"Well, sir, because I was drafted, but not by the United States. I was drafted by Death."

There were several more beats of silence. "Death?"

"That is correct. Death. The Grim Reaper. Whatever you want to call him. I am apprenticed to him and he sent me here to learn my craft."

"How in the hell did you get drafted by Death?"

"I don't know why I was chosen, only that I was. Every night for a month, Death left orchids on my pillow, as a warning that he was coming."

"Orchids?"

"Death hates them, apparently. He fears their strength, and so he has made them his calling card."

"How'd you pass your psych test?"

"Alas, I didn't take a psych test."

Reginald took off his reading glasses. Rubbed his eyes. Jesus. "Look, Horowitz, you can't keep acting like this. You're worrying the other soldiers. You keep being a strange son of a bitch and it might be you push one of them too far and they stick you with a knife. I can't have that."

"I was sent here to reap one soul in particular. My very first assignment. Would it give you comfort to know who I've come for?"

Reginald shifted in his seat. "Wouldn't that upset some sort of cosmic balance?" he said, a twinge of panic sparking through him.

Horowitz stared at him for a while and then nodded. "I suppose. Still. This is a dreadful line of work."

"So is war. Tell the Reaper to get off our backs, would you?"

"I assure you, my master does not listen to me."

"What does he need an apprentice for anyhow? Why can't he do his own dirty work?"

"I am to become Death when he is gone."

"Oh yeah? Where's he going?"

"Death is dying."

"Death can't die."

"What monstrous creatures humans would be if they could not die. It is no different for Death. Death dies because he must, because everything does. He's on vacation in the Mediterranean at the moment. I hear it's nice this time of year. He has left the war in the charge of his apprentices, which, as I have explained, I am one of."

Reg stared at Horowitz for a moment, unable to quite think of what to say. "Okay, well, just do me a favor and reel it in a bit, would you? Don't talk about any of this Death shit with the others. Dismissed."

Horowitz nodded and stood and made his way down the darkened alley back toward the bustling streets of the city.

"Horowitz?" Reg called, just before he rounded the corner. "Hold up for a second."

"Yes, sir?"

"If you really are Death's apprentice, then it shouldn't be too hard for you to tell me . . ." He couldn't help the small grin that spread across his face. Just because he didn't believe didn't mean he could resist asking. "How do I die?"

"It's a terrible thing, to know for sure. The knowledge is a curse that would drive most men mad."

"I think I'll manage."

"You drown, sir."

Reg had to laugh—he was an excellent swimmer. "Well, now I guess I'm never getting in water again."

"And thus by knowing it, you have already changed your fate, and with it your death. Well, maybe."

Reg's grin widened. "The drowning thing's a joke, isn't it?"

"Perhaps. But would you risk it, knowing what you know?"

"Hmm." He thought for a moment. About the swelling breakers of the ocean, and the way the salt seared your throat and nose after a wave dumped you on a beach. About the screaming, desperate burn of your lungs when you dived too deep and black spots that started forming in your vision as you kicked for the surface. People thought drowning was peaceful, but Reg had spent enough time in water to know it would be otherwise—it was not the way he'd want to go.

"Dismissed."

Jack Horowitz went AWOL the next day, the same day the war ended for Reginald, because he was shot in the heart.

Reg, while recovering in a makeshift hospital before his journey home, thought of Jack Horowitz, and then, when he returned to the US, he thought of him more still. Whenever he went to the beach or took a bath or went fishing, a niggling fear began to bite at the back of his mind. *You drown*, this fear whispered to him every time he was caught in a rip or knocked down by a wave or his chest began to ache from being under for too long. *This is how you will die.* For a time, the rational part of Reginald's brain argued with this voice. For a time, it won.

Reginald Solar was a sensible man, after all; he did not believe in ghosts, or curses, and he especially did not believe in the Grim Reaper.

But what if?

What if?

Soon the fear bit a little harder, and the rational voice grew shaky, and Reginald stopped going to the beach.

Stopped fishing.

Stopped taking baths.

Slowly but surely, day by day, the curse of knowing his fate settled into his head and there it made a home for itself. Reg moved away from the coast, began to circumvent storm drains, wouldn't go outside when it rained. Each day he avoided water, he fed his fear, and each day, the fear grew a little stronger, a little crueler, until it metastasized into something fat and ugly and totally in control of his life. When his children were born, so great was his fear that he passed it down to them, so that each of them would know, without knowing how they knew, exactly how they would die, and they would fear this knowledge with the same intensity he had.

And still, he wondered what had happened to Horowitz. Reg believed he'd simply deserted after the escalating threats of harm from his fellow soldiers, but he found out five years after the war from a rather intoxicated and remorseful Private Hanson that a group of them had bound and gagged Horowitz in the early hours of the morning, weighted his feet with stones, and dropped him into the depths of the Saigon River. Horowitz, Hanson reported through his sobs, hadn't fought back at all, had serenely gone along with the whole thing like it was a Sunday afternoon trip to the beach.

By this point in time, Hanson was dying from emphysema from sucking back two packs of cigarettes a day—a habit he picked up in 'Nam—and all the other men involved in Horowitz's murder had perished before the end of the war. There was no one left to court-martial. Still, Reg went to his superiors and explained what had happened, only to be told that there was no record of a Private Jack Horowitz ever having served in the war, let alone a birth certificate or social security number as proof of his existence, which Reg found very fucking strange indeed (but not strange enough to believe the dead man had *actually* been Death's apprentice, mind you).

Hanson died a month later, in excruciating pain, drowning in his hospital bed from the fluid in his lungs. A just death, Reg thought.

Horowitz had no grave, no memorial, no place for Reginald to go and mourn the unfortunate man he'd known for only a matter of hours, the man whose mental illness had cost him his life.

It was quite a shock for Reginald, then, when a very not-dead Jack Horowitz showed up on his doorstep in 1982 and asked him to be best man at his wedding.

14

4/50: SMALL SPACES

THAT'S HOW it began. Esther wasn't entirely sure how seeing Jonah went from a Sunday-only thing to something else, but after the day at Storage King, he came to her house in the afternoons most days after school and helped her bake. He tutored her and Eugene in Shakespeare, which they sucked at, and they tutored him in math, which he sucked at. They sat on the uncomfortable, badly upholstered couch and watched *The Babadook* and *Evil Dead II* and *The Birds*, thinking up new ways they could lure Death, taking notes on Esther's semi-definitive list about all the reckless things they could try.

The ridiculous cat followed Jonah everywhere, tongue lolling out of one side of its mouth, but he treated her like she was the best cat he'd ever seen, lugging Fleayoncé around in his arms like a baby and talking to her like she was a person and—occasionally—wearing her as a scarf, which she especially loved.

Sometimes Jonah called Esther in the afternoons before his

dad got home, to talk about the list, or Reginald's scrapbook, or the Harvestman, or who took everything from the storage unit and why. He never talked about his school or his parents or his house, which was fine by Esther, because she didn't want to talk about her school or her parents or her house either. He put her on speakerphone while he repainted the walls, or helped Remy with her homework, or worked on Esther's portrait, and even though she hated phone calls (they were on her semi-definitive list at number forty-one), with him on the other end of the line it was kind of okay. Not quite okay enough to take off the list—she still couldn't call strangers—but okay.

She could always tell when his dad got home, because Jonah would mutter, "I gotta go," or the line would suddenly go dead, and Esther knew not to call back. When this happened, she spent the rest of the night thinking about him and Remy in the room where the walls were alive with movement and color even though the house it was attached to was dead and dark and hollow.

On the Sunday of 4/50, Jonah came over in the morning to visit Fleayoncé and "hold her paw" as she had her cast taken off. It was the second time in four weeks that Esther had been down in the basement, and although he didn't say anything, she could tell that Peter was buzzing with happiness (which might have had something to do with the 9:00 a.m. glass of gin he was downing, but almost definitely something to do with the presence of other humans). He shuffled around his junk stacks like a mad magician, pressing old photographs into Esther's hands as he worked on the cat, telling Jonah stories about when she was a kid, stories that seemed like fiction now because they were so normal and so far removed from anything that resembled her life.

Esther and Eugene at the playground with Dad, before he became agoraphobic.

Esther and Eugene in Reg Solar's orchid greenhouse, one twin on each hip, his mind still whole.

If something was once true but now wasn't, was it ever true?

Jonah cooed at the cat and asked why she was mewling as Peter took approximately seven times longer to remove her cast and do a checkup than was necessary. Fleayoncé's tongue still lolled sideways out of her mouth, and she would never have the coordination to climb a tree or catch a mouse. Jonah didn't seem to mind that, by all measurable standards, his cat was a sucky cat. When her examination was complete, he scooped her up and held her in his arms like a baby, like he always did.

Esther sat on the couch and tried not to touch anything. Tried not to glance at the framed photographs of her and Eugene that Peter kept on his bedside table, windows into a long-faded past. She couldn't remember exactly when they'd stopped coming down here. It used to be fun when they were eleven, like Christmas all the time with the star-spangled trees and scent of old books. What she could remember was that Eugene had stopped first. When Peter missed another baseball game, another birthday party, another parent-teacher night, despite how much Eugene begged him to come. As they got older, and the whole situation got sadder, it was harder and harder to be around their father, so they just . . . stopped.

She sank back into the conversation in time to hear Peter say: "Would you like to come down for dinner one night? I don't cook much—I've only got the gas hotplate—but we could order in, all three of us. I'll save up for something special."

"Sure," said Jonah, shaking Peter's hand, clapping him on the back. "Sounds good."

"You don't have to eat dinner with him if you don't want to," Esther said quietly as they left the house on their way to film 4/50, which she was particularly stressed about because she worried that Jonah was going to seal her in a coffin or something. "Don't feel any pressure."

"What? Your dad's all right. I like him."

Esther swore she felt her heart grow a full three sizes larger, like the Grinch.

It was another long moped ride to some surprise destination. When the drive was over, they dismounted and wandered for twenty minutes through scrubland that clawed at her costume (Indiana Jones, complete with whip, hat, and brown leather jacket), pulling tendrils of hair out from her ponytail to fall unkempt about her shoulders.

At first she thought Jonah had again brought her to another abandoned prime location for murder, but the farther they hiked, the more and more people they started to see. People with helmets and lights strapped to their heads. People with ropes and carabiners attached to their harnesses. Only upon reaching the mouth of a cave did Esther know for sure what Jonah's plan was, and it was so, so much worse than she could've imagined. Before she could protest, he'd gone to collect equipment from the dude running the show, who was wearing a T-shirt that said JESUS LOVES THE HELL OUT OF YOU.

"I'm drawing a line," she said as soon as he got back and handed her a helmet. "I'm drawing a line in the goddamn metaphorical sand." And then, because Jonah didn't seem to understand the gravity of the situation, she dropped the helmet, picked up a stick from the undergrowth and drew a line in the literal sand with it. They were standing twenty feet from the mouth of a cave, into which Jonah had organized a guided spelunking tour.

"Not an option," Jonah said, already buckling his caving helmet.

"I'm serious. I should've set some ground rules. And rule one is no caves. *Ever.* Have you not seen *The Descent*?"

"No."

"Well I have, and I know how this story ends, and there is no way—*no way*—I am ever going in a cave."

"All right, people, everyone make sure your helmets are on and then follow me into the mouth for our safety briefing," said the Jesus-shirt guy, who entered the cave and walked casually toward his death. A small child, decked out in caving gear, ran past them and plunged into the darkness after him.

"You gonna let that kid out-spelunk you?" Jonah said.

"That child is going to be viciously hunted and eaten by

troglofaunal flesh-eating humanoids." The child in question's parents overheard her say this. "Sorry," she said. "Have you not seen *The Descent*?" They both shook their heads. "I'm sure he'll be *fine*. Just *fine*."

The kid was definitely going to die.

"Did you memorize the Wikipedia page for that movie?" Jonah asked. "Look, are you even afraid of small spaces, or are you just scared of what you think might be *in* those small spaces?"

"I'm afraid of going in a cave, getting stuck in a tight tunnel, and having a creature start eating me from the toes up while I can't move, because I'm trapped in a small space. It's a bit of both. Hence, I'm not going in the cave."

"You're going in the cave."

"No."

"Yes."

"*No*."

"You really want this week's video to be thirty seconds long? You want the last frame to say, 'Esther failed after only four weeks because she's chickenshit'?"

"What are you doing with these videos anyway?"

"Never you mind. Get in the damn cave."

"But . . . I'm scared."

Jonah picked up her helmet and put it on her head over her Indiana Jones hat and rapped his knuckles against it twice. "That's exactly why you gotta do it."

"I really hate you."

"So hurtful. Get in the cave."

So she did. The grapnel anchor was wedged firmly through her spine, scraping against the inside of her sternum and making it hard for her heart to beat properly, but she did. She turned her helmet's light on and kind of wandered toward the cave's mouth in a trancelike state, because her legs were shaking and she couldn't feel her body—but one couldn't be dressed as Indiana Jones and then refuse to go in a cave, she reasoned, so she drew on the power of the costume to help her feel strong.

"Never gonna meet Death at this rate," Jonah muttered from behind her. "Damn tricycle flesh-eating something somethings. Girl watches too much damn TV."

The antechamber was not immediately as bad as Esther had thought it would be. For starters, there were about a dozen other people on the tour with them—all potential bait for the monsters, so she wouldn't be the first one eaten at least—and secondly because it was, naturally, attached to the mouth of the cave, which had garlands of sunlight spilling through. Jesus-shirt dude, who turned out to be a young priest named Dave, introduced himself and talked them through how to stay safe on their two-hour expedition underground. He mentioned a lot of stuff, but nothing about cave-dwelling carnivores, which seemed like a huge oversight. There would be some tight squeezes, he said, some water in places, but nothing too challenging, nothing to be too concerned about.

Thousands of people had done this before; none of them had been eaten.

After the briefing, Priest Dave came up to Esther personally and told her that Jonah had informed him about her claustro-phobia. Esther grimaced. If there was one thing worse than being stupidly afraid of something, it was having other people *know* you were stupidly afraid of something. But Priest Dave was cool about it and told her that he, too, had pretty bad claustrophobia and she could stick with him at the front of the group if she wanted to, which yes, that sounded good, because then he could lead her out of the cave to safety while everyone else got eaten.

Esther made Jonah go behind her and said, "I expect you to sacrifice yourself for me if the need arises. I am not even kidding about this."

To which Jonah replied, "Nah, I'll just toss the monsters the kid." The kid's parents overheard this, too, and decided to relocate to the back of the group, as far away from them as possible, which was reasonable.

The tour started off not so bad. The tunnel was tall enough to stand up in and wide enough that Esther couldn't touch either wall with her arms outstretched. They didn't walk on rock or dirt, but instead on a metal platform, which quelled some of her anxiety because it was solid proof that humans had been here before and lived long enough to erect infrastructure. They wended their way through the insides of some giant limestone beast, observing the snaking white tubes of its bowels, the rust-red blood of its veins, the stalactite toothpick teeth jutting from its jaws, sharp enough to skewer skin and bone. Esther moved quickly beneath these hanging death traps, sure that an earthquake would shake them loose at any moment.

The deeper they went, the cooler it got. Whispers began to echo. The light from camera flashes moved strangely, licking at the shadows but unable to remove them. Priest Dave stopped from time to time to point out different cave phenomena. Stalagmites. Underground rivers. Glowworms that clung to the roof and gave the whole tunnel a blue haze. When they reached another chamber, the metal platform still blessedly beneath them, Dave told them to turn their headlamps off so they could experience "cave darkness," a darkness so absolute that you apparently couldn't even see your own hand in front of your face (or the approach of bloodthirsty predators).

Esther's light was the last one on. By then everyone was looking at her, waiting, and she could feel their judging gazes boring hot cavities into her skin. Her cheeks burned and her palms grew sweaty, like they always did whenever she thought people were judging her, except this time everyone was *really, really* judging her. She could practically hear their thoughts echoing in the dark. *Chicken, coward, fake,* they chanted. She didn't want to turn the light off, but she couldn't be the only one who didn't when there was a goddamn six-year-old who wasn't scared.

"Hold onto me if you want," Jonah said quietly. Esther wrapped her arms around his waist and pressed her cheek to his chest and held onto him as tight as she could, like he was an anchor and gravity was about to be switched off. Which, in a way, it was. Then she jammed her eyes closed and flicked off her light. The change in perception wasn't immediately palpable, because her eyes were still scrunched shut, but everyone began talking about how amazing the absolute dark was. Esther kept waiting for a set of long fangs to sink into her neck.

"Damn, that's awesome," Jonah said. "How you doing, Esther?"

"I'm good."

"You haven't looked yet, have you?"

"I'm *good*."

"Open your eyes."

"Stop telling me what to do."

Then, very slowly, she opened her eyes. It was hard to tell the difference.

It was dark. Like really, *really* dark. She moved her hand in front of her face and couldn't see it. She poked a finger toward her eye and couldn't sense how close it was until it brushed her eyelashes. Absolute, disorienting, impossible blackness. Esther wasn't even sure Eugene could be afraid down here. It wasn't the darkness itself that bothered him so much, but the flicker of things he saw *in* the darkness. A wing here, a limb there, a clawed hand emerging from the closet. You couldn't fear that down here, because you simply couldn't *see* it.

It made her think of the first few months Eugene had become afraid of the night, when the only way he could sleep was if he was holding Esther's hand. The tether that bound her to her mother might have degraded over time, but whatever magic she shared with Eugene was still there. Still strong.

After a few minutes, the spelunkers turned their lights on again and continued the tour, their eyes burning from the sudden brightness. They left behind the safety of the metal platform in favor of smaller, tighter tunnels that bore no sign of human survival. Esther had to crouch. Then she had to crawl on her hands and knees. Then—Lord have mercy on her circulatory system—they each had to worm their way through an opening barely large enough to accommodate Priest Dave's shoulders and belly.

This would be the worst of it, Priest Dave assured her from the other side of the hellhole. This would be the only tight squeeze on the entire adventure, and after that, everything would feel like a breeze.

Esther was still at the front of the group. She had no choice; she had to go first.

She lay down flat like Dave had and started to army crawl forward. The rock pressed against her helmet, her shoulders, slanted up slightly to press into her stomach and thighs. The space tightened as she moved through it, seizing up to swallow her body.

Her goal was not to screw around. Get through the hole before the cave collapsed (which, in her head, was inevitable). Survive for two weeks underground by eating Dave, who would (tragically) die in the accident. Write a book about her grand tale of survival, and then write the screenplay for the film adaptation. Maybe win an Oscar for screenwriting. A Golden Globe at the very least.

There was a slight bend in the tunnel up ahead, and a puddle of water about two inches deep. (Of course, of course, *of course* she was going to get wet *again*.)

"Goddamn you, Jonah," she muttered to herself as she navigated the turn, trying and failing not to think about earthquakes and cave-ins and flash floods. "Damn you, damn you, damn you."

The tightest part of the tunnel was just on the other side of the bend, where the roof dipped down and Esther had to turn her head sideways to keep her mouth and nose out of the water. She shuffled forward another foot before both of her arms became pinned beneath her, elbows bent, and she couldn't lift her cheek more than an inch from the pool of muddy liquid.

Fuck.

Don't freak out.

She tried to push one of her arms forward and unpin it from under her, but this crushed her ribs. She tried to scrabble her legs against the rock to squeeze herself through, but couldn't find a foothold. Backward. Go backward. She tried to use her elbows to force herself back, but her body was still half wedged in the turn in the tunnel.

Fuck.

The hyperventilation started before she even realized she was panicking.

"Hey, hey, hey, hey, hey," said Priest Dave, who was there suddenly, in front of her face. (It reminded her how quickly things could sneak up on you in caves.) "Slow your breathing. Listen to me, slow your breathing."

"I'm stuck," Esther managed to strangle out. "I'm stuck."

"You're not stuck. I'm gonna help you out of this, okay?"

Esther nodded. Dave already had his hand underneath her cheek so she could rest her neck without drowning.

"Have you seen *The Descent*?" she asked him as he gave her a moment to catch her breath.

"Yeah. That's what got me interested in spelunking in the first place, actually."

"What is *wrong* with you?" she choked out.

Dave laughed. "The opportunity to see things that humans have never seen before. To discover secrets that were billions of years in the making, it was too good to pass up. Plus I was scared shitless of small spaces, but I didn't want to let my fear get the best of me, so I found a way to enjoy it."

"You can't say shitless. You're a pastor."

"Priest, actually. Look, Esther, I've been through this cave system a hundred times, okay? Haven't been eaten once. Not even nibbled. So what do you say we get you out of here so you can check out the beautiful cavern on the other side?"

Esther thought of the package Jonah had brought her after 1 of 50. *Everything you want is on the other side of fear*, it had said. She'd never particularly wanted to see a beautiful cavern in a cave system, but she did want to be in an open space, so she supposed that what she wanted *was* on the other side of fear, in a way. She nodded again.

"Shuffle forward for me, okay?" said Dave. "Just like you've been doing. Tiny little army crawl steps."

As Esther moved, inch by inch, she felt less and less trapped.

Her arms became freer, the rock let go of its crushing hold on her rib cage and—a couple of minutes later—the tunnel spat her out entirely, into a cavern that was every bit as picturesque as Priest Dave had promised. And there, on the other side, was the most beautiful thing she'd ever seen: the return of the metal platform. Humans had been here, and they hadn't all been consumed.

"Good work!" Dave said as he clapped her on the back. "Why don't you take a look around while I help the others through?"

Esther stood up and took several deep breaths. It was over. She'd done it. The tunnel hadn't collapsed, she hadn't drowned in a flash flood, and she hadn't even been eaten by troglofaunal flesh-eating humanoids. As she left the damp darkness of the tunnel, still uneaten by the monsters from *The Descent*, Esther thought she understood, for the first time, the quote Jonah had written on the newspaper after 1/50.

Esther had never before believed that there was anything nice or useful on the other side of fear. Fear was a sensible barrier that kept the living from becoming the dead, and it shouldn't be crossed under any circumstances. Yet as she stood up in that room built by the hands of the Earth itself, she found a hole punched through the cavern roof where green-tinted sunlight rushed in, and directly beneath it, a peridot-colored pool where millions of years of rain and wind and floodwater had carved away at the rock. Emerald-bright plants and moss grew from the walls, devouring the daylight, and birds spiraled down to their nests to bring their chirping chicks fat worms.

She'd passed the fear barrier, and she'd lived, and she'd discovered not certain death, as she'd imagined, but impossible splendor.

What other beautiful things had fear been hiding from her? What else had the curse long kept her from discovering?

For the first time in a long time, she wanted to find out.

THERE ARE SOME MORE DIRECT ROUTES TO DEATH THAN MOTHS AND LOBSTERS

ESTHER SAW them on a Tuesday morning before school, during the week before 5/50. The bathroom door was ajar, and Eugene was shaving his measly excuse for facial hair in the mirror. As he lathered his shaving cream, turning his wrists this way and that, she caught sight of a flash of red—a series of long cuts running down the length of his arms.

"You should see the other guy," said Eugene when their eyes met and he caught her staring, and then he shut the door. He wore long sleeves that day. In fact, he'd worn long sleeves every day for months, even in the summer.

Esther felt sick. How could it be that someone you loved could be in pain for so long without you noticing?

Of course, this wasn't the first time that Eugene had been sad. Depression was a real sneaky asshole. Like that baby girl doctors thought they'd cured of HIV after aggressive antiretroviral treatment, because her viral load was undetectable, but as soon as they took her off treatment, the disease came back. Like HIV, depression was a king at playing hide-and-seek. It concealed itself in reservoirs deep inside the mind, waiting for the walls you built around it to eventually erode. Depression could be at undetectable levels for months or years. You'd be all happy and stable and think you were cured, you were a survivor, and then BAM, out of nowhere it resurged. Imagine, like, surviving the sinking of the *Titanic* or something and thinking you did it, you lived, you won the game against death, but then a few years passed and the *Titanic* started hunting everyone who got away, killing them one by one on the streets of New York. We're talking an *I Know What You Did Last Summer*–style revenge horror movie, but with a 46,328-ton passenger liner as the crazed murderer, floating around in a sea of fog. *That's* how irrational depression was.

Eugene was afraid of darkness, and so he'd die of it. That was how the curse worked. Esther had always wondered exactly how darkness would kill him; it took until that morning, the image of his scored wrists burned into her head, to understand that darkness could live in a person and eat them from the inside out.

So, while she waited for Rosemary and Eugene in the car, Esther did something she deeply hated doing. She made a phone call.

Jonah picked up after three rings.

"Solar, what's up?" he said. It sounded like he was eating cereal.

"I'm so scared of losing Eugene. That the curse is going to kill him before I can break it. We aren't trying hard enough."

Jonah was quiet for a beat. "If you're really worried about

him, maybe he should see a therapist or something." Which is what people always said when they knew people were mentally ill. Like it was so easy to treat and fix and cure. Esther thought about who she could tell. Thought about who would care enough to do anything to help Eugene. Their parents? People so weighed down by their own fears that they could barely function? Or a school counselor perhaps? Someone who'd look at her brother and not see him as the complex, brilliant human that he was, just a problem to be solved, a sickness to be medicated, a darkness to be locked away.

Breaking the curse made just as much sense to Esther as seeing a therapist did. Maybe even more.

When Esther didn't say anything, Jonah changed tack, his voice light and playful once again. "Look, it's not my fault you're scared of some dumb Mothman who's never gonna attract Death's attention."

"I'll have you know that the Mothman precipitated the deaths of forty-six people in the Silver Bridge collapse of 1967."

"Why're you calling? I normally have to call you. I thought you hated making phone calls. It's on your list."

Esther checked the weather app on her phone. "I think I might have an idea for Sunday. Something insanely dangerous that will in all likelihood result in our untimely demise."

Jonah crunched his cereal. Swallowed. "*Now* we're talking. I'm in."

Eugene might be looking for Death, but she'd be damned if they weren't going to find him first.

16

5/50: LIGHTNING

TO ATTRACT the attention of Death, you couldn't just be afraid. It didn't matter how deeply into your bone marrow your fear got. You had to truly *believe* you were going to die. It was like a beacon, that belief. A ping sent out to the Reaper that added you—even if only temporarily—to his list.

Come find me, it said. *Come and take my soul.*

At least, that was Esther's theory, which could be totally wrong. It could be that your death was predetermined, and the Reaper knew the exact time and place that you would die, and didn't bother paying any attention to you until your time came, but she couldn't work with that.

The Sunday of 5/50 happened to coincide with the forecast for a wild weather warning in the afternoon. A thunderstorm, a remnant from the fast-dying warmth of summertime, was set to roll across the outskirts of town, and even though number forty-six wasn't lightning (it was graveyards), Esther asked Jonah if they could swap the fears and—much to her surprise—he said yes.

She didn't bother with this week's ridiculous excuse. ("I'm making millinery, sorry.") She ran out to Jonah's moped when he arrived, climbed on the back, and gave him directions to a field directly in the radar path of the storm. She was dressed as Mary Poppins—white shirt, black skirt, red bow tie, and an umbrella. They drove out together to the flat plains of grass that surrounded the town, miles and miles and miles of nothing. Not even so much as a scraggly tree. Jonah had brought a picnic, and they ate in the afternoon sunshine, checking the weather radars on their phones again and again to make sure the thunder and lightning were still coming their way. The sun-bleached grass swayed around them, a sea of blond hair. When they got bored, they listened to "Bohemian Rhapsody" over and over again, yelling the line: *Thunderbolts and lightning, very very frightening me!* every time it played.

And then came the first distant growl of thunder, which made them stop and stare for the first time at the storm that had been gathering like folds of gray silk on the horizon.

"Shit," Jonah said slowly, hitting pause on Queen. "Would you look at that."

They sat in the swelling darkness, watching the cell roll across the plains. Out there on a horizon unencumbered by houses or mountains or trees, the edge of the storm seemed alive and hungry. It sucked and grumbled, shaking the ground beneath the duo as it came toward them like a wall.

"This is really stupid," Jonah said. "Like, we could *actually die* stupid."

"That's the point." Esther pulled him down into the grass

next to her, because they couldn't be standing, couldn't even be sitting, not if they wanted to survive as the storm edged over them and started to send its electric fingers out before it, searching for somewhere to strike.

"Remind me again why I agreed to let you plan this week?"

"Because you thought I'd wimp out."

"I'm gonna have to seriously rethink that opinion."

The air went cool and still, as if the storm was drawing all the power from the atmosphere to feed itself. The world grew darker. Rain began to fall, no more than a mist at first, then droplets so large and fast they stung Esther's skin.

"You're getting wet around me again," said Jonah.

"It's *still* not funny."

"But it *is* true!"

And then came the lightning. Esther had never been in the immediate vicinity of lightning before. She'd always had to count the seconds—four, five, six, seven—before the thunder to figure out how many miles away the strike was. There were no seconds between strike and thunderclap here. Brightness tore across the sky at the same time her eardrums shuddered and the ground beneath her lurched. It was so sudden, so violent, that the world seemed to blink in and out of reality for a few moments, and thunder rumbled away and away and away from them, going to warn all the people of the town that the storm was coming. But they were there, at the epicenter, at the beginning of the sound that wouldn't hit counting children for three, four, five seconds. It started with them.

Jonah took her hand, because this really *was* stupid, but they couldn't run now. They had targets painted on their souls that stretched up into the heavens, begging the lightning to funnel through them to the ground. More brightness came and she understood for the first time why lightning was called a strike. It stabbed down through the air to violently connect with the earth. Esther jammed her eyes closed. If Death was coming, she didn't want to see him. So she and Jonah held hands tightly, and their closeness made her skin shiver with delight, and every time the lightning struck, he said some iteration of, "Holy fucking shit that one was close did you feel that my God woman you will be the literal death of me!"

The strikes grew further apart, and the thunder grew distant. The rain cleared and they didn't die.

When the rain stopped altogether, Esther opened her eyes and sat up. They were gloriously, miraculously alive, but for a moment, a flicker, a heartbeat, she swore she saw a dark figure moving away from them through the grass across the plains. It was not Death as folklore imagined him, not a tall, gaunt skeleton in a cloak with a scythe in hand, but a small figure dressed in a dark coat and black hat.

Death as her grandfather described him. Jack Horowitz.

Esther blinked and the figure was gone, swallowed by the tall grass shivering on the horizon, but she was very nearly almost certain that she wasn't hallucinating.

How Esther imagined it in her head: That morning, a woman who wasn't supposed to die until May 5, 2056 forgot her office keys on the way out her front door, requiring that she reenter her house to find them, which added twenty-five seconds to her daily walk to work. Twenty-five seconds might not seem like a lot in general day-to-day life. Generally, not much can be achieved in twenty-five seconds. You can reheat a cup of coffee in the microwave. Hold a yoga pose. Listen to just under half of the instrumental opening of "Stairway to Heaven." Small victories, accomplished again and again by people every single day without killing them.

The woman in question was not to be so lucky. In the finely tuned business of death, twenty-five seconds was the difference between arriving to work still breathing, and being buried almost four decades before your time. As it happened, this unexpected exercise of free will threw off Death's careful calculations, and the woman was in exactly the right place at exactly the right time for a piece of metal shrapnel thrown up by an industrial lawnmower to decapitate her.

A gruesome freak accident, if ever there was one, that would have the people of the town speculating about the cruel *Final Destination* nature of Death for many years to come. How meticulous the Reaper must be, they'd say, to so finely tune, so perfectly time a woman's death, so that if she had left home one second later or one second earlier, or not stopped to retie her shoelace, or not bothered to go back for her office keys, or this or that, she might still be alive. There's much that could be said here about predestination—the reason why no house was built on the lot, how the shrapnel in question came to be hidden in the long grass, how the mowing was scheduled for the afternoon, but the maintenance worker operating it had a custody hearing then and so had shifted the work to the morning. How, if his wife hadn't discovered the text message from his mistress revealing their two year affair, then there would be no custody hearing, and so on and so forth. Hundreds and thousands of choices and chances in one unending string leading to that very moment, when a two-foot-long piece of pipe got caught in the mower blade and sheared its way through the woman's left temple and out the other side.

Little did humans understand that Death, too, was surprised by death sometimes.

Because of this unexpected change to his schedule, an infant due to die of SIDS was not reaped. (His parents were successfully giving him CPR by the time Death arrived; the baby would go on to live to the age of seventy-seven.) Thus Death found himself with a fifteen minute smoke break from his duties. Having given up his pack-a-day habit many years earlier, he instead decided to wander the countryside and think—about life, and death, and everything that happened in between. It was then, during this unexpected and unplanned solstice, that the Reaper happened across two teenagers laying in a field, a lighting storm going on above them. He momentarily panicked. He'd already reaped one soul just that morning who was not supposed to die, and here, again, were two more. Was this the beginning of some cataclysmic anarchy against death? How much extra paperwork would this require? Would he still be able to take his vacation to the Mediterranean if the entire circle of life went to hell?

And so the Reaper, quite powerless to intervene, did the only thing he could do: He stood in the long grass and watched them from afar, eating trail mix and hoping they wouldn't be struck by lightning and cooked from the inside out. He watched them as the storm passed without touching them, and then he moved farther away and watched them some more as they helped each other to their feet and ran in crazed circles around the empty field, throwing their hands in the air and screaming to the high heavens about their immortality. The girl, he thought, might have seen him, but humans tended not to focus for too long on things that frightened them, and she was quickly distracted by the boy at her side.

Death recognized her, though. The shape of her eyes, the red tinge to her hair, the storm of freckles across her face and—perhaps most telling of all—an almost wolfish glint of defiance in her eyes.

Reginald Solar, over the years, had caused a considerable amount of disturbance to Death's work and so his granddaughter was someone to be paid attention to, if only to be sure that she was not also causing shenanigans, which she clearly was.

Back to reality: Esther didn't tell Jonah that Death had possibly been there, that he'd come to watch them. All she said, as they helped each other to their feet, both drenched and dripping, was, "It's totally working."

17

6/50: CLIFFS

THE NIGHT before 6/50, Esther couldn't sleep. She was lying in her bed, drifting off, when she got one of those jolts your body gets that made it feel like you were falling down stairs. The sensation brought her back to full consciousness, and her brain suddenly fed her the image of a wave of water crashing into her house. Windows shattering, debris pinning her to the walls. A tsunami. They lived an hour's drive from the coast, so the fear was totally irrational and she *knew* it was totally irrational, but that didn't stop it from replaying again and again and again in her head, a wave (ha) of adrenaline surging through her each time.

After two hours of failing to save Eugene and drowning in the murky water of her bedroom, she gave up on sleep, collected her bedding, and went to lie on the kitchen bench, which seemed a moderately safe place to be in the unlikely/impossible event of a tsunami. (Wood floats, after all.)

This was not a new phenomenon. The first time the fear cascade happened, she was about eleven, and the irrational dread that kept her awake was that a cougar (not native to that area—never so much as *sighted* in that area) was going to slink in the back door (which was locked), make its way to her bedroom door (which was closed), and maul her to death. She spent the whole night in Eugene's room, sitting in a corner, staring at the door, waiting, waiting, *waiting* for the moment the big cat came to eat them.

She'd been so *certain* it was going to happen. It did not.

When Jonah arrived in the morning, Esther still hadn't slept. Her eyes were burning and she didn't feel like doing whatever stupid, reckless thing he had planned for the day. (The fear was "cliffs"—it was always going to be bad.) So she *did* employ her "get out of doing the fear for a few hours" ridiculous excuse of making millinery. She sat with Jonah on their yellow couch and made hats out of cereal boxes, toilet rolls, and wire they salvaged from the trash. He even stuck little paper flowers and butterflies on his, and made a feather out of tissues.

"Show off," she muttered, shaking her head when he put his hat on and started prancing around the living room sipping tea from an imaginary cup.

Then it was time to tease Death. Jonah told her to change into beachwear. The only thing she had was a swimming costume she'd bought at a thrift store, an early twentieth-century style knee-length monstrosity complete with pale yellow stripes, Peter Pan collar, and a large bow at the back. When she changed, he spent a solid two minutes facedown on the floor laughing at her outfit.

"The finishing touches," he said when he finally recovered, and he removed his cardboard hat from his head and placed it on hers and fastened it under her chin. "Ready for a day at the beach in the year 1900."

"What's my acceptable excuse next week?"

"You're too busy going on a date with Jonah Smallwood to be bothered with cornfields."

"I don't date boys who laugh at my excellent swimwear choices."

"I'd be wary of anyone who *didn't* laugh at your swimwear choices."

"Jonah. Be serious. We have to focus on the list. I'm worried about Eugene."

"So bring him along, get him in on the nightmare action. It would do him and Hephzibah good. And I *am* being serious. Go on a date with me."

Jonah was staring at her, waiting for her answer. Esther felt a strange sensation in her chest, like a thread around her heart had just been pulled taut. It was something she'd felt before, when they were in elementary school, and Jonah would sit with her at recess to stop the mean kids from taunting her about her hair or her freckles or her clothes. Esther remembered the way his brow wrinkled and the ferocity in his brown eyes. They said, "Nobody screws with you when I'm here." They were saying that again now, and Esther wanted to believe them, because Jonah was beautiful and good and smelled like bliss condensed into the shape of a person.

But he'd made her feel safe once before, and then he'd left, and she still hadn't forgotten how much it hurt to rely on somebody and then have them let you down. "I'll have to consider how desperate I am to stay away from cornfields," she said finally.

"Desperately avoiding fear. That's how I get all the girls to date me."

"Dated lots of girls, have you?"

"Don't try and slut shame me, Esther Solar!" he yelled out the window. "I will not be slut shamed!"

Esther clapped her hand over his mouth. "Christ, all right, let's go do this."

Jonah grinned underneath her hand. "Bring your bro."

"Eugene hates the ocean."

"All the more reason. You go get him while I organize this," he said, unzipping the black duffel bag he'd brought with him. Esther noticed for the first time that it had mesh panels.

"What's that for exactly?"

"Oh, didn't I mention it earlier? I bought it for the cat. I'm bringing her on our adventures." Then he scooped Fleayoncé off the couch, lowered her carefully into the carry bag slung over his shoulder, and went on his merry way, feeding her bits of dry cat food and whispering to her as he went. Esther thought the feeling that rocketed through her heart at the sight was something very close to love.

And so, on the sixth Sunday they spent together, Esther invited Eugene and Hephzibah to join them on their quest for Death.

The beach was an hour's drive from their town, which still

wasn't quite far enough for Reginald Solar, who feared water's immensity so greatly that he hadn't so much as looked at a swimming pool since shortly after the war ended. Esther feared the ocean too, mostly because her grandfather did, but also because it contained sharks, piranha, and potentially Cthulhu.

They drove to the coast in Eugene's car. Fleayoncé sat on Jonah's lap, purring madly. Heph was dressed in white, long ribbons threaded through her ashen hair. Eugene was quiet as he stared at the flat road ahead. Sometimes, when the mottled sunlight hit him strangely, his fingertips curled around the steering wheel looked like glass.

The beach was bleak and deserted when they arrived. The craggy coastline of cliffs plunged into the flat blue ocean. People came here for cliff diving in the summer, but today the sun was washed out and a cold breeze rose from the water, carrying with it the scent of seaweed and brine. There were no trees for as far as the eye could see. No houses, no stores, no developments of any kind. Just flat grassland that sank suddenly and dramatically into the water.

The four got out of the car and walked abreast toward the cliff's edge, Fleayoncé on a leash at Jonah's side. Five feet before the verge, Esther stopped. She couldn't help it. In that moment, in front of her friends, she wanted so badly to be brave, but her feet stopped working and she shook her head. She found heights actually, physically repulsive. Once she'd watched a YouTube video of two Ukrainian guys climbing the Shanghai Tower; it made her throw up.

She felt a sudden need to have as much of her body touching solid ground as possible, so she lay down flat on her back.

"How you doing?" Jonah asked when he appeared over her.

Esther flopped a weak-wristed hand in his general direction. *I'm fine*, the gesture was supposed to convey, but was doing a poor job. Jonah sat cross-legged next to her.

"You can do this, Esther," he said. "Think about everything you've done so far."

"I'm not like you. I'm not fearless."

"You think I'm not scared? Man, I was nearly shitting my pants in the cave. I watched *The Descent*, by the way; I'm never going spelunking again."

"You filthy *hypocrite*."

"Look, fearless people are stupid, 'cause they don't even understand what fear is. If I was fearless, I'd jump out of a plane without a parachute, or eat your mom's cooking again." Eugene laughed at this. "Yeah, there we go, he knows what I'm talking about. Point is, you gotta be scared. Fear protects you. You gotta be scared right down to your bones"—he touched his fingertips to her collarbone—"for bravery to mean anything."

Esther looked over at him. "What if I die?"

"What if you live?"

At that moment, Esther heard a scream. Out of the corner of her eye she caught a pale blur, a tall ghost dressed all in white.

"Was that—" was all she had time to say before Hephzibah Hadid barreled off the edge of the cliff, shrieking and fully clothed, her long limbs flailing in the air for a moment before she disappeared out of sight.

"Holy *shit*," Esther yelled as they all scrambled to their feet and bolted to the cliff. Heph was in the water far below, a halo of white lace fanning out from where she broke the surface. She floated on her back, kicking lazily to the rocky shore like a figure in an impressionist painting.

"You okay?" shouted Esther. Hephzibah gave two enthusiastic thumbs up. "Heph's a daredevil?" She sunk to her knees so she could get a better view over the edge without the fear of being sucked down to her death. "How did I miss that?"

"Heph's a wild animal," Eugene said. "How could you not have noticed?"

Esther sidled away from the edge and turned to scale down the path that led to the ocean to help Heph out, but Jonah shook his head and said, "I'll get her. You jump." Then he slung Fleayoncé around his neck and she lay there, limp and smiling, the world's ugliest taxidermied stole.

Esther forced herself to her feet, the wind curling her red hair around her body like a firestorm. As she stood on the precipice, she felt something she'd never felt before. The old fear was there, the grapnel anchor lodged in her chest, the thing that wanted to pull her back away from the edge and whisper *no, no, no*. Yet there was a new thing: a lure. Something down in the water that whispered *yes, yes, yes*. Go forward, onward, into the unknown. It felt like something between destruction and thrill.

Everything you want is on the other side of fear, she reminded herself. What was fear hiding from her this time?

Here was the thing about adrenaline: She'd never realized, before, how addictive it was. Until recently, adrenaline had been an enemy, something pushed into her veins against her will. She'd never understood how jumping off a bridge with a glorified elastic band strapped around your ankles could in any way be classified as enjoyable. But now she could see that it was about control. Choosing when and where and how the adrenaline spiked, as opposed to waiting for it to find you in your bed as you fell asleep.

Esther still wasn't sure which force would win, which force would be stronger, until Eugene came to stand next to her on the ledge and said, "Jonah just gave me a pep talk."

"He thinks he's a philosopher. What did he say?"

"Something about a dragon and a knight."

"Of course. A classic."

"So. We doing this or not?" Eugene extended his hand to her. Always careful to keep his sleeves covering the skin of his wrists.

Far below, Jonah pulled Hephzibah from the water and shouted that he had a good, clear shot lined up with the GoPro and they could jump anytime they wanted.

Esther took Eugene's hand; his skin was corpse cold against hers. "I curse the day I met that boy," she said of Jonah, and then sister and brother counted to three, and then they jumped with a scream as one. As she fell, Esther wasn't worried about being blown off course and plummeting into the rocks below. She wasn't

164

worried about hitting the shallows and pin diving to the ocean floor and shattering her spine. She wasn't even worried about Cthulhu. (Okay, maybe a little.) What she worried about was Eugene's willingness to jump. The way he glanced down at the water far below and looked at it like it was home. The way he stepped lightly from the cliff's edge, and the way he fell through the air faster than she did, dragged down by earth's magnetic field. The way he flickered in the sunlight as he hit the water, the same way Tyler Durden flashed on-screen four times before you saw him solidly. Foreshadowing the twist to come.

Eugene was afraid of demons, and monsters, and above all the dark, but he was not afraid of death. That scared her more than anything.

Esther hit the water feetfirst and was sucked down, down, down by momentum and her body weight. The shock of the cold splintered into her bones and made her lungs constrict. By then her brain was yelling *up, up, up*. Eugene was gone. Everything was gone. It was just her and Cthulhu in the deep cool dark. She scrambled for the surface and broke it at the same time as her brother. They each drew in a huge breath. Eugene was laughing, howling, splashing her with water. She swam to him, pushed him under playfully, noted the way the light passed through him and turned him clear when he was submerged.

How long did she have? How long until he evaporated for good? How long until he flickered out and never came back? Not long enough.

"Hey," she said to him when he resurfaced, placing a palm on each of his cheeks. There was a strange magnetism in his skin that made her feel calm whenever they touched, some twin enchantment perhaps. "I love you. Don't ever forget that."

"Stop being a weirdo," he said with a grin as he pushed her away. "I want to go again. Let's find somewhere higher."

Esther smiled too, eager to attract Death's attention with their wildness. Maybe he would come here to watch them being reckless, just as she believed he'd watched them once before.

The four of them spent the rest of the afternoon plummeting off the cliffs, getting bolder each time. Higher each time. They ran and jumped. They somersaulted. After lunch, Eugene drove to the Walmart up the coast and bought four inflatable dolphins that they rode off the cliff and into the water, like they were going into battle against Poseidon. The footage, Jonah said, was incredible.

And in the water, Esther discovered the beauty that fear had indeed been hiding from her: the tidal pools filled with orange starfish and green coral, portals to another world; the schools of fish that danced a ballet around her body every time she dived; the salt that dried in swirling patterns on her skin.

They didn't meet Death that day, but Eugene and Hephzibah seemed happier and younger than Esther had ever known them to be, and for that she was immeasurably thankful.

"See you on Sunday for cornfields?" Jonah asked on the drive home. She was sitting next to him in the back seat, her head resting on his shoulder, Fleayoncé a salty heat source on her lap.

"Sorry, can't," said Esther sleepily. This close to him, she felt the sudden desire to press her lips to his cheek and wrap her arms around his neck, which was not a desire she was used to feeling for anyone.

"Why not?"

"I have a date."

Jonah grinned about as mischievously as she'd ever seen him grin. "See you on Sunday."

18

7/50: CORNFIELDS

IT WAS the weekend of 7/50 that the furniture started to vanish.

On Saturday morning when Esther woke, the microwave and dining room table were gone. She'd learned not to question these sudden disappearances, so she made her oats on the stovetop and locked her laptop in the chest at the foot of her bed, just in case.

On Sunday morning, the TV was gone. The landline phone. The slow cooker. Reg's old armchair.

Eugene preferred to ignore these things and give Rosemary the benefit of the doubt—maybe she *wasn't* selling all their stuff on Craigslist again—but Esther liked to watch their mother sometimes, just to make sure things weren't getting too bad. To this end, she had constructed a specially formulated gauge to calculate how broke they were at any one point in time:

DEFCON 5. Rosemary ordered takeout = not so broke. Normal readiness. Action required: none.

DEFCON 4. Ramen for dinner more than two nights in a

row = moderately broke. Above normal readiness. Action required: general observation of situation. Intervene where possible.

DEFCON 3. Food was not provided. If lack of food was mentioned, Rosemary suggested they get jobs = pretty broke. Increased readiness. Action required: attempt to prevent large appliances and furniture from being sold online.

DEFCON 2. Distant relatives started calling the house looking to be paid back the money they lent = flat broke. Extreme readiness. Action required: cry to said relatives about how Rosemary had lots of bills and Dad couldn't work and they were absolutely, definitely, positively not broke because she'd been hitting the slot machines more than usual. Lock the bedroom to prevent pillaging of remaining family heirlooms.

DEFCON 1. Maximum readiness. Rosemary's engagement ring gone for "cleaning" = pretty damn broke. This had happened only once before. Eviction from house imminent. Action required: hide valuables. Like, really well. Say you lost them when Rosemary asked where they were. Suffer her wrath. (Reg's service medals, Esther's most prized possession, were currently buried in Heph's backyard to prevent Rosemary from selling them.) Pack all remaining valued personal belongings in suitcase, ready to move in with Hephzibah or any number of angry relatives at a moment's notice. Prepare to become a ward of the state.

There was no food in the house on Sunday morning. When Esther asked her mother about the grocery shopping, Rosemary suggested she get a real job instead of selling cake, so Esther hid her late grandmother's jewelry in a loose floorboard under Eugene's bed. Then she dressed as Claude Monet's *Woman with a Parasol, facing left*, and went outside to wait for Jonah on the porch steps, as had become her routine.

She'd been swept up in a moment of giddy appreciation when she'd agreed to go on a date with him and now she kind of hoped that he would both a) not remember that she'd said yes, and b) never mention it again.

When he arrived, though, he was dressed in a pressed brown suit with a custard-colored shirt and patterned bow tie. It was easily the most hideous ensemble of clothing Esther had ever seen, but Jonah somehow made it look adorable. He kind of made everything look adorable. That was part of the problem. It would've been far less panic-inducing to be around him if he wasn't quite so charming.

He'd made her a paper corsage (complete with a dead moth corpse glued to one of the petals; so romantic) to mark the occasion, so she could hardly change her mind now.

Still, cornfields were far less terrifying than going on a date, so she insisted they do that first.

"Cornfields aren't scary," said Jonah as he parked the moped under a tree and they started to walk toward the distant farm. "What did corn ever do to you?"

"It's like the dark," Esther explained as she used her parasol as a walking stick, her long white dress hitched up in her free hand. "It's what's *in* the corn that's scary."

"What the hell is in the corn?"

"Children. Crop circles. Scarecrows. Serial killers. Tornadoes.

Aliens. Seriously, cornfields are messed up. They may actually be the epicenter of all evil things."

"How come corn got the bad reputation, and not wheat or sugarcane? All this discrimination against moths and cornfields makes me sick."

"I had my first panic attack after watching *Signs* when I was thirteen." Esther wasn't sure why she told Jonah this; she'd never told anyone before. Talking was easier around Jonah, somehow. The muscles in her shoulders that were constantly clenched around other people seemed to loosen in his presence. He calmed her. Made it easier to talk about scary things.

"Yeah, well, Mel Gibson *is* a frightening dude."

"Eugene and I watched the movie at Heph's house. I didn't sleep that night. I swear I could *hear* something outside the window making that clicking noise the aliens make on the baby monitors. When we got home in the morning, I decided to go for a run, just around the block, just to burn off some of the anxiety. One of the aliens started following me."

"What, you were hallucinating or something?"

"No. I never saw it. I wasn't even *near* corn or anything. I just *knew* it was there. I *knew* it was right behind me. I ran until I collapsed, and then I crawled under a car to hide from it. Took me two hours to get home. I had to run from car to car, hiding from this alien. Scratched up my knees and arms until they were bleeding and I was bawling my eyes out, shaking. I *knew* I was going to die."

"Man, you're more messed up than I thought."

"Thanks."

When they reached the edge of the corn, Jonah knelt and fished a drone out of his backpack. A goddamn *drone*.

"Do I *even* want to know where you acquired that?" she said.

"Probably best you don't ask questions about this one," he said as he attached a camera to the device and sent it up into the air.

Then they sprinted together through paths in the cornfields, the drone cruising along above them, dipping and whirling as they ran. Esther imagined what the footage would look like: the long green ribbon of her hat trailing along behind her like seaweed in the air, mint umbrella at her side, the billowing skirts of her dress threatening to launch her into flight. Then she thought of that long, terrible morning she'd spent running for her life, the first time fear really got its claws into her. The first time she felt what Eugene felt every single night as she sat hunched over and hyperventilating in the gutter next to a car, tears streaming down her face, knowing logically that she was in no real danger but unable to shake the certainty that death was imminent.

They turned. The drone followed. The corn began to sigh in the breeze as though breathing. Whispering even. Jonah slowed, and then they stopped completely to listen. The sun beat down. A bead of sweat rolled down her spine. The drone circled above them, strangely threatening. Something made her eyes water.

"We shouldn't be here," she said quietly. The corn was definitely whispering. *Run, run, run,* it said to her. *Something is coming for you.*

The cornfield was a sea and they'd swum far away from safe

shores. The stalks were taller than their heads. A sea of corn had drowned the world. It was everywhere, everywhere, and they were sinking in it, being pulled down. Esther felt a surge of panic, that same panic that jolts through you when you're underwater and scrabbling for the surface but aren't quite sure if you'll make it before your lungs involuntarily suck in a flood of water.

Get out, get out, get out, sighed the corn. Or maybe the warning was from the irrational part of her brain. The same part that made her worried about sharks in swimming pools, murderers lurking behind shower curtains, and sudden velociraptor attacks.

"I need to get out!" she said, and now she was panicking, turning, looking for an easy escape. The corn was whispering, hissing, snagging her hair, pulling at her clothes. Creatures were moving through the stalks. She could feel them. She could see the shadow trails they left behind, and the corn was trying to trap her so she could be eaten.

This was the point where most people said, "Breathe." This was the point where most people said, "Calm down." This was the point where most people said, "Aliens don't exist."

Jonah Smallwood was not most people. He put his hands on her shoulders and said, "The curse doesn't make you interesting."

The statement was strange enough to rip Esther right out of the panic quicksand. "What?"

"You think the curse is the most interesting thing about you, but it isn't. It doesn't even make the top five. You being scared of cornfields and aliens doesn't make you some special snowflake. Everybody's fear sounds the same in their head."

"How dare you," she said sarcastically, panting as she came back to herself. "I *am* a special snowflake."

"You really wanna let M. Night Shyamalan do this to you? That's like crying to a Nickelback song. Have some self-respect."

She gave a shaky laugh. "What are the top five?"

"Top five?"

"Most interesting things about me."

"Narcissist."

"Shut up."

"I'll make you a deal. I'll tell you number five right now, but I'll save the other four for later when you no doubt have other freak-outs about all the fun stuff we'll be doing."

"Okay."

"Number five: your hair color."

"Strawberry blond isn't interesting."

"Nothing strawberry or blond about it. It's peach. Hair like an orchid in summer," he said, and then he had a strand of that very same hair threaded through his fingertips.

"You read too much Shakespeare."

"How about you tell me a story. I wanna hear more about that Jack Horowitz dude."

"Okay," she said, and as her breathing settled into a manageable rhythm, she told Jonah Smallwood about the second time her grandfather met Death.

19

A NICE DAY FOR
A WHITE WEDDING

IT WAS late morning on October 4, 1982 when Jack Horowitz, the Man Who Would Be Death, rang the doorbell of Reginald Solar's house and asked him to be best man at his wedding. Reg, now the father of two sons and a daughter, took one look at the familiar pockmarked face on his porch—who, as you might remember, he believed to be long dead—and promptly fainted. When he regained consciousness half a minute later, Horowitz was crouched over him, fanning him with a handkerchief.

"Goodness, I thought I scared you to death. It would have been very awkward if my master had arrived to reap you. I called in sick today. Hello, Lieutenant."

"You're dead," Reg said, staring up at Horowitz's ghost, which looked remarkably *alive*. The scars on his face were red and pitted and far more inflamed than the skin of a ghost should be. Could ghosts even *have* skin?

"Quite the opposite." Horowitz extended his arm. Reginald didn't take it, instead remaining stationary on the floor.

"I don't understand. You were murdered. You drowned in a river in Vietnam."

"Oh no. I was down there for some time, though. They tied me tight, you see. I was down there fumbling around in the rocks, looking for one sharp enough to cut my bindings for quite some time indeed."

"You . . . Why are you here?"

Horowitz smiled serenely. "I find myself in the position of needing a witness at my wedding. A best man, if you will. You were the first and—I hope you'll forgive me for admitting this—only person I thought of. I don't have a great deal of friends." Horowitz glanced at his still-extended hand. "Do you intend to spend the rest of this conversation horizontal?"

Reg let Horowitz help him up, then said, "Best man? Horowitz, you don't *know* me. We only met once, the night before you died."

"Yes, but you mourned me. You fought for my honor to be reinstated. I suppose I have developed something of a soft spot for you, Reginald Solar. And since the state requires there be a witness at my wedding—someone who knows who I am—I would like for that person to be you."

"I thought you'd been murdered on my watch."

"Alas, as I tried to explain to you in 1972, I am very hard to kill."

Reg, of course, still did not believe that Horowitz was Death's apprentice—even if his survival was remarkable. Still, he invited him inside and they drank milk together as Horowitz explained that Death, too, could love, and indeed, he had swiftly fallen for the young Vietnamese woman who'd discovered him floating facedown in the river, too weak to swim to the bank after several days of trying to free himself.

"Several minutes, you mean," corrected Reginald.

"I assure you, Lieutenant, it was several days."

Reginald shook his head and poured them both another round of milk. Horowitz continued. It was frowned upon for the Grim Reaper to take a lover, he explained. During his tenure as Death, he would be granted long life and immunity from the messy business of dying for as long as his term of service lasted, but his partner would not. This, as you can imagine, had caused some problems in the past. Horowitz couldn't confirm it for sure, but there was a rumor that the Black Death of 1346–53 was the direct result of the Reaper becoming depressed at the sudden and unexpected demise of his young boyfriend, who was killed in a freak accident—the kind that even Death cannot predict. Plagued by despair, he walked the streets of Europe for seven years, rats infected with the *Yersinia pestis* bacterium scuttling behind him by the dozen. In his state of mourning he touched the cheeks of young lovers as they slept so that they, too, might know his sorrow.

Horowitz described the ordeal as a "logistical nightmare." Still, he loved the woman, Lan, and every single person who dared to love risked losing their beloved anyway, so why should he be any different? He thought himself very unlikely to go on a rampage if she died, and besides, she was young and fit and healthy, so why should she perish anytime in the next fifty years or so? He would remain a young man while she aged, and then, when she passed peacefully in her sleep surrounded by her children and grandchildren and great-grandchildren, he would train an apprentice, and then retire and join her in the afterlife. Even as Death he'd have to die eventually, but he'd get to choose how and where and when—one of the few perks of the job.

The two men spoke until early afternoon, mostly about the war and the years that had passed since it ended. Reginald showed Horowitz pictures of his wife and children, and Horowitz showed Reginald pictures of the little white house he'd bought in Santorini. It had blue window frames and a blue door, and a small goat grazing in the yard, perfect for making cheese. Lan, his betrothed, loved olives and sunshine and waking to the sound of waves crashing against rock, so that was what Horowitz was giving her.

"You'll be happy there, I'm sure," said Reg as he handed back the Polaroids.

"I must ask you, Reginald, to keep a terrible secret for me."

"Uh . . ."

"My beloved, she . . . Well, she doesn't know who I am. Or what I am, rather. I know it's deceitful of me not to tell her, but who could love such a thing as me if they knew the truth?"

"If you haven't told her, I certainly won't," Reg said, even though he believed that a person had a right to know they were probably marrying a basket case who had delusions of being the Grim Reaper. If the woman hadn't figured out by now that Horowitz was delusional and possibly psychotic, he wasn't going to be the one to tell her.

Horowitz's wedding took place the next afternoon, in the town's local chapel. Lan wore a pale pink sundress with a strand of pearls at her throat, and the Man Who Would Be Death dressed in a lavender tuxedo with shiny white shoes and a ruffled shirt. Reginald thought the supposed Reaper really ought to have more style about him, but then again, Horowitz was born in the South and raised on a farm—or so he said—so style wasn't exactly expected.

Esther's grandmother, Florence Solar, also attended the wedding, though Esther never got the chance to ask her about what she thought of the Reaper and his bride; she died the very same night her grandfather first told her the story. Esther wondered if she knew Horowitz was Death. Wondered if, at the moment of her last breath, she was shocked to find the pockmarked young man whose wedding she'd attended almost three decades earlier come to collect her immortal soul.

The two men parted ways again after the wedding, Reg Solar still no more convinced that Horowitz was indeed Death but glad to know that he was alive and stable and happy, for the time being.

While Esther told her story, Jonah absentmindedly weaved a crown of cornhusks and placed it atop her head. "Queen of Death," he said when she finished. By then, the sun had sunk low and the drone's battery had run out and the corn was still whispering, urging them to leave.

"Do you want to go on that date now?" she asked him, and he said yes, so they did.

"THERE ARE FOUR STEPS to wooing the ladies," Jonah explained to Esther an hour later. They were standing in front of a Mexican food truck called Taco the Town. "First I buy them Mexican food, then I buy them beer, then I take them to my favorite place, and then I whip out my secret weapon."

"I sincerely hope the secret weapon is *not* your genitals."

"Ugh. Get your head out of the gutter, Esther. Honestly."

"Wait, are you saying you're trying to woo me right now?"

"I've been trying to woo you since elementary school. You're just too distracted to notice. You think I'd reupholster a couch for just anyone?"

"Abandoning someone and not contacting them for six years is hardly an optimal wooing technique."

"Touché."

"Where did you go by the way? You haven't told me."

"You haven't asked."

"I'm asking now."

"It's a long story that involves time travel and a failed attempt to kill Hitler. Trust me, you don't want to know."

They ate their burritos while sitting in the gutter next to the taco truck, then drove until they got to the WELCOME TO sign on the outskirts of town. They sat on the other side of the sign, huddled close to keep warm, officially outside the boundaries of the place that held them in like a black hole. It was amazing—Esther could breathe there. No more than two feet beyond the edge, and the straps around her chest had loosened, the metal plate that encased her brain had dissolved.

"Salud," Jonah said, passing her a warm can of beer from inside his jacket.

"Does this technique *really* work for you?" she asked him. He didn't answer. Instead they cracked open their drinks and watched the highway that led out of town, all the cars that moved beyond the event horizon like it was nothing, nothing at all, the easiest thing in the world to escape. Esther didn't have to ask Jonah why this was his favorite place. They stared at the cars, each one plunging off into an unknown that they wouldn't know for years. Might never know.

Esther thought about what she wanted for herself after school, but as hard as she tried to visualize herself as a college freshman, or maybe traveling through Asia on a shoestring budget with nothing but a backpack, all that kept coming back to her was a single thought: Eugene. Eugene was an anchor. A small, dark part of her knew that he wasn't stable enough for college, and wouldn't be able to leave home after school. As long as Eugene was sick—as long as the curse had him—she was going to be stuck here.

Esther wanted to save his life, but she also wanted to give herself a chance at her own.

"Tell me about your parents," Jonah said. "What were they like before the curse?"

Esther smiled as she thought of Rosemary and Peter as they

had once been. "My dad's favorite things in the world were poetry and Christmas. Just so embarrassingly nerdy. I've never seen a grown man so excited for Christmas morning. And the poetry—he used to recite limericks to us every morning on the drive to school. A new one, every single day. I have no idea if he wrote them himself or found them on the internet and memorized them, but they were always terrible, and they always made us laugh."

Jonah smiled. "And your mom?"

"Mom used to grow plants in boxes outside our windows. Said they were gardens for fairies that would keep us safe while we were sleeping. She still works as a horticulturalist, but it's not the same. I mean, she used to be able to grow *anything*, anywhere, without sunlight or water. She used to be magic. I was obsessed with that woman. We went everywhere together, and she used to talk to me about everything. She was my best friend. And then . . . nothing. Bit by bit, she kind of shut down and fell away and left us on our own."

Jonah reached out and held her hand, and she was too tired to stop him, too tired to stop herself from wondering if this was what people felt in the beginning, if this is what *she'd* felt like before, when they were children. Esther had loved him once, in the way kids love, of that much she was sure. For a small amount of time, he'd been the bright light in the darkness.

And God, the way he *smelled*. She'd bottle that scent and touch his perfume to the pulse slipping beneath the skin of her neck every day if she could. As they drank warm beer, Esther supposed that it would be very easy to fall in love with Jonah

Smallwood again. It would be very easy to let him become a part of herself again, and therein lay the problem. Esther had no illusions about who or what Jonah was: he was a pickpocket, a skilled petty criminal, an underage drinker (then again, so was she), a public nuisance, and also—undoubtedly—the very best person she had ever met. Jonah was *good* in a way that baffled her, and she feared that if she let him get too close, came to rely on him as a shield once more, the way she had before when she was a little kid, that he would disappear again, and she would be left to mend the broken bits on her own.

Esther could have fallen in love with him that night, but it was safer not to, so she did the only thing she could do: she rested her head on Jonah's shoulder, drank the beer he had brought her, and dreamed about the day she would be flung beyond the event horizon at the speed of light, never to return.

"I'm still waiting for the secret weapon," she said after a while.

"Just you wait," he said. And that's when Jonah Smallwood stood and started dancing in the middle of the road.

"Sweet Caroline, bah bah bah," he crooned as he moved, "good times never seemed so good. Oh sweet Caroline, bah bah bah. The last girl I brought here was Caroline andIdidn'thavetime-tolearnanewsongforyou." The last part of the sentence he tried to squash into a single word to make it fit the tune.

Esther shook her head. "I cannot believe any girl, ever, has been impressed by you."

"Come dance with me, bah bah bah."

"Absolutely not."

"Why not, Esther Solar?" Still to the tune of *Sweet Caroline*.

"Because they did that in *The Notebook* and it has therefore been done."

"They didn't dance like this, bah bah bah."

"I *know*. I'm aware. That's why it looked good."

"That cut me real deep," he sang, but didn't stop dancing. Esther took out her phone and started filming him, which only made him really turn it up. "SWEET CAROLINE, BAH BAH BAH," he screamed to the night sky. "I WISH I'D LEARNED A SONG FOR ESTHER."

"You're embarrassing yourself. I won't be part of this tom-foolery. Please stop singing that god-awful song."

"Only if you join me."

"The people driving past will see me."

"No they won't. They'll see *Woman with a Parasol, facing left*. Nobody is going to care."

"*I* care."

"Too much. About too many things."

"You're a ridiculous human being," she said, but she supposed he was right. She watched the cars as they passed, and thought about what they'd see if they looked out their windows: a ghost dressed in white, a flash of red hair. Not enough, she hoped, for anyone she knew to identify her. Finally she stood and finished her drink and fell in line next to him. "Don't watch me."

"I won't. I promise."

Then she started line dancing, just the way her grandmother had taught her when she was little.

Esther knew the exact moment Jonah broke his promise and peeked at her, because he collapsed face-first onto the asphalt, his favorite move whenever he found her particularly preposterous. "You dance like Elaine from *Seinfeld*," he said a minute later when he could finally speak again through his laughter.

"I hate you," she said, but she didn't stop dancing, and he didn't stop dancing either, not for a while, not until he held her hand and spun her around and pulled her close to him so they were in the waltz position. Jonah hummed as they slow danced, his head resting against hers. Esther liked the way he felt against her. Liked the way he made her stomach flutter like a storm of orange butterflies.

And that, of course, was the problem.

Esther put her hand on his chest and gently pushed herself away. "I can't do this," she said quietly, unable to look at him. Her heart felt strange. Painful, somehow.

"Why not?"

"Because . . ." Why? So many reasons. Because she wasn't good enough. Because something inside of her was rotten and broken and unlovable. Because Jonah would figure this out eventually, and why bother starting something if the end of it was inevitable? Because he'd had to leave once before, and it had sucked, and maybe it had only sucked because eight-year-olds can be real dicks and the bullying that happened in his sudden absence had left its mark somewhere deep in her soul. Whatever the reason, she couldn't fathom giving anyone that kind of power over her again.

Esther tried to tell him all of this, but some error occurred in the translation of thought into speech, and all she could manage to say was, "Because . . . I just can't, okay?" Sometimes it was better to not get what you wanted. Sometimes it was better to leave beautiful things alone for fear of breaking them.

"Okay," Jonah said quietly, and he stroked her cheek with his thumb but didn't say anything more, because you couldn't convince someone to love you if she wouldn't.

The hurt in his voice killed her, because pain was a language she'd learned to speak well, but she couldn't give him what he wanted. Couldn't give herself what she wanted either.

"Sweet Caroline, bah bah bah," they sang together, much softer now, because they were almost the only words they actually knew. "Good times never seemed so good."

20

8/50: OPERATING AUTOMOBILES

"SO YOU'VE never even been behind the wheel of a car before?" Jonah asked.

Esther was sitting in the driver's seat of Holland Smallwood's hideous squash-colored '80s station wagon, refusing to start the engine because she didn't want to a) kill herself, or b) get murdered by Jonah's father. "I tried once, but I had a panic attack, so I added it to the list and never looked back."

"Let me get this straight. As soon as you come close to failing at something, you decide to never do it again?"

"Exactly. Then I can feel really, really good about never having failed at anything. It's all perfectly psychologically healthy. I'm a genius."

"You're gonna learn today," he said, nodding at the gearstick. "Holland drives stick."

"I cannot drive stick."

"Man, my dad is halfway retarded and he can drive stick, so you can too."

"You can't say retarded. It's politically incorrect. Besides, if I crash Holland's car, he'll kill me."

"Nah, he'll kill *me*. Then you. Then your family. So you got enough time to flee to Mexico before he starts hunting you. Start the engine."

"No."

"Esther, look at your costume. Look who you are today. Would *Kill Bill* have been interesting if the Bride refused to so much as drive a car?"

Esther looked down at the yellow and black leather ensemble she'd chosen for today and took a steadying breath. "Channel Uma," she said with a nod. "Channel your inner badass."

It didn't go too badly at first, to be honest. Esther wasn't as terrible a driver as she remembered being, and although she didn't have even one-fifth of the coordination required to operate a motor vehicle, she didn't crash into anything. Jonah kept her out of traffic and away from intersections so she wouldn't have to stop and start too much. They mainly stuck to the smaller roads on the outskirts of town, ones that were long and straight and had no traffic lights or stop signs.

The day might have ended very differently if it weren't for the erection of a mall out in the boondocks and the subsequent roadwork that was taking place to facilitate the white behemoth's construction.

A woman in a high visibility vest brought them to a stop while a truck crossed from one side of the construction site to the other. Esther found herself at the front of a line of cars. While she waited, she adjusted her rearview mirror so she could count them all. There were six, with more braking behind her every few seconds.

"I can't do this," she said quietly as she made mirror eye contact with the man directly behind her. "Swap seats with me."

"What?"

"There are too many people *watching* me. They're all *looking* at me."

"No one cares, Esther."

"They're all going to get angry if I stall."

"Look, she's telling us to go. Come on."

And she was. The construction worker had flipped her STOP sign around to SLOW and was waving them through.

Esther shoved the car into first but let the clutch out too quickly and it lurched forward, stalled. The man behind them beeped. The construction woman took a step back and laughed.

"I told you I couldn't fucking do it!" Esther said. The eyes of the drivers behind her were like a spotlight, heating up her blood.

"Yes you can, Esther," Jonah said, and she must have looked panicked, because he was clasping her shoulder and speaking low and clear. Her skin strobed between warm and freezing. There was a familiar tingling in her fingers. "Listen to me. You *can* do this."

The driver in the car behind them leaned on the horn again. Jonah rolled down his window. "You want me to come back there? I will come back there, asshole! She's learning!"

Esther restarted the car and put it into first gear. A strap around her chest was tightening, squeezing her ribs smaller and smaller. She tried to ease the clutch out, but her legs were shaking and she was sweating inside her yellow leather outfit and the sun was beating down through the windshield, searing across her skin. There was no air.

The car jolted forward and the engine gutted out. A violent stall. Several drivers behind them beeped in unison. Esther didn't realize she was hyperventilating until she couldn't breathe. Her hands were shaking and she couldn't breathe.

Couldn't breathe.

Couldn't breathe.

Jonah was already out of the car, leaning across her to unbuckle her seatbelt. The car was an oven and her skin was prickling all over and everyone was watching her, everyone could see. The tingling in her fingers rolled up her arms to her neck, where invisible hands clamped down on her esophagus.

You're dying, you're dying, oh God, you're dying.

This was it. All these weeks they'd been looking for Death, and finally he'd decided to show up to the party, and all Esther could think about was what a stupid idea this was and how much she really didn't want to die.

The car was moving then and her cheek was pressed to the hot, cracked leather of the back seat. She couldn't remember how she'd gotten there. Time had warped. There came the sound of running water every few seconds, which she soon realized was her vomiting. There was no heaving. It leaked out of her without effort and trickled into the footwell.

You're dying, you're dying, you're dying.

Then the car stopped and Jonah was pulling her out of the back seat. He left her under a tree.

"I'm sorry, I'm so sorry," she managed between sobs, but Jonah was already gone, and she wondered if he was going to leave her for dead like Bill had done to the Bride, which was fair enough, she supposed. She did vomit in his father's car.

Actually, she was kind of surprised it had taken this long for him to get sick of her. There were only so many times you could have panic attacks in front of people before they wrote you off as a lost cause. Too fragile. Too much hassle. Too painful to be around. Hadn't she done the exact same thing to her father? Why did she deserve any different?

Esther looked around, sure that Jack Horowitz would be there waiting to snatch up her immortal soul, and her panic folded in on her again.

But then Jonah was back with a bottle of cold water in one hand and a box of tissues in the other, and he sank to the ground beside her as she peeled off her yellow jacket and lay down in the grass and tried to slow her breathing.

"You're okay, you're okay," he said, pressing the damp tissues to her forehead.

Maybe it wouldn't be this time, or the next time, or the time after that, but Jonah would eventually get tired of her. Eventually get so frustrated by her inability to be normal that he would leave. Maybe if she was sexy, or confident, or her skin wasn't covered in a minefield of freckles, then she could justify being crazy and broken and weird. As it stood, there wasn't anything alluring enough about her that she could imagine making him want to put up with her bullshit for any great length of time.

People got tired of mental illness when they found out they couldn't fix it.

"Your bedroom," he said.

"What?"

"That's number four. On the list of most interesting things about you. Your bedroom."

"That's really lame. You're making this up as you go along, aren't you?"

"Yeah. Trying not to get too sappy with this shit either, you know."

"Number one's probably gonna be like 'The shape of your toenails' or something."

"Nah, that's number three for sure. You do have some lovely toenails." When she finally felt well enough to sit up, Jonah said, "I'll take you home."

Esther shook her head. "Not home."

"Okay. Uh . . . I showed you my favorite place. How 'bout you show me yours?"

They got back in the now vomit-smelling car (Jonah drove, of course) and she directed him to the parking lot of the local mall.

"Yeah . . . this is a parking lot," he said as he parked.

Esther was still shaky and sweaty and generally a mess. Man, fuck panic attacks. "When we were eleven, Mom brought us here on Christmas Eve morning."

"Last-minute shopping?"

"Not quite. She explained to us in the car that she hadn't been able to buy us any presents that year. It'd been two months since Dad went into the basement, and Reg was already in Lilac Hill, and she'd been laid off from her job, and we didn't have any money. Like, *any* money. Not even enough for food."

"How's this a happy memory?"

"We spent the whole day here together, just the three of us. We walked up and down the lot in a grid, going from level to level, picking up any loose change that we could find. We didn't collect much, only a few dollars, but by the afternoon we had enough for a gingerbread man each. Mom didn't have enough left over for herself, so she kept the two quarters she found; she said they were lucky. She wouldn't even take a bite of our dessert, and later, when we went home, she cried all night."

"Stop me if I'm missing something here, but still kinda struggling to see this as a fun time."

"It's the last memory I have of her being *her*. The last time we were really a family, you know? Even though Dad was in the basement, for some reason, Eugene and I really believed he'd come out on Christmas Day and surprise us. Dad loved Christmas more than we did, and he'd never missed one before. We didn't care that we weren't getting any presents, or that we'd spent Christmas Eve scrounging for coins, because we had Mom, and Dad was coming back to us the next day, and we got gingerbread for dinner. Life was pretty great."

"Your dad didn't come outta the basement."

"I think that's what broke her. Christmas Day. Waiting and waiting and waiting for something that wouldn't come. We ate at my Auntie Kate's every night for a week, and then Mom won three grand on a slot machine. The lucky quarters she found really were lucky. God, she came home with *so* many late Christmas presents: cell phones and books and a feast, everything she'd wanted to buy us but hadn't been able to. The only thing she got for herself was a tiger's-eye necklace for good luck.

"I don't hate her for what she's become. I want to, but I can't. I love her too much. That's the problem. That's what's wrong with love. Once you love someone, no matter who they are, you'll always let them destroy you. Every single time." Even the very best people found ways to hurt the ones they loved.

"The car accident my mom died in was just after Remy was born," Jonah said quietly. "The day I disappeared from school. Valentine's Day. That's why I left. I got pulled out of school before recess. Everything fell apart after she was gone."

"Jesus, Jonah. I had no idea. Shit. I'm so sorry." All these years some dark little voice had been whispering to her that Jonah had left because of *her*. Because all the other kids had called her names and been so mean and he'd grown tired of being the only thing that stood between her and their cruelty. Of course that wasn't true. Of course Esther had made herself the center of the universe. Anxious people always thought the world revolved around them, but knowing the truth didn't make it any easier to stop believing the lie. "Tell me more about her."

Jonah smiled. "She taught literature, but she'd always wanted to be an actress. That's why she loved Shakespeare so much. Man, I swear, she was reading me Shakespeare before she was reading me picture books. And she bought me my first paint set when she saw that I was good at art. She was the only person who didn't laugh at me when I told her I wanted to do movie makeup when I grew up. I told her about you, you know."

"No way."

"Yeah, I did. Told her about you being picked on at school, because it upset me. She sat me down and read me that quote, the one that says, 'All tyranny needs to gain a foothold is for people of good conscience to remain silent,' then explained what it meant and what I needed to do. I sat with you for the first time the next day.

"Ruined my dad, though, her dying. He was a good guy before that, but then I guess the grief turned to depression and the depression turned to booze and the booze is what makes him mean."

Esther didn't know what to say, so she did the only thing she could do: put her hand on Jonah's shoulder and leaned her head against him.

"One day," he said, "everybody's gonna wake up and realize their parents are human beings, just like them. Sometimes they're good people, sometimes they're not."

Before Esther and Jonah went home, they each bought a cookie from the same store Rosemary Solar had taken her children to six years earlier. Esther made a mental note to add gingerbread men to the roster of illicit treats she sold at school.

Near the car, they spotted a quarter glinting in the dark, but neither of them stopped to pick it up.

THAT NIGHT, Jonah decided to stay for his bro date with her dad, which she was, he informed her, invited to. Esther tried to talk him out of it—it wasn't Jonah's burden to carry—but he refused, saying he'd already promised Peter he'd come, and besides, he didn't mind spending the evening in a musty basement if it meant he didn't have to go home. Holland wasn't cruel to Remy, Jonah said. In fact, he barely acknowledged her existence.

Jonah left around sunset and returned half an hour later with an expensive bottle of Scotch. Esther didn't ask how he acquired it. Then he scooped up his cat and slung her around his neck like a scarf, like always, and they went down to the basement.

Once they were downstairs, she was glad Jonah had wanted to stay. The junk, normally stacked up in perilous columns, had been pushed to the sides and neatly arranged. The floors had been cleaned. A table had been set up with three chairs around it, a strip of fabric usually hung on the walls used as a tablecloth. Peter was shining, the petrified half of his body gleaming like polished wood in the low light. Esther could see the age rings that had formed beneath his skin, the opaline veins of white glitter that threaded through the darker wood.

Peter had washed his hair and trimmed his beard. He told them how he'd eaten nothing but beans and rice for four weeks so he could justify spending his carefully rationed savings on this one meal. Esther and Jonah offered to pay for the Thai food they ordered, but Peter wouldn't hear of it.

They stayed for hours. Jonah was the Jonah she'd first seen at the nickel refinery, the one with a drink in each hand, telling some grand story to a crowd of people. The one who painted the brightness of the galaxy to hide the darkness that lived inside him.

Peter adored him, that much was clear. "We should do this again sometime," he said, raising his good arm for a toast. "To new friends."

They raised their glasses of Scotch too. "To new friends," she and Jonah said together.

Esther thought, as she watched them, that perhaps she'd judged her mother too harshly for not leaving her father despite the constant pain he caused her.

Perhaps falling and remaining in love with people, even if you didn't want to, was not the great disaster she'd always imagined it to be.

21

9/50: SATAN INCARNATE

AKA GEESE

ON THE Sunday of 9/50, before Jonah could even ask, Esther held up her hand and explained to him why she avoided geese: "a) Canada geese brought down the plane that crashed into the Hudson River, and b) geese are generally just terrible, horrible, satanic beasts."

"For once," he said, pulling oven mitts out of his backpack and taping them around his wrists, "I agree with you." He looked her up and down, taking in her Stormtrooper armor. "I brought you gloves and goggles, but it doesn't look like you'll need them."

"I have battled a goose before," she said as she put on her helmet, praying to the Great Pit of Carkoon that it would be enough to protect her face from being mangled. "I will not meet them unprepared again."

"You ready?"

"For geese?" Her voice was muffled and her breath was warm against her face, but she didn't care, because *geese*. "No. Let's go."

They walked to the park near her house, where the local

geese were made of beaks and hatred. The pond had been cordoned off for the better part of a decade, ever since the birds tried to maul a small child to death. There were signs pegged into the lawn everywhere that read WARNING: AGGRESSIVE GEESE.

They were going to die.

"Geese are the only birds to have killed a man," Esther said as Jonah strapped his GoPro to his forehead.

"That's not true," he said.

A goose locked eyes with her and hissed, even though they were fifty feet away. "I'm *pretty sure* it's true. They're ready for us."

Jonah crossed himself and took a breadstick out of his backpack. They nodded at each other in understanding that this may very well be the end.

How Esther saw it in her head: an establishing shot, her and Jonah on one side of the screen, the goose horde, on the other, as they marched toward the birds to the tune of Carl Orff's epic "O Fortuna." They began running; so did the geese. There were battle cries from each side. Jonah held up the breadstick and screamed "FOR HUMANITY!" Then a sweeping aerial shot, showing the armies about to collide, and how the two mammalian warriors were vastly outnumbered. A close-up of her Stormtrooper helmet. A close-up of a goose's face, its expression bloodthirsty (aka resting goose face). And then the shot this had all been building toward: their armies meeting in the middle of the screen, two tsunamis slamming into each other, feathers flying everywhere as the geese set upon them.

Back to reality: Esther lost Jonah in the carnage, but she

heard him scream, "Take the bread you sons of bitches! Just take the bread!" The birds were everywhere, snapping at her plastic suit, trying to find the weaknesses in her armor. They were hissing madly, necks outstretched, wings flapping wildly, as they tried to decide whether to eat the breadstick or murder the intruders or both.

"There are too many of them! Retreat, retreat!" Esther yelled. That's when a goose bit Jonah's ankle and brought him down. He screamed and collapsed in a heap, his chest and arms exposed to the fury of a dozen beaks.

"Go on without me!" he said between goose bites. "Go on without me!"

"That's a negative, Ghost Rider!" Emboldened by adrenaline, Esther dove into the demon bird tornado and grabbed Jonah under the arms. But the geese were fast and knew how to hold a grudge, so even though she dragged him halfway across the park, they still followed, hissing and biting and flapping like some symphony of evil. The geese finally decided they were far enough away from their territory and went dead still on the lawn, sentries waiting for the duo to regroup and strike again. Esther dropped Jonah and sank to her knees, heaving breaths inside her helmet. She yanked it off, and then her gloves, so she could tear open Jonah's shirt to check for injuries. He was moaning and writhing on the ground, mumbling over and over, "I can't feel my legs." There were three blood blisters on his shoulders and a dozen on his ankles and legs where the geese got their beaks into him, but apart from that, she couldn't see any lasting damage.

She stared at the geese. "O Fortuna" started playing in her imagination again. "It isn't over," she said, shaking her head. "They'll come for us when we least expect it."

Jonah stood, limping. A goose hissed at him and he jumped. "Man, fuck this. Fuck geese."

22

AND ADULTS WONDER WHY TEENAGERS DRINK

THE UPGRADE to DEFCON 2 came a few short days later. The house had been slowly drained of furniture, which meant Rosemary was on a bad losing streak, but this was nothing new. Money from the slots was like the tide: it came in, it went out, it came in, it went out. During a high tide the house overflowed with furniture and electronics and food, and then slowly began to recede again as the money ebbed and the slot gods took back what they'd given. Even with the salary from Rosemary's horticulture job, the past due notices on personal loans began to accumulate.

Auntie Kate rang at 5:00 p.m. to talk to Rosemary, which she only ever did when Rosemary owed her a considerable sum of money. Esther did what was required of her: she cried. It wasn't hard. She didn't even have to fake it. She could feel the tide rushing out faster than ever before and sucking everything from her life with it. A tide like that meant only one thing—a tsunami was coming, and it would destroy everything in its path.

Once Kate finally hung up, Esther waited for Rosemary all

afternoon and most of the evening. There was no food in the house, literally nothing, and her mother had promised to bring home pizza.

"She's not coming, Esther," Eugene said when she called Rosemary for the ninth time. "If she was coming home, she'd be here by now."

At eleven o'clock, her stomach growling, Esther decided to send her mother a passive-aggressive message.

ESTHER:

Don't worry about dinner if it's too much hassle.

ROSEMARY:

Okay x

ESTHER:

Oh so NOW you see your phone?

ROSEMARY:

Sorry, busy x

Esther wanted to send her texts that said things like, *Don't you realize how much you're hurting your family?* and *Fuck you for being so selfish!* but she knew it would only make Rosemary cry, and then Esther would feel bad, and it wouldn't help anything anyway.

The whole situation made her so angry that she wanted to rip something, scratch something, tear something to pieces. She wondered if this was the feeling Eugene got before he slid a razor blade through his skin. She thought about trying it. There had to be *some* reason he did it. Maybe it felt good? In the end, she settled on knocking back a quarter bottle of vodka until she was in a different type of pain, an oh-god-there-goes-my-liver kind of pain. What better thing to destroy than yourself?

She messaged Jonah.

ESTHER:

What are you doing right now?

JONAH:

Painting. What are you doing?

ESTHER:

Contemplating alcoholism as a legitimate form of teenage rebellion.

JONAH:

Bring some of that rebellion over here.
No one should rebel alone.

So she did. Eugene drove her to Jonah's and they parked four houses down from his and snuck into the backyard, which was unnecessary, because Jonah's dad wasn't home.

They drank behind the house in the cold until everything was funny, and Jonah painted page after page of watercolors that went from bright and beautiful when he was sober to formless, swirling masses when he was drunk. Eugene described to him the apparitions he saw in the dark, and he painted those too, monstrous things with bright white eyes and skin made of dripping tar.

For a while, Jonah worked on his portrait of Esther. Eugene

peered over his shoulder and said, "It's just a mi—" but Jonah shushed him.

"Don't spoil the surprise," he said.

"I don't get it," Eugene said, frowning, but Jonah shook his head.

"*She'll* get it, man," he said as he looked up at her. "*She'll* get it."

Esther blushed and pressed her lips together to stop from breaking into a smile.

Later, when the portrait session was over, Jonah sat next to her, his paint-flecked fingertips tracing circles on her palm. Esther sipped her vodka and let her anger spill out. She told them that tomorrow would be the day she confronted her mother. She was going to do it, she was going to do it, she was going to say something.

They drove home at sunrise without having slept. Esther didn't ask Eugene if he was sober enough to get behind the wheel of a car, because she thought if he wasn't—if he was intoxicated—that maybe that would finally attract Death's attention.

Eugene *was* sober, or at least sober enough to drive without hitting anything, so they made it home without any visits from the Reaper. It was a cool morning—she could tell from the lace of frost strung across the fallen leaves in their front yard—but she couldn't feel anything, even though they drove with the windows down. Rosemary's car was parked in the drive, which meant she'd come home and either a) found her children missing and hadn't given a shit, or b) hadn't even bothered to check if they were in their beds.

Esther wasn't sure which was worse. She slammed the door of the car and stalked barefoot through the tinkling nazars up to the house, fired up and full of alcohol and ready to tell her mother exactly what she thought of her.

"Esther, don't," Eugene said as he closed the car door.

"Why the hell not?"

"You don't think she feels bad enough? You screaming at her isn't gonna help anyone."

"It'll help *me* feel better."

Inside, though, she found her mother curled up in the hall with a pillow under her head, a hand pressed to the orange door that led down to her husband's tomb. All the acid went out of Esther. Rosemary's other hand was tucked tight against her chest, clasping the locket that contained a picture of her and Peter on their wedding day. Scattered on the wood beneath her pillow were sage leaves with wishes written on them. *Set him free*, they all said. *Set him free, set him free, set him free.*

Here was solid proof of the ruin love could sow. A reminder of how letting someone under your skin only gave them the power to destroy you in the end.

Esther wanted to wake Rosemary. She wanted to make her feel bad for what she'd become. She wanted to know why she stayed in a relationship that had halfway ruined her. She wanted her venom to burn in her mother's veins and hurt her from the inside out. But then she noticed how the tips of her fingers had been eaten away.

How Esther saw her mother in her head: All over her

skin—her ears, her nose, her neck, everywhere—there were little holes of decay, as if she were termite-ridden. Houses infested with termites became hollowed out and started to collapse under their own weight. Esther wondered if it was the same for people.

"Do you see that?" she said to Eugene as she touched the brittle ends of Rosemary's fingers. Flecks of skin and bone chipped away in small chunks. "Our mother is made of wood."

Back to reality. Eugene was gone. Esther searched the whole ground floor for him, and the yard, but he'd vanished. After half an hour of searching, she gave up and dragged a blanket off Rosemary's bed and covered her mother. She stirred but did not wake.

"Do you want to go to school?" Eugene said when he reappeared from the ether three hours later. It was the longest time he'd spent invisible. When he returned, he smelled of damp soil and wood and some dark, unearthly scent Esther couldn't place. She wondered where he went when he wasn't there; she wondered if she wanted to know.

"It's almost midday already," she said, looking over at him from where she'd been waiting on the couch, Fleayoncé a puddle of fur and warmth curled up on her stomach. "So no."

Eugene checked his phone. Esther saw him flicker for several seconds before becoming solid again. "Huh." He looked around. "I must've lost track of the time."

Then he meandered to his room and they did nothing for the rest of the day except sleep off their hangovers. Their mother, even when she woke, never came to check on them.

23

THE COLD KISS

OF DEATH

THE HEATING gave out the weekend before Thanksgiving. Esther woke shivering in her bed, her breath a cloud that hung over her mouth. The house was cold and gloomy—even the lamps and candlelight didn't seem able to shift the weight of the dark. Eugene was hovering in her doorway, a vengeful spirit woken by the frost; it looked like he'd been crying.

"No heat," he said. "Everything is darker in the cold."

"Can't sleep?" Esther asked.

Eugene rubbed his arms, the skin beneath his hands covered with goose bumps. "I never sleep. Can I come in here?"

Esther nodded and Eugene came and curled up with his back to her. He was shaking. Sobbing, she realized. There were small tremors from the other side of the bed, aftershocks of whatever terrible thing had made him desperate enough to come into her room. She put her palm against the thin ribs protruding from his back and hoped he could feel the calm they'd always been able to pass between their skin.

"Why are you sad?" she whispered. A superfluous question, perhaps. In the broken remains of the Solar family, there were so many reasons to choose from. Still, despite how bad the situation had gotten, Esther didn't feel the need to drag blades through her skin.

Something more plagued Eugene. Something deeper.

"I don't know," he whispered back. "It's just the way I am."

Esther couldn't fix that. She couldn't help him. She couldn't change Eugene being sad any more than she could change that his eyes were brown or his hair was black. There were temporary fixes for those things—hair dye, contact lenses—but underneath, really, they were what they were. She couldn't help him, didn't know *how* to help him, and that killed her.

Not for the first time, she wished that his injuries were more obvious. That whatever swollen, infected thing inside his head that made him feel this way could be seen, could be sliced away, could be stitched up and covered with a bandage like any other wound.

Eugene was always waiting for the jump scare even though it never came. Always waiting for a face to appear in the mirror behind him. Always waiting for a demon to snatch at any ankle skin not covered by a blanket. Always waiting for the lights to flicker out and a serial killer to be watching him with night vision goggles.

To the kids at school, the ones who were drawn in by his magic, he was tall and dark and beautiful, a boy witch made of mystery.

To Esther he was a reedy figure, like taffy stretched too thin. And behind him, dragging him back, dragging him down, a thick black mass, a swelling tar creature that he fought with all his might but could never beat. There was no Eugene without this darkness. And maybe that was the problem.

Maybe Eugene wasn't afraid of what was in the darkness.

Maybe Eugene was afraid of the darkness that was inside himself.

WHEN ESTHER WOKE AGAIN IN THE MORNING, the hall was white with frost. Rosemary was sitting in the kitchen, wrapped in a blanket, her hand curled around a steaming cup of coffee. Fred's head poked out from beneath the layers, and four soft rabbits nestled into her legs.

"The heating," she said, motioning to the frosted patterns spreading on the walls, as though Esther might not have noticed, "is broken."

The rest of the week was unnaturally cold. A bitter freeze crept across the state, slipping its way under doors and through the cracks in windows, shifting blankets off feet so it could turn the pink and tender flesh of toes to stone overnight. Death was busy, with the elderly, alone in their houses, and with the homeless on the street. He was busy rocking the cradles of newborns, kissing their cheeks to infect their tiny lungs with pneumonia. He was busy wandering through thickets of dying woodland, laying his fingers on all the squirrels and rabbits and raccoons and foxes that would rot and bloat in their holes when the warmth returned, their small bodies unable to fend off the cold.

The cold came for the Solars, too. It wandered the increasingly barren halls of their gloomy home. It seeped into their bones and made them shudder as they slept.

By Monday, Esther had a cough and could no longer feel her fingers.

By Tuesday, she gave in.

"Call someone to come fix it," she told her mother through chattering teeth. All along, this had been a game, who could stay cold the longest. Hardly fair when you were up against a ghost boy and a woman made of wood. "I'll pay for it. I have some money saved. I'll pay."

Rosemary actually smiled when she told her this. She smiled because she knew she'd won.

THE HEAT GUY came the day before Thanksgiving while Esther was home alone after school. She let him in and stood in the kitchen close to the steak knives in case he got any ideas, but he wandered around the house without attacking her, so she relaxed a little. He didn't normally work so close to Thanksgiving, he explained, but he knew Rosemary from the casino.

It was a bad situation, heating-wise. The guy poked and prodded at the house's guts for ten minutes before asking her where her mom was. She started to give him Rosemary's cell number but he said he already had it, then stepped outside onto the porch to call her.

Esther listened through the mail slot. She heard only half of the conversation, from the guy's end: "The whole system's dead. It'll need to be entirely replaced. I've never seen anything like it," he said. Then: "Two thousand," he quoted for the job. "Two thousand, minimum, and that's with a friend discount."

Esther left before he'd even finished talking. She rode to Jonah's. They were supposed to go hiking, but she couldn't muster the energy for it, so they sat in the bitter cold in the gutter outside his house and looked out at the whole wasted world—the trees stripped of leaves, the cars stripped of paint, the damp trash collecting on people's lawns, the bleached and hazy sky.

What a shithole.

Jonah put his arm around her shoulder even though he knew that wasn't allowed.

Esther said: "I hate it here."

And he said: "Tell me about it."

She said: "Do you ever feel like a rose that grew from a compost heap?"

And he said: "No." Then: "Do you think your family is the compost heap? Or this town? Or me?"

"How could you think I mean you're the compost?"

"Because I'm not a rose. So I must be part of the heap."

"You're a rose. The most beautiful one I've ever seen."

"Stop trying to woo me." He elbowed her playfully, then took a strand of her hair and twisted it around one of his fingers and stared at it contemplatively. "You're gonna get out of here, Esther."

"I'm gonna take you with me."

"Sure."

They didn't say anything more for a while because they were both such terrible liars.

WHEN THE COLD got its long fingers inside their jackets, they went inside. Jonah worked on her portrait for a while, and Esther tried not to let him see her cry. Two thousand. Two hundred would've been too much, but two *thousand*? Two thousand would break them.

Jonah was quiet as he packed up his paints and came to lie next to where she was curled up in a blanket. He wiped a tear from her eyelashes and put his hand on her cheek, but there was nothing he could say to make it better, any of it, so he didn't try. They fell asleep together, huddled close to ward off the cold, both dreaming of another life any life—that wasn't the one they'd been dealt.

When Esther woke, it was with a start. The sun had gone down, and a man was standing over her, screaming. She couldn't make out most of what he was yelling, except for "SLUT" and "PREGNANT." Jonah was pushing her roughly toward the door and chanting, "Go, go, for fuck's sake Esther, go." She moved as if in a dream, desperate to go faster but unable to get her heavy, sleepy body to do exactly what she wanted.

Remy was in the backyard, hiding in the long grass behind the house, crouched and unmoving. She watched Esther as she stumbled toward the side gate, her scarf bundled up in her hands. When she finally stopped shaking, she texted Jonah.

ESTHER:

Fuck.

I'm so sorry.

Fuck fuck fuck.

We shouldn't have fallen asleep.

Are you okay?

Please let me know you're okay.

Then she waited at the end of the street until the streetlights came on and the sun slid below the horizon. Fall sunsets were her favorite, so crisp and cool, a vast pane of clear glass tinged with green in the last moments before the whole sky blinked into blackness. This was the only time of year and the only time of day that magic, the kind from storybooks, felt like it could be real. The buttery sunlight of summer dissolved from the world, leaving the light thin, the atmosphere thin, the space between realities thin.

Impossible things from other realms could slip through the sky on nights like tonight, Esther was almost sure of it.

Something smashed inside Jonah's house. Glass. Esther

sucked in a breath of cold air. It was strange that such beauty should exist alongside such ugliness.

Jonah didn't come out. He didn't message her back. The windows of his house stayed unlit. Nothing impossible slipped into our world from the sky.

Esther walked home in the dark, wondering if she was more of a coward for not calling the police, or for still dreaming of magic in her senior year of high school, when it was pretty damn clear that there was no magic now. At least not for her.

The nazars whispered welcomes to her as she threaded through the oak trees. The house, as always, was bursting with light.

Rosemary was curled up on the couch, asleep, her face puffy from crying. She looked so small, like a child, the rings that dripped from her fingers slipping over her skinny knuckles. There were bowls on the ground beside her, each filled with water and some herb meant to bring prosperity: basil, bay leaves, chamomile. Tonka beans spilled from her hands. Emergency measures, meant to bring money their way in a hurry.

Seeing her mother cry made Esther want to cry. She hated not just that they were broke, but that everything they touched seemed to turn sour and curdled, breaking to pieces in their hands. She hated their life. She hated the bits of it they'd chosen for themselves and the bits of life that had fallen on them like dandruff, unpleasant and unwanted. She hated that she couldn't pull her father from the pit of sludge that had become his existence, that he would drown there and she'd have to watch his last gurgled breaths because she wasn't enough—strong enough, smart enough, brave enough, enough, enough, enough—to save him.

Not enough to save Eugene. Not enough to save her grandfather. Not enough to save Jonah. Not even enough to save herself.

If Dad dies, she thought as she watched her mother, *it will be the end of her. If he dies, she'll unravel, and our family will be over.*

Esther wanted to ignore her. She wanted to walk past her into her bedroom and close the door. But she couldn't. She couldn't. Rosemary was lying there on the couch, her cheek resting heavily on her hand, as still and pale as a statue, and she wanted to yell at her and tell her it was her fault, her fault, all her fault, but she couldn't do that either. Whatever primordial magic that bound them whispered to Esther and said, *Comfort her.* So Esther pressed her hand to her mother's clammy cheek, still wet and warm with tears. Rosemary opened her eyes wide and looked up at her as a small, sleepy smile spread across her face.

"Hi, baby," she whispered, still somewhere between sleep and waking.

"Hi, Mama," Esther whispered back. She crouched next to her and rested her head on the sofa and let Rosemary run her fingers through her hair, like she'd done when she was a child. Esther breathed in the scent of her mother and tried to remember exactly when they'd started drifting apart. The rift hadn't been a sudden thing, more like something that happened inch by inch, so you couldn't see how far apart you were until the distance was insurmountable.

"I'll pay for it," Esther mouthed. She said it twice before she realized no sound was coming out of her mouth, only breath. She cleared her throat. "I'll pay for it."

"No, you won't," Rosemary said, but Esther could feel the way her muscles relaxed in her hands. "You worked hard for that money. That's for your college fund."

"Is there anyone else." It wasn't a question, because questions were things you asked when you wanted an answer, but she already knew the answer. "Anyone else who could loan you the money."

"No."

That night, Esther used her phone to transfer her mother the money to have the heating fixed. Two thousand dollars. Just about all the funds she'd saved from her baking business. As Rosemary kissed her cheeks, her eyelids, her forehead, Esther wondered if they would ever find their way back to each other, or if the continental drift that separated them would only continue to wrench them apart, so slowly that neither of them felt enough pain to try and stop it.

"I'll pay you back," Rosemary assured her daughter as she rinsed her hands in chamomile tea. "I'll pay it all back to you, I promise."

How could you save people who were drowning in themselves?

24

JONAH HAD messaged Esther on Thanksgiving to let her know he was okay, but that he couldn't hang out again until Sunday. Now it was Sunday morning, and Jonah had been at her house since sunrise, lying on her bedroom floor and helping himself to all the books on her walls like he owned the place.

Esther hadn't asked him why he was there so early. Why he crawled in her window, thinking she was asleep, and cried for a little while on the floor until she'd sidled out from under her covers and laid down next to him, her palm pressed gently to the bruise swelling darkly along his cheekbone. Jonah was a talented makeup artist, but he wasn't *this* talented. His skin bulged out beneath her touch. His eye had been consumed by his face, too vicious to be fake.

"I've figured out another way we could meet Death," he whispered to her as she traced her fingertips along the fresh bruise. "We could cut out the middle man. Bring Death right to us."

"Oh?"

"I could kill my dad." Only half joking.

Esther shook her head. "Don't throw your life away. Not for him. You're so close to finishing school and going away to college."

Jonah pulled away from her touch and looked at her like she might be an idiot and laughed this kind of bitter laugh. "You think I'm going to leave Remy in that house with him? You think Holland's going to let me leave? Don't you get it? There's no way out for me. Until Remy's grown up, this town . . . it's all there is for me."

"But . . . you're so talented. You told my mom you wanted to go to Hollywood."

"Yeah, well, you can't exactly tell someone's parents that you have no career options except working full-time at a fast-food joint until your baby sister is old enough for college. This is all I've got, Esther. This"—he motioned to the film equipment he'd brought with him—"is probably the closest I'll ever get to working in movies, at least until Remy is old enough to get out."

"That's a long time."

"Shorter than a prison sentence for murder, though. Those are my only two options at this point." Esther could tell he was trying to make her laugh. She didn't. "Would you leave Eugene?" he asked eventually.

They both knew the answer.

No. No, she wouldn't.

Esther told Jonah to ice his swollen face and then she went back to sleep, thinking about how, for the past few months, she'd believed this boy thought he was saving her, which she hated, because she was not a damsel in distress. All along she thought he thought he was saving her, but she could see it now; they had both, each of them, been saving little bits of each other.

At 10:00 a.m., after Jonah had poked and prodded her for half an hour and draped Fleayoncé over her face, Esther finally got out of bed and they made their way to the kitchen and she cooked them breakfast (which was difficult, because the Solars still had very little food). They didn't talk about what they'd discussed earlier in the morning, or the bruise on Jonah's cheekbone, or anything that would only make them sadder. Instead he asked her, for the fortieth time, how exactly they were going to see dead bodies.

Esther had decided to plan 15/50, partly because she had a good idea and partly because she thought Jonah might dig up a grave and drag a fresh corpse into her house if she left him to his own devices.

"Never you mind," she said as she made a smiley face on a plate out of the last of the oatmeal.

"I don't want to see, like, dead puppies or anything," he said, sitting on the kitchen floor because all the chairs were gone by then. Esther thought that the rabbits were doing a very poor job of being lucky. "I'll be very upset if you take me to see dead puppies."

"There'll be no dead puppies." She paused. "At least I'm pretty sure. There might be dead babies though."

"You take me on some really weird dates."

Esther tried to suppress a smile; you had to admire his perseverance. "We are not dating."

Jonah chuckled. "Why do all my girlfriends keep saying that?"

Esther dressed as Rosie the Riveter and then gave Jonah directions to the School of Medical Sciences, a small research university that had somehow ended up in their town. The campus was quiet on a Sunday morning after Thanksgiving. The odd student or two bustled about, but for the most part, the place was deserted.

"Oh, I know what we're going to see," Jonah said as they walked toward the college library. "Med students don't actually count as dead people Esther. They may look like zombies but they still have a pulse. Shocking, I know."

Tucked behind the library was the small, squat building they'd actually come for. The sign above the entrance read THE MUSEUM OF HUMAN DISEASE.

"What's this?" Jonah asked.

"It's a museum," Esther explained, "of—wait for it—human disease."

"Thank you, Captain Obvious."

The Museum of Human Disease, as it turns out, was also not a happening place on Sundays. Or maybe ever. The caretaker was asleep in her chair and Esther had to ding the bell to bring her lurching back to consciousness.

Jonah paid for their tickets. They were warned by the woman to show respect to the specimens. Each of the three thousand bits and pieces inside came from real people, real humans with lives as rich and complex as their own, and to mistreat them would be disrespectful to their memory and the generous donation they'd made upon their death.

Inside, the place felt more like the cold, stark halls of a hospital than a museum. It wasn't a particularly upmarket affair. Esther had been expecting wooden floors and dark walls and bloodred hearts suspended in glass jars. The reality was much more clinical: green linoleum floor, white walls, plastic shelving, and monochromatic tissue specimens, all turned an unappealing shade of pus-yellow thanks to the preservation process. Each sample was preserved in formalin, encased in clear glass rectangles, and stacked on the shelves like morbid figurines.

Esther and Jonah walked quietly around the place, stopping every now and then at the more disturbing displays: an arthritic hand, curled in on itself like a dead spider; a lung as black as pitch, taken from a coal miner in the early twentieth century; a gangrenous leg, the flesh rotten and buckling from ankle to kneecap; a uterus with a tumor growing its own teeth and hair.

And everywhere, everywhere, signs of Death. His handiwork on every muscle fiber, every shard of bone, every cell born and grown only to die by his hand in the end. The shadow of him was on everything in the building. Esther shook her head at the destruction of it all, at the incomprehensible scale of it.

Each one of them had once been a human being. The aggregate of all their happiness and sadness had been immense. The memories they'd held in their collective heads could have overloaded all the servers in the world. That severed foot used to be a living, breathing, walking, real human with thoughts and memories and emotions. That slice of brain had once stored the cumulative thoughts acquired over decades that had made the donor the person they'd been.

So much work for nothing. That a living thing should be there and then gone just seemed so impossible. So impractical. So . . . wasteful, somehow.

Because where did it all go, in the end? Esther understood the first law of thermodynamics, that nothing was created or destroyed and all the little bits and pieces that made up a human would be redistributed elsewhere when they died, but where did the memory go? The joy? The talent? The suffering? The love?

If the answer was "nowhere," then why the hell did we even bother? What was the point of these fleshy globs of consciousness that ate and drank and loved and rose from cobbled-together bits of the universe?

"I think I'm gonna puke," Jonah said, gagging at the aforementioned uterus when they were about halfway through the collection.

"Why don't we get out of here and get something to eat? How about Taco the Town?" she said, pointing to a severed foot with a huge plantar wart growing like a cauliflower out of the sole, which looked strangely reminiscent of the quality of food available at the taco truck.

Jonah looked at it, then vomited on the floor in the middle of the hall, bits of his budget oat breakfast splattering on the formalin-encased remains of the diseased dead people. Esther sat him down and ran to fetch him water, like he'd done for her when she'd been sick. And that's how, on a Sunday afternoon in early December, they were banned forever from the Museum of Human Disease.

25

17/50: DOLLS

IN THE week before Christmas, the world grew as bitter and gloomy as Eugene's fitful nightmares. The last of the leaves dropped away from the trees, the cold came in blankets to settle over the town, and Esther and Jonah continued their search for Death, despite the ever increasing pressure from school to STUDY HARD AND DO WELL OR YOUR LIFE IS GOING TO SUCK SERIOUSLY YOU GUYS WE'RE NOT EVEN JOKING WITH THIS.

The four of them met on Sunday—Christmas Eve—at Hephzibah's house, partly because she had the creepy dolls they needed to film 17/50, but mostly because her house was the nicest, and her parents spoke softly to each other, and one of her grandmothers always brought around freshly rolled rum balls on Christmas Eve which were strong enough (when they'd been in elementary school anyway) to get them halfway tipsy. The other grandmother brought over latkes topped with applesauce in an attempt to out-grandma the other grandmother, so the real winner was their stomachs.

It always felt like Christmas was supposed to feel at Hephzibah's: warm and fragrant and festive and distinctly Middle Eastern (the baby Jesus was from there after all). The Hadids, half Christian, half Jewish, were big believers in Chrismukkah, and decorated accordingly.

For the decade before her birth, Heph's parents had been foreign correspondents and lived in half a dozen cities. Their house was a catalogue of where they'd been in the world: hand-woven Afghan carpets covered the floor, heavy Balinese chairs with intricately carved backs sat in the dining room, and the lounges were Scandinavian, their minimalist design clashing with the Japanese room divider and all the Peruvian pottery scattered about the place.

Hephzibah had been born in Jerusalem but spent the first few years of her life pinballing between Paris, Rome and Moscow, and had even done her first year of school in New Delhi before her parents came to the United States and decided to settle down. They still travelled for work sometimes, mostly to Mexico or Canada, and Daniel, Heph's dad, had even covered the early days of the Syrian Civil War until journalists became afraid to go there, but mostly they worked from home.

The four of them filmed 17/50 after dinner, when the night was dark and cold and the basement where Hephzibah kept her childhood toys was appropriately horror-movie-esque. The toys had been moved down here at Esther's request sometime in late elementary school, when she'd started sleeping over at Heph's and found herself quite unable to close her eyes in the same room as dolls that were clearly created for the main purpose of becoming receptacles for demonic possession and little more.

Jonah made her stand surrounded by the dolls for five minutes with the lights off. Esther almost started hyperventilating at first, thinking of all the dolls she'd seen in movies that came to life and tore out people's jugulars, but the longer she spent with them, the slower her breathing became. They didn't move. They didn't blink. They didn't reach out with their creepy little porcelain fingers to gouge her eyes out when she wasn't looking.

In the end, when the five minutes was up, she felt sorry for them. Little girls, frozen in time and left alone in the dark, smiles painted on their still faces. Esther was the one who'd condemned them to this cage years ago, just as Death had been the one who'd condemned her family to live in fear.

When Jonah flicked the light on, she carried each of them, one by one, back up to the world above.

ESTHER AND EUGENE spent Christmas morning at Lilac Hill. It was not a good day. Reginald had fallen the night before—a bout of syncope—and today he was in pain and couldn't remember why. It was a terrible thing to see. Like when babies or animals were sick and you couldn't explain to them what was happening, so they cried and cried and it made you want to cry too because there was nothing you could do, nothing at all. There was a bruise, the nurses told them, from his hip to his armpit, splashed down his side like a watercolor storm cloud, and he had difficulty breathing or sitting up or moving too much. Four broken ribs, they said.

Reg's hands shook so violently that he couldn't feed himself; Eugene had to do it. He choked on his food because the disease was eating away his ability to swallow and he cried most of the time his grandchildren were there, though he didn't seem to notice their presence or recognize who they were. Eugene sat and glowered out the window for most of the visit, looking how Esther felt. Like, if she met Death in a dark alleyway, she would take no prisoners.

These are the things she remembered about Reg that day:

- The story Rosemary had told her, that when she and Eugene were babies, Reg would come by unannounced almost every day to see them. The way he'd pick them up from their cribs and wake them even when they were sleeping just so he could read to them or play with them or take them for a walk through the garden to see the birds and the flowers and the trees.
- The way he loved Johnny Cash, and would sing "I Walk the Line" to Florence Solar on a regular basis, even though he couldn't hold a tune.
- The way, whenever Esther wanted to run away from home, she'd call her grandfather, and he'd come and pick her up and pretend he was helping her escape great tyranny. The way they'd sneak out together like

spies, even though Peter and Rosemary knew very
well he was there, and go back to Reg's and Florence's
house for fish sticks, Esther's favorite food as a child.

Before they left, the nurses pulled them aside and informed
them that his hallucinations had worsened, that he scared the
other patients when he told them that Death was there with them,
that he visited him once to play chess, that his time was very close
to being near.

"Death comes here?" Esther asked. "Have you seen him?"

The nurse looked at her like she was crazy, then explained
again that Lewy body dementia caused recurrent visual hallucinations, and that nothing of what Reginald said should be believed.
Eugene raised his eyebrows and looked at his sister.

"She means now that he's sick," she said when the nurse
was gone.

"No, she means *ever*."

"You're not allowed to believe in demons and not Death,"
she reminded him.

Eugene turned to stare out the window again. "Again: I believe what I can see."

WHEN THEY GOT HOME, there were no presents to be opened;
there was no tree and no decorations, unless you counted the ones
permanently set up downstairs. Esther sat at the top of the basement stairs and listened to the Christmas carols jingling from the

record player and wondered if she should tell Peter that his father was coming undone at the seams. Would it make a difference? Would he be any more inclined to unstick himself from the basement and venture outside, or would the imminence of his father's death only drive him further underground?

Jonah snuck into her room sometime after midnight, his lip busted.

"Let me call the police," she said as she pressed the sleeve of her sweatshirt to his mouth, but Jonah shook his head.

"If we get taken by the state, they'll split us up. I might never see her again," he said. "Tell me a story. That's what I need right now."

And so, with his head in her lap, her fingers in his hair, her sleeve pressed to the split at his lip, Esther told Jonah about the third time her grandfather met Death.

26

THE BOWEN SISTERS

ON THE morning of September 30, 1988, Christina and Michelle Bowen, seven and nine years old respectively, were waiting at the school bus stop only two hundred yards from their home when a man in a mint Cadillac Calais pulled over and told them the bus had a flat tire and wasn't coming and he could give them a lift if they'd like. They accepted—the man didn't *look* like a stranger, not the ones their mom had told them about, the kind that offered candy and had a cute puppy to lure them into an unmarked van. Besides, his car was nice and clean, and all the windows were rolled down, and he wasn't wearing a long dark coat, which was what the girls assumed all strangers wore.

The Bowen sisters climbing into the Cadillac Calais was witnessed by a neighbor, who thought nothing of it because the girls went willingly. They were seen alive only once more, half an hour later, by a gas station attendant as the man driving filled up his car. By this time they were miles away from the school and both girls were in the back seat crying, but the attendant assumed that the man was their father and thought nothing of it.

They were reported missing in the afternoon when the siblings failed to return from school, right around the time that an anonymous tip came through to the police station that a strange man had been seen dumping trash in a dry creek bed on the outskirts of town. The person assigned to investigate was homicide detective Reginald Solar, who normally wouldn't have covered such things, but his shift was over and he lived near the dump site and everyone was far too busy with the missing Bowen children to pay some trash-dumping miscreant too much attention. So Reg clocked out for the day, sure that the Bowen girls would be discovered at a friend's house, and went to Little Creek to see what could be done about the illegal dumping.

It was early fall and the river had dried up from years on end without rain, leaving only a wide expanse of sand and trees and scrub. From the bridge, Reginald couldn't see any sign of the garbage, so he parked his car, a secondhand Toyota Cressida, on the roadside and scaled down the steep riverbank in his suit. It was late afternoon—crickets were chirping and a breeze pulled through the carved-out canyon, not quite cool enough to stop a bead of sweat from slipping down Reg's spine. He took off his suit jacket and folded it over his arm. The place smelled at once of campfires and tree sap and stagnant water that boiled up from the underground stream and found itself with nowhere to go but to sit and grow putrid.

There was a difference between good detectives and born

detectives, Reginald once told Esther. Good detectives were the ones who took in what they heard and saw and smelled. Born detectives did this too, but they had another sense, something in the gut or the soul that guided them even when their senses couldn't. Reginald stopped and listened to the silence, his eyes watering. He knew, without knowing how he knew, without having even seen them yet, that the Bowen sisters were there in that riverbed. He couldn't explain it, except to say that dead bodies had a sound, a kind of ominous buzzing silence that he felt in his teeth and the lining of his stomach when he was close to one.

That's when he saw the footprints in the sand, two and sometimes three sets of them. There were scuffles between the three, and whoever belonged to the smallest set had refused to walk and so had been dragged for a time. Reg followed the footprints without obscuring them and put on gloves to pick up the trinkets he found along the way: a locket, the clasp snapped open as though it had been snatched from a neck, a child's hat; a copy of *A Light in the Attic* by Shel Silverstein; a backpack with the name *Christina* emblazoned across the pocket in glittery gold letters.

And then, what he knew he would find from the moment he looked out at the riverbed from his car on the bridge, not because he could see them, but because he could feel them, the echo of their lives: the Bowen sisters, both naked and facedown in the sand. They were ten feet apart, the elder girl with her arm outstretched toward her sister.

Esther didn't go into the details of what had been done to them, a courtesy she wished her grandfather had extended to her.

All she said was that their hair had been brushed, and their school clothes neatly folded beside them, and their socks tucked into their shiny black shoes. To look at them from that angle, there were no signs of violence. That's not to say they could be mistaken for sleeping—far from it. Their chests didn't rise with breath, and their faces had been pushed into the sand.

Reginald stood frozen for some time, just staring, until his body betrayed him. He dropped to his knees, vomited twice, and felt hot tears streak down his cheeks. And then, with his blood pounding through his body in revulsion and horror, he caught the movement of a shadow out of the corner of his eye. He quickly drew his weapon and pointed it at the man, who was dressed in a dark coat and black hat and was sitting on a piece of bone white driftwood, staring at the dead children. The man, her grandfather was shocked to see, was none other than Jack Horowitz.

"What the fuck are you doing here?" Reg said to him.

"Why do you think I am here?" he replied.

"Horowitz, I'm going to need you to put your hands in the air."

"I must ask you, at this precise moment, not to be an idiot."

"You're at the scene of the crime. I *have* to take you in."

"I have been at the scene of many crimes today, Reg. Too many. I am not in the mood for humans at the moment."

Reginald Solar didn't lower his gun. It hadn't escaped him that Horowitz, now thirteen years older than when he first met him, hadn't aged a day.

"Do you really believe I killed them?" said Horowitz, looking up with big eyes framed with black lashes. There, in the afternoon sun, his scars were worse than ever—they bubbled beneath the surface, distorting his features. You might think his parboiled skin made him monstrous, but it had the opposite effect. Most found him to be a sympathetic figure, felt sorry for him, felt a need to protect and follow him when he asked. It would make the former private, in the decades to come, a very successful Reaper.

Reginald did not believe that Jack Horowitz had killed the children. He thought it *very fucking strange* indeed that Jack Horowitz was here in this dry creek bed and staring at their bodies, but no, he did not believe he had killed them. So this was what he did: he holstered his weapon, called for backup, and sat down on the driftwood next to his sort-of friend, the Man Who Was Now Death, and he too stared at the little blond girls who lay facedown in the sand.

"Fuck me," said Reginald after a moment, partly because of the horror of the scene before him, but partly because, for the first time, he found himself genuinely believing that Horowitz was who he said he was. Horowitz was Death incarnate—why else would he be here? Reg pulled off his hat and wiped away several hard-wrung tears. "Fuck me. How long have you been here?"

"Since it happened. I find myself quite unable to move."

"What?"

"I believe I am suffering a panic attack."

Reg looked Horowitz up and down. He was sitting quite rigidly on the driftwood, hands balled into fists on his knees, but apart from that he exhibited no signs of distress. "Are you sure?"

"Oh yes. My heart is beating rapidly, I am short of breath,

my limbs are numb, and I feel very much like I am about to die of a heart attack, which I know for a fact to be incorrect. I am not on my own list, you see."

"Sure." Reg cleared his throat and patted Horowitz on the back a few times. "Breathe deep, old friend."

"Why do you do this to each other?" Horowitz said. Reg noticed for the first time that he was, indeed, struggling to get his words out through his strangled breaths. He hadn't looked away from the little girls, and even though Reg wanted nothing more than to stand up and go home and hug his own children, he looked back at them too. They hadn't been dead for long. Faint bruises—liver mortis—had started forming across their ribs and arms and shoulders, but from this distance, if you squinted, it might only be a flush on the skin from the heat.

Reginald stood—he was here to investigate, after all, not to provide cold comforts to the last person who should need them—and started to cordon off the crime scene. "You might be in the wrong line of work," he said to Horowitz as he worked, who'd since gone pale and was now breathing between his knees.

"Did you ever think that Death might not want to be Death?" said Horowitz.

"So don't be Death."

"As I told you in Vietnam, I was conscripted. I do not have the luxury of making that choice. We are somewhat short-staffed, apparently."

"You got shanghaied into a gig as the Grim Reaper because the afterlife was running low on skilled workers?"

"There are more humans than ever before. More deaths than ever before. We are overworked."

"And underpaid, I suppose."

"The remuneration *is* less than you might think." A beat. "She died, Reg. Lan died."

Reg thought back to their wedding day. Lan, smiling broadly in her pale pink sundress, a strand of pearls at her throat, white lace gloves on her hands. They'd spoken only once, and briefly at that—but he knew how much Horowitz adored her. Could see it in the way he looked at her, the same way Reg looked at his own wife, Florence. "When?" he asked sadly. "How?"

"Death came for her while I slept. I was still his apprentice. Nothing I could do. We had only been married a month, and living in our little home in Greece for even less. A wave took her out to sea, and the sea kept her."

"Jesus."

"Now I am become Death, the destroyer of worlds," he said, quoting the *Bhagavad Gita*; it was, Reg knew, the same phrase J. Robert Oppenheimer had thought as he watched the first atomic bomb detonate.

"I don't suppose you'll tell me who did this?"

Horowitz shook his head. "You will not catch him."

"I could. If you told me."

"If I told you who he was, you would kill him, but I cannot, because it is not yet his time."

"Bullshit, Horowitz. Bullshit. You know this asshole deserves to die, so give me a name."

"You want a name? How about Eden Gray? Arjuna and Rathna Malhotra? Yukiko Ando? Carlotta Bianchi? These are the murdered children I have reaped today already. These girls will not be the last. They are not special."

"How about you get to the next murder a few minutes earlier and stop it from happening?"

"I will not give you the name."

And that is when Reginald Solar—quite calmly—curled his fingers into a fist and punched Death square in the jaw, proving that the Reaper, too, could bleed.

On the way home to his wife and two young children, Reginald stopped at the roadside greenhouse of a local woman who grew orchids, where he bought enough plants to fill up the entire back seat and trunk of his Toyota Cressida. When he arrived home, he went straight upstairs to his children's rooms, where they were playing before dinner. He sat with them for a long time, watching them, noting the distinct color of their eyes, the way their hair fell across their faces, the shrill sound of their laughter.

After dinner, he went out to the garden and started constructing a greenhouse in which to grow his new orchids. It began raining at 9 p.m., a torrential downpour from a storm system that would last several weeks and cause a flash flood at the scene of the crime, where the coroner and a forensic photographer would be swept away, their bodies to be found downriver more than a week later. The Bowen sisters were not found at all.

Reginald worked through the deluge despite his fear of water, and the greenhouse was complete at dawn. After moving the orchids in, he went back to the police station to begin the long and arduous murder investigation, not knowing, yet, that this would be the one case that would haunt him for the rest of his life.

What he didn't tell anyone—not his colleagues, not his captain, not even his wife—was that two young girls, both pale and gossamer as spider's silk, had begun to follow him everywhere. They stood at the end of his bed that night, dead-eyed and unblinking. They followed him to the police station in the morning and hid under his desk, each curled up like the bud of a ghostly flower. They wandered around his greenhouse with him in the afternoon, whispering to the orchids to make them grow. And when he visited the now-raging river two days after their deaths—the closest he would come to a large body of water ever again—they screamed and screamed and screamed, but only he could hear them.

27

18/50:

GRAVEYARDS

NORMAL TEENAGERS, on New Year's Eve, might be planning a number of things:

1. Getting drunk and making poor life choices. A very popular pastime.
2. Wishing they were getting drunk, but going to watch the fireworks with their parents instead because they couldn't get alcohol.
3. Ignoring the institution of New Year's Eve entirely, because there was far too much pressure on you to have the Best Time Ever, which usually resulted in a terribly disappointing night.

The group had collectively decided that since the holiday coincided with 18/50: graveyards, Esther, Jonah, Heph, and Eugene would spend their New Year's Eve at Paradise Point Cemetery.

The cemetery was the oldest in town, packed full of graves that rose from the earth like crooked concrete teeth. People were still buried there now, so the headstones were a strange mishmash of styles going from nineteenth-century gothic behemoths to these weird black marble blocks that seemed to be the hot ticket in the '80s and '90s to the graves of today, which were sleek and white and minimalistic.

There seemed to be no discernible pattern in the way bodies were buried. Two-hundred-year-old graves were next to corpses that had been interred just months ago; remains seemed to be kind of squeezed in wherever they fit. They walked along a trail through the older part of the cemetery shrouded in trees, where the graves were moss-covered and the headstones cracked and every second statue looked like one of the Weeping Angels from *Doctor Who*. Then they walked through the newer part, dotted here and there with mausoleums and glossy marble slabs alike.

The fireworks went off at midnight. The four watched them from perches on the cemetery walls, bright dandelions that burst like stars and were blown away into the night. Jonah stood behind where Esther sat on the wall. When the clock struck twelve, he placed his hands on her waist and pressed his lips to the small patch of bare skin at the back of her neck, only once, quickly enough that Eugene and Hephzibah didn't see. Esther closed her eyes and savored the feeling, as though the kiss might melt through her like a red-hot ball of nickel dropped into her flesh.

They hadn't planned to sleep in the churchyard. It was freezing, for one thing. Each of them was wrapped in half a dozen layers to stave off the cold and had to rub their hands together and breathe on their fingers to stop them from going numb. For another, Eugene couldn't be expected to remain in the open dark for any stretch of time, *especially* not in a cemetery. He needed walls. He needed electricity. He needed all the things humanity had invented to separate themselves from the old wild, a time and place that was full of monsters now forgotten by all but those who were still hunted by them. The dozen flashlights and solar lamps they carried between them weren't enough.

But it was Eugene who found the small graves of the Bowen sisters, Christina and Michelle, their little rectangular plaques set side by side in the grass. The girls were not actually buried there, of course. The ground beneath the markers was still waiting for their bodies, which Little Creek had claimed and kept for decades. It was Eugene who built and lit the fire. Eugene who knelt in front of the plaques and suggested that they should stay there and drink instead of retreating back to the Solar house.

They didn't mean to fall asleep, but the fire was warm and the wine was strong and the whispers of ghosts lulled them into fitful slumber.

Esther woke sometime later to Eugene clawing at her wrist. The fire had smoldered down to embers and now gave off only fleeting flickers of light. Eugene was panicking, tearing at his throat, eyes coin-wide as he tried to breathe. "Esther. Esther. *Esther,*" he whispered, trying not to wake the others. "There's something out there in the dark. I can *hear* it."

"Hey, you're okay. There's still light. You're fine here, you're safe."

The fire popped. A twig snapped at the base of a nearby tree. Eugene gave a strangled sob. "It's gonna kill me."

"Hey, hey, look at me. Eugene, look at me. Focus. Ground yourself. Remember. First five things you can see. List them." It was an old trick from when Eugene used to see a therapist, but sometimes it worked. "Come on, Eugene, list the first five things you can see."

"Hair. Grass. Shirt. Grave. Fire."

"Okay, good. Really good. Now list four things you can touch."

"Stone," he said, placing his palm flat on the empty grave of Michelle Bowen. "Dirt." Touched the ground. "Fabric." Esther's sleeve. "Skin." Her cheek.

"Three things you can hear."

"My heartbeat. Your voice. A party happening somewhere nearby."

"Two things you can smell."

"Burning wood. Your dirty socks."

"You cannot. Liar."

"Can too."

"Ugh. Last one. One thing you can taste."

"Impending doom."

"Survey says: not an option."

"I don't know. Saliva? I haven't eaten all day."

They sat cross-legged on the grass as Esther finished setting up a spread of baked goods she'd brought with her. There was very little left of her savings after paying to have the heating fixed, but she'd been determined to start again, and so the smuggling of treats into her high school continued.

"Do you remember how it started?" Esther said around an inhaled piece of caramel shortbread. "Your fear of the dark. I'm not even sure I really remember starting my list."

Eugene didn't look up from his food. "I remember."

"Can you tell me?"

"You don't remember that night? The night everything changed?"

"The night Grandma died."

Eugene nodded. "We were in the car on our way to Pop and Grandma's house for dinner, and we were listening to the radio, and this story came on the news about a little girl who'd been missing. Alana Shepard. Do you remember her? She was our age, like ten or eleven. She'd been gone for three days or something, and they ended up finding her in a dam way outside of town. She'd been raped and stabbed with a screwdriver and weighed down with bricks. I'd never really paid attention to anyone dying before. I didn't even really know what dying meant yet. But I can still see her clearly, the way I did in my head. Her body weighted down among the lily pads. Forever trapped in shadow. I'd always been scared of the dark, but after that night, I never slept without the light on again."

Esther closed her eyes. She, too, remembered the story well, not because she'd heard it on the radio, but because they'd arrived at their grandparent's house to find Reginald Solar crying. Reg, who was born in the 1940s, a time when being a man meant rubbing dirt in your wounds, drinking whisky for breakfast, and having the emotional intelligence of a wet dishrag. Guys didn't cry, and Reginald Solar *definitely* didn't cry, so Esther had been incredibly dismayed at the sight of him weeping as his old radio played a fuzzy recording of Johnny Cash in the background. The house was overflowing with vases full of orchids, their heady scent drifting through the halls. The place smelled like a florist, green and fresh; even the scent of the garlic and rosemary lamb roast in the oven was overpowered by the fragrance.

Reg had surrounded himself with purple blooms, just as Eugene would surround himself with lamps a few weeks later. A safety blanket. A shield from fear.

Florence Solar looked panicked. Peter wanted to call 911.

Reginald was crying for two reasons:

1. In his gut, he already knew what it would take
    forensics several weeks to piece together: that the
    DNA collected from the body of the murdered girl
    would match a cold case that had haunted him for
    more than a decade.

WHOEVER KILLED THE BOWEN SISTERS had never been apprehended. The investigation had been such a disaster that the case had come to be thought of as cursed, a sort of modern-day tomb of King Tut. The police captain had vowed not to stop working until the murderer was caught—he died of a heart attack five sleepless nights into the investigation. Files went missing.

Evidence was mishandled. The two witnesses of the abduction gave conflicting reports on every detail of what they'd seen (to the point that the gas station attendant was certain that one of the sisters had been a boy and the man who kidnapped them reminded him of a harvestman spider, all limbs). The police sketch artist lost an eye in a car accident immediately after drawing the suspect. And at the precinct Christmas party some months after the murders, three quarters of the staff had to be hospitalized after drinking eggnog that later proved to be riddled with salmonella.

Some sixty-four men were brought in for questioning, but no suspect was ever named. DNA evidence, first used in a criminal conviction in the US in 1988, was collected but never matched to anyone. Without evidence, without motive, without a murder weapon, without a suspect, and without any leads, the case—much to Reg's great despair—went cold.

It took five years before a bunch of kids who went down to the riverside to drink during school hours unearthed the murder weapon—a screwdriver—not far from where the girls had been dumped.

The case was reopened, and the moment the lid of the box was removed in a puff of dust, the curse began anew. A reporter who made copies of the case files was strangled in a mugging on her way home. Again, the police captain died of a heart attack. Some supposed evidence of the curse was so far removed that the case for a curse became a little thin (one of the cop's cousin's daughters was diagnosed with leukemia on the same day the case was reopened), but everyone connected every bad thing that happened to everyone they even vaguely knew to the curse, and thus to Reginald Solar, the discoverer of the bodies.

Everywhere he went, Reginald carried the mark of death. People could feel it on him. Smell it on him. They knew, without knowing exactly how they knew, that bad luck was centered on him, channeled through him, seeped from his skin as pus would seep from an infected wound. And maybe it was true. Maybe Death did leave his mark on Esther's grandfather, but all he was to her was a good and gentle man left halfway broken by the terrible things he'd seen and a terrible truth that had left him unable to sleep at night. He'd never caught the Bowen sisters' murderer, and now, for the second time—and possibly many more times than that—the murderer had struck again.

2. The second reason her grandfather was crying was because he knew with utmost certainty that his beloved wife was hours away from dying of a catastrophic brain aneurysm and was—understandably—quite upset about this, too.

REG STOPPED WEEPING SOON after they arrived and sat them on his lap and tucked orchids behind their ears and told them, at eleven years old, about the Man Who Would Be Death, about the war in Vietnam and some of the more terrible things he'd seen humans do to each other. He told them about the danger of strangers, about how the boogeyman was real and that it lurked in the dark, waiting to prey on wayward children. He told them about the Bowen sisters, what had been done to them, in as much detail as he thought appropriate for eleven-year-olds, which was far too much. He told them about the ghosts of all the children who followed him, the ones he couldn't save, the ones that had died because he wasn't a good enough detective to catch their murderer. When they'd been born, only the Bowen sisters appeared at the foot of his bed. By the night Alana Shepard was found, seven spectral children haunted his every waking moment, asking for their parents, asking to be fed, asking him to read to them, crying when he didn't.

That night, their grandfather taught Esther and Eugene that monsters were real, and they looked just like them. They didn't doubt—they had no reason to. They sat and listened and soaked it all up, because they were children and no one had ever taken them so seriously before.

Reginald told them of his cursed life in less than an hour, and instilled their tiny, wildly beating hearts with the kind of fear children didn't normally stumble upon until they were older, when they came to understand mortality through the death of an older relative. They knew of their grandfather's primal fear of water already, how he no longer so much as showered but washed his body with a damp cloth for fear of slipping in the tub and drowning. But it was on that night, the night they learned the curse would kill them, that the curse Death had given Reg when he told him he would drown became real in their heads.

Esther and Eugene ate their roast dinner in silence, both horrified, in their own way, to learn that Death was real.

Florence died the next morning, of a brain aneurysm, just as Reginald had known she would. One week later, when the story of the curse had fermented in Esther's brain into something much larger and darker than her grandfather had perhaps intended, she started writing her semi-definitive list of worst nightmares to protect her from the Reaper's spell.

What were the ingredients of a well-founded curse? Mix one part Death's apprentice with twenty years of war and the unexpected death of a beloved grandmother, and then sprinkle the concoction with the serial murder of children by a man who came to be known as the Harvestman.

Then, ladies and gentlemen, you've got yourself a curse.

28

21/50: ABANDONED BUILDINGS

IN LATE January, Eugene, Heph, and Esther met Jonah in the late afternoon outside Peachwood General Hospital. Abandoned in the mid-'90s when the new public hospital opened across town, Peachwood was purchased shortly thereafter by a developer, who wanted to renovate the entire complex and sell old wards as apartments to rich people for millions of dollars. The public laughed—who'd want to live in a building where thousands of people had died?—and the developer went out of business and hanged himself in the remains of the psychiatric ward. Three weeks passed before anyone found him; by then, wild dogs had eaten his feet.

More than twenty years after the property had been abandoned, Peachwood was being digested by nature. Greenery swelled at its base, sucking the dead hospital slowly back into the earth, suffocating it from the bottom up. Peachwood was gutted for parts like an old car long ago: window frames, air-conditioning systems, hospital beds . . . everything of value had been stripped and plucked and stolen, leaving only a shell to rot in the elements.

The building sat on an open plain now, the parking lot that once surrounded it cracked and blistered by weeds.

Jonah picked the lock on the chain-link fence that cordoned off the property. Again, no one saw how he did this—he simply cupped the padlock in his hands and it seemed to fall open for him with a sigh, as if it had been waiting knowingly for his touch, as if it shuddered with delight at the feel of him after all this time. Esther was always surprised by how easy Jonah was able to open locked things; she had a feeling he had the same knack with locked people.

They walked across the lot toward the white building, Hephzibah running ahead of them, her hair trailing behind her like smoke. She looked like she was going home. A patchwork of gray frost was scattered on the ground amid the winter-bleached grass, and their breath bloomed out in front of them, but Esther was too hyped to feel the cold. Fear 21/50 was abandoned buildings, and Jonah had brought them to the most haunted place in the whole town, a place where even teen vandals feared to tread after two of them vanished from the ruins just before she and Eugene were born. The cops found the kids' spray cans and their backpacks and their half-eaten school lunches scattered around a ward, but they never found the boys. More children snatched up by the Harvestman, the rumors said, though the police could never confirm it.

Esther zipped up the jacket of her Amelia Earhart costume. Dressing as the most famous disappeared woman of all time suddenly seemed like a bad idea.

Eugene made it all the way to the broken basement window before his legs stopped working and he shook his head vigorously from side to side.

"I can't," he said breathlessly. "Too dark."

"I got you, man," Jonah said to him, placing a hand on his shoulder. Eugene, like the lock, seemed to soften at Jonah's touch. "I've spent all afternoon setting up something just for you."

"You came here by yourself?"

"Only got harassed by poltergeists, like, twice. Piece of cake."

"Okay," said Eugene. He drew three more quick, deep breaths, then looked at Esther. "Okay."

They climbed into the basement one by one, Hephzibah first because she was the bravest, the wildest, the strangest. Jonah next, and then Esther, and then—when all were holding the lit oil torches Jonah had prepared earlier—Eugene slid into the dark too, flashlight in one hand, his back pressed to the brick wall as his eyes adjusted to the change in light.

"All right, man?" said Jonah, handing him a fourth torch, the light from the flame making Eugene look waxen.

Even Hephzibah stayed close as they made their way deeper into the basement of the hospital. The walls spoke as old walls often do, sighing as they passed. Wind sang through windows with no glass, and the concrete shifted and moaned. Water dripped from pipes long gutted by rust. An orchestra. The building was alive and knew they were there, feeling the intruders like a splinter in its flesh.

Jonah led them to the psych ward, where the developer had

been found swinging. It was even better lit than the Solar house. A generator hummed in some far-off hallway, breathing life into a hundred yellow bulbs laid out in a grid on the floor.

Eugene grinned. "Never should've doubted you."

"Yeah, this is only half of what I set up." Jonah knelt in a corner and produced three sleeping masks, the kind worn on airplanes. "You're gonna wait here and wear these while I turn the lights off."

"You can't joke about that shit, man."

"I'm not joking."

"Like hell you aren't."

Jonah took Eugene's face in his hands. "Hey, hey, hey," he said. Eugene grabbed Jonah by the wrists but didn't try to push him away. "Do you trust me?" Eugene thought for a moment, then looked to Esther, who nodded.

Eugene swallowed hard. "If she trusts you, I trust you."

"Then *trust* me," Jonah said as he lowered the blindfold over Eugene's eyes. "I won't let anything happen to either of you." Eugene's shallow breathing was all Esther could hear as she too lowered her blindfold. "I'll just be a minute," Jonah said as he squeezed her hand. "Leave your masks *on*."

Eugene held onto his twin like she was a buoy in the middle of a stormy sea. There was no one he wanted more when he was afraid than her, and she felt the same way. Whenever she'd been scared as a child, she had always run to Eugene, not her parents. There was some kind of magic in his skin; whenever she pressed her palms to his back or his arms or slipped her hand into his, everything bad went away. Maybe it was all the light he soaked up at nighttime that made him so enchanted.

The sound of the humming lights went dead and Esther could almost feel the darkness crash into her. Eugene gasped. Actually *gasped*. His fingers tightened around hers and she thought at any moment that he would scream and be attacked and dragged away from her, but he wasn't.

Then came the sound of footsteps as Jonah returned. "Blindfolds off," he said breathlessly.

They took their blindfolds off.

The lights were out and it was dimmer than before but it wasn't dark. Not by a long shot. Eugene was silent, his mouth open as he turned in a slow circle to take in the ceiling, the walls, the floor. A dozen black lights had been set up along the bases of the walls, and beneath their neon glow, every surface of the ward was ablaze. UV paint in purple and pink and green and red and orange had been splashed everywhere, a galaxy of bright stars to illuminate the dark. Planets and stars and spaceships and nebulas and ethereal creatures floated in the abyss.

Jonah had painted the universe.

"I brought this too, if you want to try it," he said, throwing Eugene a tube of paint. Eugene caught it and looked at the tube, confused. "UV body paint," Jonah explained. "Light on your very skin. You'll be able to move through the dark without a flashlight or fire or anything."

Even though it was freezing, Eugene stripped down to his boxers and they all painted him in an elaborate geometric design so that every inch of his exposed skin was set alight. He looked like a wild neon demon from another dimension. Esther painted a bright heart of red and white on the center of his chest, a shield against fear and the demons the curse sent to kill him, demons that lived inside his head.

"Do you think this is going to work?" he said quietly as he stood at the edge of the doorway that led into the darkness.

"I'm sure of it," Esther said. She squeezed his painted hand.

Jonah had set up black lights in the halls surrounding the glowing galaxy room so that Eugene could, for the first time in living memory, move unencumbered through blackness. He put his painted fingertips against the barrier that had held him back for six years and let his hand sink into the terrible dark, baiting the monsters to see if they would dare take a bite.

They didn't.

Esther was glad for the semidarkness; it almost hid her tears as she watched her brother step out into the unlit hall, like an explorer discovering the depths of the ocean in the very first atmospheric diving suit. The black lights set his skin ablaze. Eugene screamed, not in pain, but in delight. He whooped and ran and leaped and laughed, awed by such unimaginable freedom. Whether he saw the monsters he claimed to be able to see in the shadows, Esther wasn't sure, but if he did, that night he paid them no mind.

Thank you, she mouthed to Jonah. He nodded, smiling casually, like he hadn't just done the most extraordinary thing in the world.

And then she did what she hadn't had the courage to do until that moment—she took a step toward Jonah, put her hands on his chest, and kissed him. His skin warm beneath her fingers, she pulled him close and tasted the glow paint on his lips and kissed him with everything she had in the bright glowing light of the universe.

29
THE DYING
OF THE LIGHT

WHEN ROSEMARY called her later that night, Esther wondered for half a heartbeat if her mother was at home and wondering where her children were.

"I just got off the phone with Lilac Hill," she said. "Reg has gone downhill very fast. The nurses think it's time to stop food and water, like he asked for."

"How long does he have after that?" Esther asked.

"Not long," said Rosemary. "Not long now."

30

24/50:

BURIED ALIVE

IN THE week leading up to 24/50, the quest to find Death was forgotten in favor of spending time with Reginald Solar at Lilac Hill. Every Sunday Esther and Jonah had gone out and faced a new fear, but each week they'd become less and less scared because cliffs and geese and graveyards didn't seem so terrifying when the people you loved started disintegrating around you.

It was also during the week before 24/50 that Peter Solar had another stroke. Again, he told no one, terrified that he would be forced to leave the basement. Jonah found him on the toilet, unable to move, two days after the fact. It was the most horrific and heartbreaking thing Esther had ever seen. Peter cried as Jonah cleaned him, pulled his pants up, helped him stand. Peter tried not to let her see him like that, but she did. Esther saw it all and it killed her.

Perhaps the worst, though, was Jonah, who by then frequently arrived at her house with fresh bruises. Sometimes she noticed them right away, and sometimes she didn't realize he was hurting until she touched his arm or chest or back and he winced in pain. When this happened, she fantasized about killing his father for him; in her imagination he was less a man, more a large mass of shadow, the evil villain from a cartoon.

"I'm not sure I need to be buried alive," she said to Jonah, Hephzibah, and her brother on the Sunday morning of 24/50. "I already feel like I'm drowning."

Esther expected Jonah to protest—they hadn't missed a single fear yet—but he didn't. Actually, he nodded. "Do you wanna, I don't know, do something normal teenagers do? See a movie or something?"

So that was what they did. People stared more than usual. People leaned into each other and whispered and pointed their fingers at them, which Esther thought was very rude until she realized they weren't staring or pointing at Eugene or Jonah or Hephzibah. They were fixated on her.

"Why is everyone looking at me?" Esther whispered to Jonah.

"Maybe because you're dressed as Mia Wallace," he said as he looked around, but he didn't seem able to feel all the eyes that were pointed their way.

After the movie, Eugene drove Heph home, and Esther and Jonah walked back alone.

"Do you think Death is afraid of anything?" he asked her.

Esther already knew that Death feared exactly two things, because her grandfather had told her. In the Mediterranean Sea and waters of Japan, there was a species of small, biologically immortal jellyfish called *Turritopsis dohrnii* that grew old and then young again, like a yo-yoing Benjamin Button. It was where Death, she liked to imagine, went on vacation whenever he had a quiet moment to spare, when there were no wars or famines or teenagers being purposefully reckless in order to attract his attention. Esther liked to imagine the Reaper floating on his back over a school of bodies that looked like bubbles of saltwater taffy. She liked to imagine that it was Death's favorite pastime, swimming among the bright, beautiful things he wasn't required or allowed to pluck from this earth.

At the same time, Esther knew that Death feared these creatures that he couldn't touch. They drifted under the sun for time immeasurable, unaware of gods or men or monsters or, indeed, Death. They were the only thing on this planet capable of making Death feel small and insecure, except for his second great love and fear: orchids.

Death kept every gift that life sent his way, but he couldn't touch this one.

"Death is afraid of orchids," she said to Jonah. He nodded like he understood what this meant, but didn't say anything. It was strange, seeing Jonah Smallwood so sad and so quiet. Like the light had gone out of him. Before he left, he kissed her on the forehead and she held him tight around the waist.

After that, she didn't see or hear from him for a week.

31

THE DEATH DOOR

ESTHER:

Are you coming over this afternoon?

Fleayoncé missed you yesterday.

Okay, I missed you too.

Are you ignoring me because my line dancing skills intimidated you?

Are you dead? If you don't message me back I'm going to assume you're dead and call the cops.

Jesus, Jonah. Please. Please let me know you're okay.

Esther had sent him a message every day for the whole week; he'd seen them but hadn't replied. On Sunday, when he didn't show up at her house at their usual meeting time, she knew she had only two choices: call the police or check on Jonah herself. Both were unappealing. If she called the cops, Remy might be taken from him, and he'd never forgive her for that. If she went over there herself and Jonah was dead in a pool of his own blood, his skull caved in . . .

Don't. Don't even think like that.

Esther went to his place dressed as Matilda Wormwood. One needed to feel formidable on days like this.

From the outside, his house looked peaceful, but in the sad way that corpses looked peaceful after they'd been embalmed and made up for an open casket. Esther pushed the side gate open; there was noise coming from inside the house. Someone was yelling. Something thudded against the wall.

Around the back, the porch door was swung wide. Most of the drywall had been ripped down, and someone had taken to the mural on the ceiling with some kind of blunt object. Remy was huddled in a corner, crying.

"Where's Jonah?" Esther asked her, panicked. "Where is he?"

Remy pointed, without speaking, into the house.

Esther pushed open the door of Death. Beyond it was a dimly lit hallway. She moved down it slowly, each of her footfalls measured. More noise. Grunting. A yelp of pain. For perhaps the first time in her life she had a fight instead of a flight response, and her adrenaline sent her careening in the direction of her fear.

In the living room, Holland Smallwood, Jonah's father, had his son by the neck, pushed up against a wall. "Do I look fucking crazy to you?" he screamed. "Is this what a crazy person looks like, huh? Look at me! Is this what a crazy person looks like?"

Jonah, who was always so tall and bright, like a hero out of a comic book, was crying. Next to his dad he was a little kid. He closed his eyes and shook and didn't do anything to defend himself except hold up his hands weakly.

"Please," he muttered. "I'm sorry."

Holland slammed him into the wall again.

"Stop!" Esther yelled, and then she was among it, part of it, scrabbling to get him off Jonah. Something solid connected with her cheekbone. An elbow? A fist? She didn't realize she'd fallen until she was on the ground, the horizon vertical in her view. The world kept slipping sideways, an old projector stuck between frames.

"Get the fuck out of my house!" Holland screamed at her. She curled into a ball and covered her head with her arms. She thought he was going to kick her, but no blows came.

Jonah's lip was split. There were dots of blood everywhere. Blood and spit and glass and pieces of a broken chair. Jonah just stared at Esther, heaving breaths.

It was the little girl who came to her rescue. Remy, dragging her up, pushing her out, whispering, "Go, go, go, go, go" as she guided Esther to the front door. She followed Esther out onto the porch and then retreated inside. Like the immune system expelling a pathogen.

Esther could hear heavy footsteps going up the stairs. She pressed the heel of her palm to the hot, throbbing lump on her cheek where some part of Holland had struck her.

Jonah came out a minute later. His lip was already swollen. Esther used her sleeve to clean away some of the blood, and then she just squeezed him. Wrapped her arms around his torso, his arms still pinned to his side, and squeezed him and squeezed him, like maybe if she applied enough pressure she could turn him into a diamond.

Jonah seemed empty. He didn't react to her touch. "I can't do this anymore, Esther," he said eventually. "I can't be brave for the both of us." Then he broke down and collapsed into her, heaving sobs that shook his whole body. Tears rolled down Esther's cheeks as she stroked the back of his neck and whispered, "I'm sorry, I'm sorry, I'm so sorry," because what else was there to say? What else was there to do? They were teenagers, and they were powerless, and until they were adults they had no choice but to let their destinies be bent and swayed by outside forces.

It was the moment she'd been waiting for for months. The moment that was inevitable. The moment Jonah realized she was more trouble than she was worth.

People only understood mental illness up to a certain point. Beyond that point, their patience waned. She knew this, because she felt it sometimes with Eugene. With her mother. With her father. The desire just to take them by the shoulders and shake them and say, "Get better! Be better! For God's sake, fix yourself!"

She'd known for a long time that this day would come, and now here it was, and she couldn't blame him, because the shit he was going through was even worse than hers. The cumulative total of their collective pain was too much to bear. It was easy enough to hurt for yourself; hurting for other people was what broke you.

"Okay," she said as she broke away from him. "Okay."

"Hey, hey, wait. Where are you going?" Jonah said as he caught up to her on the lawn and ran his thumb over the bruise forming at her cheekbone. His jaw wobbled and jutted forward as he touched the swelling; she had never seen him so angry before.

"You just said . . . you couldn't do this anymore?"

Jonah shook her head, then kissed her injured cheek softly. "Not you. I didn't mean you."

Esther collapsed into him. What had she done to herself? How had she let this happen? How had she allowed the boy who pickpocketed her at a bus stop become a person who could make her come undone?

"I'm sorry I'm crazy," she sobbed. "I'm sorry you got sucked into all this. I'm sorry I can't fix all of this for you."

"Hey. You're not crazy. And I didn't get sucked into anything. We started this together," he said. "We're gonna finish it together."

They waded out into the long grass behind his house, far enough that they could no longer see any lights but the half dozen solar garden lights they carried with them, stolen from a neighbor's yard. Jonah set the lamps in a ring, like a fairy circle out of myth. The sky above them was heavy and thick with magic, and all around her, Esther could sense a danger that she could not see. An old danger, from a time before electricity and cars and the internet had made people forget what lurked in the dark. It stalked around them, a swirling mass of unknown menace. It sent goose bumps up her arms. It made her take small, shallow breaths through her mouth. It made her eyes water because she couldn't bring herself to blink.

"I'll never be rid of this fear," she said as Jonah drove the final light into the ground. "I was stupid to think I could break the curse."

"How about you fuck off, you giant bitch?!" Jonah yelled, and for a second she thought he was talking to her, but no—he had his hand cupped around his mouth and was yelling at the shadows. "Yeah, you, thou currish onion-eyed maltworm! I see you, dickwad. Take a hike!"

"You're going to swear and shout Shakespearean insults at the dark?"

"Got a better idea?"

Esther turned back toward the gloom. "Piss off," she said weakly.

"Come on, Solar, you can do better than that. Thou foul defacer of God's handiwork!" Jonah boomed. "Thou mewling rump-fed clodpole! Suck my dick, thou frothy dread-bolted scullion!"

"Yeah!" Esther added. "Screw you, you piece of shit. You . . . uh . . . bucket of dildos!"

"Thou frothy dismal-dreaming horn-beast!"

"Douchenozzle!"

"Thou mewling crook-pated canker-blossom! The power of Christ compels you, bitch! Thou art unfit for any place but hell!" Jonah looked over at Esther, a lopsided grin on his swollen lips. "Better?"

Esther smiled. "Better." She took a breath. Steadied herself to ask a difficult question. "Why do you stay? Every time I think you've had enough of me . . . you come back for more."

"You really don't know?" Jonah took a step back. Rubbed his eyes. "Because I . . . I kind of love you, Esther."

"*Why?*"

"Why? Because . . . you're so much braver than you realize. Look, I lied about not remembering how we met as kids, okay? I remember you being bullied. I remember the way you used to grit your teeth and stick your chin out and keep doing whatever you were doing even when you were being tormented. Most kids would've cried, you know, but you? You've got guts, Solar. You always have."

"The only reason you like me is because you don't see who I really am."

"I *see* you."

"Then let me see the portrait. Let me make sure."

"Some paint on a canvas isn't gonna make any difference if you don't know by now. I knew this would be hard for you but . . . I thought you'd feel the same way."

"Eugene flickers in and out of existence, sometimes for hours at a time. My father is turning to stone. My mother is being eaten by termites. I can't be sure if Hephzibah is even real or not. You're the only person I care about who's solid and I don't want to . . . to ruin you."

What Esther didn't say, what she didn't add, was that she

didn't want to give Jonah the power to ruin her either. Love was a trap, a sticky trap of molasses meant to bind two people together. It was a thing that couldn't be escaped, a weight that people strapped to their own legs before they waded into the water and wondered why they drowned. Esther had seen it time and time again. She'd seen the thing people called love, the thing romantic movies were made about, and the power of it scared the shit out of her.

Her grandfather had loved her grandmother, and the loss of her had sent him mad. Her mother had loved her father, and the disappearance of him had eaten her up, turned her into termite-eaten wood.

Despite the clear and present danger Jonah posed, Esther let him tuck a strand of her hair behind her ear. She let him lean close to her and press his swollen lips to hers. She pulled back, tried not to hurt him, but Jonah didn't seem to care. His hand was in her hair, pulling her closer to him, pressing her mouth harder against his. He kissed her like he was going to war and didn't expect to kiss anyone ever again.

Then it was over and he was resting his forehead against her. "Please prove me wrong," she said quietly, her lips against the skin of his hand.

"Man, you're wrong about so many things, I can't pick where to start proving you wrong. What do you even want me to prove you wrong about?"

"Death, mostly. And love."

"No way I can prove you wrong about love, unless you've gone and fallen in love with me too."

As soon as you admitted to loving someone, you suddenly had a lot to lose. You freely gave them a way to hurt you.

There was never a single, grandiose moment of realization. Esther certainly noticed the big things: his goodness, his strength, the way he protected her when no one else would. But it was the little things that accumulated over time that made Jonah Smallwood extraordinary. The way he grinned when he was planning something mischievous, how he looked at her with wide, excited eyes in the moments after she'd faced a fear, the way his hips wiggled when he danced, and how he collapsed to the ground whenever he found something really, ridiculously funny.

A thousand little moments had made Esther fall more and more in love with him, without her even noticing. A thousand little pieces of his soul had splintered off and dug themselves into her.

"You got the hots for me, Solar?"

Esther didn't answer.

"Well I'll be damned."

"Prove me wrong," she whispered.

"You are *so* wrong," he said, and then he kissed her forehead, the tip of her nose, her lips. Esther supposed, as they held each other under a threadbare carpet of stars, that this was how it must always feel in the beginning. Yet even there, next to him, the most excellent person in the universe, she couldn't stop herself from thinking that love was a pitcher plant. Sweet with nectar on the outside, but once you caught the scent and took the plunge, it ate you whole.

Soul and all.

32

EUGENE

THEY SLEPT in the closed-in porch, curled up together under a blanket beneath a galaxy of painted stars. Esther awoke in the early morning to twenty-three missed calls, all of them from her mother, and two text messages:

MOM:

Call me immediately.

It's Eugene, Esther. It's Eugene.

33

THE SHADOW BOY

MERCY GENERAL Hospital, the one built to replace Peachwood, was a big, geometric puzzle of a building, all glass and steel and concrete. Though its outsides were modern, its insides could be from any hospital in any decade: long, brightly lit corridors devoid of warmth or comfort, ugly industrial flooring, and the acid smell of bleach trying (and failing) to veil the stench of death.

Esther walked through the halls with grass from the night before still in her hair. Her Matilda Wormwood costume was ripped and dirty. She looked thoroughly out of place in such a sterile environment, a feral girl who'd wandered in from the jungle.

Or maybe, here on the mental health ward, she looked just right. Maybe this was where she belonged.

Rosemary had explained it to her on the car ride over, after she'd picked Esther up from the end of Jonah's street. There had been a power outage on the street, and Eugene had disappeared into the sudden darkness. Whatever had snatched him and dragged him through the ether spat him back out, sweating and screaming and smelling of damp earth and decay. Smelling of the grave, Esther realized.

It had only taken him a minute or two to calm down once the lights were back on. Rosemary made him tea and tucked yarrow behind his ear.

He said he was fine. He said it was getting easier, now that he was older. He said she should go to the casino, if she wanted. He said he'd be fine on his own.

He said he'd be fine.

It was Peter who found him. It was Peter who, like his father, had a sixth sense for death. When he still took part in the world above, this extrasensory perception had made him an excellent veterinarian. He knew, without knowing how he knew, which animals to treat and which ones Death had already laid his hands on. Which ones were already marked and thus beyond the help of medicine. All he had to do was be near the dying to hear the dark, buzzing silence that was the symphony of Death.

The same symphony he heard when Eugene sank a veterinary scalpel into each of his wrists in the bathroom above the basement.

Eugene Solar was seventeen years old when he died.

"Aren't you coming in?" Esther asked when Rosemary stopped at the door.

"You know he'd only want you."

She nodded. She would be the same. If she was sick, or sad, or dying, or all three, Eugene would be the one she would ask for.

Esther watched her mother walk back down the hall toward

the nurse's station. She was rake thin and her skin fell in soft drapes across her cheekbones

Inside the room, Eugene was lying on his back in the bed, his eyes open but lifeless. Esther knocked on the wall. Eugene broke out of his corpse pose and looked over at her.

Eugene Solar was seventeen when he died. He was also seventeen when the EMTs brought him back from the clutches of the Reaper against his will—twice.

"Hey loser," he said croakily.

Peter had gotten there in time. Just. Despite three strokes and a fear so great and terrible it had driven him underground for six years, their father had dragged himself, half paralyzed, up the basement stairs and gotten to the bathroom just in time to save his only son. Thirty more seconds, the EMTs said. Thirty more seconds and they wouldn't have been able to bring Eugene back at all.

"Apparently you suck at dying," Esther said. "Finally, something you're not good at."

"Oh no, didn't you hear? I died *twice*. I'm just fine at dying. It's the staying dead part that's tricky." Eugene stared at the ceiling again. "Well, this is not a conversation I was hoping to have. Now everyone's gonna think it was a cry for help."

"Our parents are so inconvenient. Never there when you need them and then right when you're trying to kill yourself . . ."

"They barge in and ruin the whole thing. God, what dicks."

"Dad really came out of the basement?"

"Yeah. I can't explain it. I was quiet. I made *sure* I was quiet. I didn't call for help or anything, but . . . he still found me. I don't know how. I don't remember much, just him stumbling into the room and practically falling on top of me. It might as well have been a dream."

"So a casual suicide attempt was the answer all along."

"Now if you develop a slight addiction to meth or something, we'll get the family back together for sure."

Esther laughed, which turned quickly to breathless sobbing. She didn't really understand how she could be crying when there was nothing left inside her body. She sat on the side of his mattress and took one of his bandaged hands in hers. "Don't leave me," she whispered. "Don't leave me here with them."

Esther wanted to make her brother understand that he was the sun. That he was bright and burning and brilliant, and without his warmth, without his gravity to orient herself around, she would be nothing. She wished they had that psychic twin thing, that she could push images into his head and make him see. Make him see that he was everything.

Eugene was quiet for a moment, until he said, "I can't stay, Esther," as he twisted the ends of her hair in his fingertips. Esther started to cry harder, because she knew he didn't mean *I can't stay in the hospital* or *I can't stay in this town*. Eugene meant he couldn't stay on this planet, not when there were so many demons and ghosts to be stumbled upon in the dark, so many jump scares waiting in mirrors and blackened hallways and the bare branches of trees at night. The whole universe was wrong for a creature like Eugene; too much dark matter, too much space between stars, too many unknowns floating in the infinite abyss.

"It'll get better," she said through her tears. "I promise it'll get better. You won't always be scared."

"Don't be lame, Esther. You're better than that. I don't want to live like this anymore."

She grasped desperately for bargaining chips, for reasons to make him stay. "You know if you die before her she's going to play that terrible slideshow at your funeral."

"That's genuinely one of the reasons I put it off for so long. I tried to find it last night but the woman keeps it hidden like it's a family heirloom."

"How can you want to leave me?"

"Oh, Esther," he said as she burrowed her face into his chest. "It isn't about you. Not at all. It never has been. You can love someone with all your soul and still hate yourself enough to want to die."

But she wasn't willing to accept his surrender.

Not yet.

Not ever.

"You've gotta fight it, Eugene. Whenever you feel like hurting yourself, tell me, tell Heph, tell Mom, tell Dad, tell Jonah, tell your friends. I guarantee you that at least one of us will say, 'Come over, I'll be your backup.' And then we fight the dark thoughts together. If you try and do this on your own, your chance of getting ambushed by your own mind skyrockets."

"Sometimes there's not a strategy for everything."

"No. Shut up. I will not compromise with this *thing* inside you that makes you hate yourself so much. I can't do that."

"The thought of finishing high school, of graduating and going to college . . . it exhausts me. It makes me so tired. When I think about the future, all I feel is emptiness. Even if things get better, I know this feeling will come back eventually. It always does."

"Give me your phone," she said.

"I don't have it. It's in a bag somewhere."

Esther found his phone in the bag Rosemary had packed for him and did a Google search and added the number for the suicide hotline into his contacts. "You *ever* wanna hurt yourself again, even if you feel like you can't call anyone you know, you call this number."

"You make it sound so easy."

"Of course it's not going to be easy. You're fighting a war against yourself. Every time either side makes ground, *you're* the one who gets hurt. But it's not about winning the war against your demons. It's about calling a truce and learning how to live with them peacefully. Promise me you'll keep fighting."

"Why should I? You don't."

"What does that mean?"

"You don't fight. You think you're so brave, but you don't fight your demons either."

"I'm *trying*. I've been *trying* for months."

"Like hell you are. You go out every week and do some stupid stunt that you aren't even really scared of. You get your heart pumping for a little while, but it's not real fear."

"We're getting close, Eugene, I can feel it. We're catching up to him. Or getting his attention. I can *fix* this."

"The Reaper isn't *real*, Esther. The *curse* isn't real. Jack Horowitz is just some guy. Pop isn't going to drown. I think that's pretty clear by now. It's a bedtime story he used to tell us when we were little kids, which—might I add—is pretty screwed up. I was close to the afterlife and I didn't see anything or anyone."

"Then why was all of this happening to us?"

"Because your life doesn't need to be cursed for it to be a totally shit time. Look, Pop told me, okay? I asked him before he went into Lilac Hill if the curse was real, if he'd really met Death, and he just laughed. Said I should know by now that it was a fairy tale."

Esther looked at Eugene, waited for him to falter, but he didn't. "But . . . that makes no sense. He . . . he told us for years that the curse is real."

"It's a *story*, Esther. A fairy tale."

"What about Uncle Harold? What about cousin Martin and the bees? What about Pop's dog? What about *you*?"

"No one believes but you. *You're* the only one it's real for. *You're* the one who keeps it alive."

Esther opened her mouth to disagree, but Eugene was either so tired or so drugged up that his eyelids grew heavy and his head nodded forward. "Move over," she said, and he shuffled to the side as best he could, and she climbed into the narrow bed with him and carefully scrabbled her way under his injured arms and into his chest.

"Eugene," she whispered into his hospital gown, beneath

which his thin ribs moved up and down, drawing breaths against his will, "you *cannot* leave me."

Eugene said nothing, just lifted a bandaged hand to place against her cheek. They lay how they did for nine months in the womb, all tangled limbs, until she felt his fitful breathing slow into the cadence of sleep. The frown lines on his forehead relaxed. The tensed muscles in his shoulders melted into the sheets.

How could death not be appealing, when the only thing that gave him comfort in life was being unconscious?

34

BETRAYAL

JONAH CAME by that morning, as soon as Esther called him. They ate breakfast together in the sad hospital cafeteria and waited for Eugene to return to the waking world he so desperately wished to leave.

"Do you think they purposefully make hospitals hideous?" Esther asked. The cafeteria had lemon walls and orange floors and all the furniture looked like it was from an old office building. A young girl, maybe thirteen or fourteen, with a cast on her arm, gave Esther a strange look as she and Jonah lined up to buy their food.

"Man, I hope they don't serve this to Eugene or he's gonna wanna kill himself all over again," said Jonah as they sat down with their trays of bland eggs and "toast."

Esther took a mouthful of food, but a strange sensation made it hard for her to chew and swallow. She looked up. The girl with the cast was still staring at her. Esther looked down at her Matilda Wormwood costume; nowhere near the weirdest thing she owned.

"That girl keeps looking at me," Esther said. "It's making me uncomfortable."

"She's *clearly* looking at me," Jonah said. "You know what, this food isn't bad. Come on, eat some more."

"Okay, she just looked at me *again*."

"Stop looking over there and she'll stop looking over here."

"Jonah, I'm not kidding. She's staring at me."

"It's probably because you wear costumes everywhere. You're being paranoid."

"I am *not* being paranoid."

"Eat your eggs, woman."

"I'm not hungry."

"How come?"

Something in Esther cracked. Her eyes welled and her throat swelled and suddenly she was crying. "Because my family is disintegrating around me and . . . and . . . and it's all my fault. I should've . . . fought harder to get my dad out of the basement. I should've tried harder to break the curse before it tried to kill Eugene."

"Hey, hey, hey, there's no way any of this is your—" Jonah began, but the girl who'd been watching them was now standing behind him.

"Esther Solar?" she said. Esther wiped her eyes and frowned. "No way! It is you! I'm such a huge fan! Sorry, I don't mean to interrupt but . . . can I get a photo with you?"

"What?" Esther said.

"Can I get a selfie with you?"

"Why?"

"I watch your YouTube channel."

"My . . . YouTube? I don't understand."

"*A Semi-Definitive List of Worst Nightmares,*" the girl explained, looking between Jonah and her, like maybe they were not the people she thought they were. "The one where you guys go out every week and face a new fear. The geese were my favorite. One bit me when I was a kid and I've never—"

Esther looked at Jonah.

"Esther," said Jonah, softly, pleadingly, but she'd already lurched up from the table and sent her bright orange tray of hospital food flying in the process. Jonah caught her at the cafeteria entrance.

"They're online," she said between gasps. She wasn't sure if her breathing was wild from panic or from running or from pure rage or from all three. "You put the videos online."

"It was supposed to be a surprise for 50/50."

"You made me look like an idiot!"

"An idiot? You haven't even seen them. You haven't even seen how much people love you."

"Don't touch me!" she spat when he tried to put his hand on her arm. "You lied to me! You promised me that no one would ever see. You promised me. You promised."

Jonah took a step back. "Yeah, okay, I lied. You wanna know why? Because what were we gonna do when we got to the number one slot? You aren't scared of lobsters or snakes or blood or heights. That's bullshit. I've known what you're afraid of since the day I met you. I've known what you're too chickenshit to write down."

"Oh yeah, and what's that, Dr. Phil? Please psychoanalyze me with all your many years of experience!"

"Are you kidding me? You actually don't *know*? You *have* to know."

"Screw you. You don't know anything about me."

"I *see* you, Esther. I meant it when I said that. You think your fear makes you so interesting and so special, but it doesn't. You think you're so unique or some shit because you carry around a list of everything you can't do, but you're not. *Everyone* is scared of exactly the same stuff. Everyone fights the same battles every day."

"You don't know what it's like living with a cursed family."

"Jesus. *Your family isn't cursed.* Eugene's been trying to tell you for months and months that he's sick, but you don't want to see it. You don't pay attention. You want a simple solution to a complex problem. Well, *there is none.* People get depression and develop gambling addictions and have strokes and die in car crashes and get hit by the people who should love them, and it's not because they were cursed by Death. That's just how it is."

"This isn't about you and your fucked-up life."

"Goddamn it, Esther," he said, and then he kicked a trash can.

So Esther said the thing she knew would cut the deepest. "Already starting to take after your dad, I see."

Jonah took a deep breath in and steadied himself. When he spoke again, his voice was low and measured. "You think so little of your family because they don't love you like you wanna be loved, but that doesn't mean they don't love you with everything they've got. Just because they aren't perfect people doesn't mean they aren't enough."

"You promised me you'd prove me wrong."

"You think this means I don't love you?"

"No. I know you love me. This just proves to me that love was exactly what I thought it was all along. The power to cause pain."

"I *see you*, Esther," he pleaded. "I *see* you."

All the times her mother should've left her father but didn't, wasn't strong enough, was too afraid of the unknown. But Esther had had practice. Months and months of practice being brave. So she was brave again then. There were no tears. She simply shook her head and walked away.

35

THE GREAT ORCHID HEIST

ESTHER AND Rosemary spent the morning in the hospital, in and out of Eugene's room as doctors and nurses came and went and told them again and again how lucky he was, how close he'd come. Esther's heart had never hurt so much before; she hadn't been aware before that day that things like betrayal and grief could hurt as much as physical pain. When she thought of Eugene and what he'd done, she couldn't breathe. When she thought of her father and how he'd been rushed to the hospital alongside his son, because he was too weak even to move, her eyes burned. When she thought of Jonah and what he'd done, she wanted to vomit.

People had seen *her*. Strangers on the internet had *watched* her in some of her most private, vulnerable moments: when she was wet and sobbing and hyperventilating and shaking and weak and a coward. It had taken so much for her to let Jonah in, and he had just *let* them see her like that. Jonah had *given* her to them willingly, against her wishes. And that, Esther thought—that was unforgivable.

More than that, she hated herself for caring about something so trivial and stupid when her brother, her twin, her own flesh and blood, was lucky to be alive.

Esther rested her head on her mother's shoulder. Rosemary looked and smelled and sounded thoroughly out of place in the washed-out hallways of the hospital. Today she was wrapped in layers of bright silk, her fingers still heavy with rings, her clothing still tinkling from all the little gold coins sewn into hems and sleeves and stitched to the inside of every pocket. Her brown hair was piled high on her head and threaded with sprigs of yarrow, and her eyes were bloodshot. Esther thought she looked like a mad seer, descended from her tower to tell of a terrible premonition.

"Oh. I forgot to tell you. Fred is dead," Rosemary said solemnly as she stared at the stalk of tea that had floated to the top of her cup. Esther knew what this beverage-based omen supposedly meant, because her mother had told her many times before: a stranger is coming.

"What? How'd that happen?"

"I don't know. All that's left of him is a large scorch mark in the kitchen. You know Aitvarases become a spark when they die."

"You think the chicken spontaneously burst into flames," Esther said slowly.

"Fred was a rooster, not a chicken. Well, goblin rooster, technically. And yes."

"Did you see this happen?"

"No, but I think he sacrificed himself to save Eugene."

"Okay."

Esther stood up. Rosemary fished out the tea stalk, placed it on the back of her left hand, and hit it with her right. After only one hit, the stalk slid off her skin and fell to the ground. "A stranger will come in one day," she said. "A man. He'll be short."

THE CALL FROM LILAC HILL came in the afternoon. Rosemary pulled Esther out of Eugene's room and told her, as they collected cans of Coke and packets of chips from the vending machine, that Reginald was close now. Very close to slipping away.

"The nurse said you need to say your good-byes," Rosemary said. "Today, not tonight. Now. As soon as possible."

Esther pressed a finger and thumb into her burning eyes. Great timing. "We have to tell Eugene."

"Absolutely not. There's no way he can leave to go and see him. Telling him would only make him upset."

"He'll never forgive us if we don't give him the chance to say good-bye."

"I will never forgive myself if I don't give him the chance to get better. You know I'm right about this, Esther. Don't even try. You've both said good-bye to your grandfather so many times already."

"Eugene loves him so much."

"I know, honey. I know. You should go, while he's sleeping."

"Will you come later?"

"Reg is a good man, but I said my good-byes to him a long time ago, too. Eugene needs me more than he does."

What Esther wanted to say: *We've all been living without you for years. What makes you think having you here now is enough to make up for that?* Instead she said nothing, but her expression must have betrayed some of what she was feeling, because Rosemary pulled her daughter in and hugged her. For a moment Esther felt the spark of the tether that bound them, the magic that had once burned bright. She wanted so badly to melt into her mother and have the world feel right again.

"I know I don't live up to most of your expectations," Rosemary whispered. "I know you think I could be better in a lot of ways, and maybe if you could pick and choose some new parts for me, I'd be a better mom."

The words stung, mostly because they were true, and Esther felt the spark waver and die. "Mom. Please." She sighed and pulled away from her embrace and leaned forward to rest her head against the vending machine. "I really don't want you to think that."

"It's okay, honey. I know, sometimes, that I'm not enough. You and Eugene make sure I know it. But I really do love you. More than anything."

Esther opened her eyes. Was love enough? If a person could offer you nothing but broken promises and disappointment, was love enough to make up for that? She thought of Jonah, and what he'd done to her—how she'd shown him all of the most vulnerable corners of her soul, and he'd taken those secrets and sold them wholesale to the masses.

Esther held her mother's hand. Rosemary pressed it to her cheek and kissed her daughter's wrist. "My beautiful girl."

"I should go," she said, and then she did.

ESTHER BORROWED HER mother's car to drive herself to Lilac Hill. The fear that'd once coursed through her at the thought of people seeing her stall somehow felt muted and dull after Eugene's close call with Death. She drove slowly, carefully, but felt very little of the dread she once had.

These are the things she thought about instead:

> The fact that her grandfather was very close to death now, and hour by hour, it seemed less and less likely that he would drown. The impending reality that the Reaper's prediction was, in fact, quite wrong, made Esther feel hopeful and sad at the same time.
> - How much Reginald had loved orchids, and Johnny Cash, and birds, and his wife, and how he would have none of those things to comfort him as he left this world, and how very unfair that seemed.

So instead of going straight to her grandfather's deathbed, Esther first made a small detour and brought the car to a stop two houses down from the one that had for many years belonged to Florence and Reginald Solar. The house remained as quaint and kempt as it was the day the Solars moved into it when Reg returned from the war. The window frames were still bright white, the twisting garden path was still flanked by bushels of flowers, and an American flag still flew from one of the posts on the little porch.

Before she got out of the car, Esther thought about the

fourth time Reginald met Death, a meeting that occurred at the very house she stared at in the evening dark.

It happened in the greenhouse in the backyard, on the afternoon before her grandmother's death. Reg had only told her the story once, the day after Florence died. Esther and Eugene were eleven. Jack Horowitz, slight, pale, pockmarked, and no older than when he'd first met Reg in Vietnam some forty years before, knocked on the greenhouse wall and waved politely through the glass.

Reginald took off his gardening gloves and opened the door for Death.

"I am here to tell you some news you will not take kindly to hearing," said Horowitz.

"I'm about to die."

"No. You will die some years from now, of dementia. You will plan to kill yourself after the diagnosis, but the disease will be incredibly swift. You will not have the time."

"The hell I won't."

Horowitz shrugged. "For decades you have wondered how you will *really* die and now I tell you and you don't care to hear it."

"I get diagnosed with dementia, you can bet your ass I'm gonna put a pistol in my mouth before I start forgetting what my grandkids look like. And I'm *still* not going near water. Why are you here?"

"In the early hours of tomorrow morning—at 4:02 a.m., to be precise—someone you love dearly will die from a catastrophic brain aneurysm."

"If you touch anyone in my family, Horowitz . . ."

"I'm doing you a favor that many would sacrifice everything they have for."

"Oh, and what the hell is that?"

"The chance to say good-bye." It was at this point that Horowitz picked up an unopened bulb. It didn't wilt and turn black at his touch, as you might expect of Death. "You will invite your family over for a meal tonight. You will cook a grand feast. Roast lamb with rosemary and garlic, the same meal you cooked for your wife the first time you brought her home."

"How the hell do you—"

"Later in the evening, when all your children and grandchildren have gone home, you will wash the dishes and pour her a glass of red wine and then you will dance together to 'Moonlight Serenade,' as you did at your wedding. Before you go to sleep, you will put freshly cut orchids by her bedside table, as you have done every week since those young girls died, and you will kiss her goodnight. It is a good death, Reginald. Better than the one you will get."

"And if I take her to the hospital right now?"

"The aneurysm will still happen. Florence Solar will fall into a coma and pass away on Friday evening. If you take her to the hospital, you will give her five extra days, but they will not be days well spent. Take tonight, my friend. It is my gift."

"I wish I'd never met you, Horowitz."

Horowitz chuckled. "Believe me, that is the sentiment of many. Why orchids?"

"What?"

"On the afternoon you began investigating the murder of the Bowen sisters, you brought home dozens of orchids. I have never been able to figure out why."

"Because of you, you miserable bastard."

"Me?"

"Cut up an orchid and plant a piece of it in a new pot and a whole plant grows out of just that severed bit. They're like hydras. Orchids are death-proof; that's why the Reaper before you used them as his calling card. He was afraid of them and you should be too. You can't get your grubby skeleton fingers into them."

"So if I plant this spike, a new flower will grow from it? Immortality. Like those wretched jellyfish that taunt me."

"Can you even grow anything? If you planted a seed, would it grow, or would it cower in your shadow, afraid to bloom? Why would you bother planting anything, knowing you'd have to reap it in the end anyway?"

"Why do you bother living, knowing you will have to die?" Horowitz stroked the bulb in his hand. It blossomed at his touch. He tucked the bloom into his buttonhole. "I have never gardened before, but perhaps I will start."

"Leave, Horowitz."

"That is the mistake most people make. To think that Death loves nothing." Horowitz smiled. And then, still eighteen years old and covered in acne scars, Death dipped his hat and turned to leave, the orchid bright and blooming at his chest. "Good-bye, Reg. We will meet twice more. At the end, of course."

"And the other time?"

"I'll visit you in your nursing home. You'll lose to me in a game of chess."

"Typical. Can't even let the dying man win."

"You were supposed to die in Vietnam, you know," said Horowitz at the doorway. "The day after we met. The bullet that tore through your chest was supposed to stop your heart."

"But . . . you said . . . I was supposed to drown?"

"To know your fate is to change it. If I'd told you the truth, you never would have been shot."

"But I *was* shot. I didn't die."

"Have you forgotten? I was otherwise occupied at the bottom of a river."

"You were sent there to reap me."

"You were to be my first. Then, on the day of my wedding in 1982, you and your lovely wife were supposed to be involved in a fatal head-on collision with a pickup truck but . . . I couldn't have that. The afternoon you found the bodies of the Bowen sisters, you were supposed to be crushed to death by a collapsing brick wall. Freak accident. You would have, too, if I hadn't phoned in a tip about someone dumping trash in Little Creek. Every time we've met, Reginald Solar, I have been here to reap your immortal soul."

Reg felt suddenly uneasy, and glanced sidelong at his gardening shears. If he drove them into Death's chest, would Death die? "And *this* time?" he said slowly.

"Relax. I'm purely here as a courtesy. To give you the time

with your wife that I did not get with mine. Death is not cruel, but it is insistent. I have learned that firsthand. I wish it were not true, but it is."

"You saved me three times. You didn't save any of them." Reg motioned to the ghost children that, even now, followed him everywhere.

"That is the other mistake people make. To think Death regrets nothing." Horowitz bit his bottom lip, thinking. "I have a second gift for you. Something I have been saving since the Bowen girls died. I've never been sure if I was going to give it to you or not, but . . ." Death drew an envelope from his coat and handed it to Reginald. "You are, I imagine, the closest thing to a friend I will ever have."

Reginald opened it. "A fucking condolence card?" he said, half choking on his anger and grief. "Get the hell off my property."

"Do yourself a favor. Don't check the news tonight."

When Death was gone, Reg tucked the little white card into his jacket without reading it and went upstairs to find his beloved wife curled up on their bed, mid-nap. He sat down next to her and stroked her hair, then replaced the orchids on her bedside table with a new bunch, freshly cut. He thought about telling her, "You are going to die tomorrow. What is something you've always wanted to do but never got around to?"

Instead, he said, "How about we invite the kids around for dinner? I feel like making a roast. Something with rosemary and garlic from the garden."

Later that evening, Esther's grandmother turned the television on to watch the 6:00 p.m. news while she crushed herbs and drank a glass of her favorite red wine.

The little girl who'd been missing for three days had been found.

ESTHER CLOSED HER CAR DOOR quietly and crept across the yard, trying to look inconspicuous and unsuspicious, which was a very hard look to achieve and usually resulted in the person attempting said look appearing both very conspicuous and very suspicious at the same time.

The greenhouse was to the left of the house, behind a hedge and a fence. Esther scrambled over. Years had passed since she'd last been there. The yard was much smaller than she remembered it. Reg's aviary where he kept doves and finches and parakeets and the occasional quail had been removed and replaced with grass. The vegetable patch that had once grown semisuccessful tomatoes and rarely-successful lettuce had been dug up and turned into a run-of-the-mill garden bed. The lemon trees where she used to play tag with Eugene looked so much closer together than they had when she was little. The yard used to be the size of a kingdom, with mountains and rivers and trolls and—if Esther would have had her way—the small bunker she'd planned to dig and live in. Now it was the size of a yard.

The kitchen windows were still covered in the stained-glass butterflies she and Eugene made with their grandma when they were kids. It used to bemuse Reg, coming home to find all the wineglasses and windows covered in stained glass, all the spare scraps of wood in the backyard painted with landscapes. This was also what he missed most about Florence when she was gone.

The front door of the greenhouse had no lock, naturally, because how often are flowers stolen? There weren't many orchids left by then. The new owner had wanted to keep some, but maintaining hundreds of plants wasn't feasible, and most had been cut up into pieces and left in green waste bins. But there were still several dozen flowers there. Esther took as much as she could carry, intending to make only one trip, but then she came back again and again for more. The flowers first, loading them pot by pot into a wheelbarrow and wheeling them quietly through a gate out to the street, where she loaded up the trunk and back seat of the car and even strapped some to the roof. The stem cuttings next, the immortal part, the death-proof blooms; these she stuffed into her backpack and pockets and scattered like confetti onto lawns and sidewalks as she drove toward Lilac Hill in the night.

The nursing home was peaceful in the low light. Esther heard nothing but the wind in the trees and the occasional calls of ghosts. She parked close to the building and carried the plants through Reg's window, then placed the flowers around the room, working quickly, afraid that her grandfather might wake and freak out or that a doctor would bust her and freak out. But the only person who came was a nurse; she frowned at the flowers but didn't say anything.

When all the orchids (bar one plant still in the car) were in the room, Esther marveled at her makeshift Eden. Every surface was carpeted in purple. In the small space of his room, the orchids seemed to move of their own accord, almost as if being in Reg's presence fed them some invisible energy.

Were there always this many? she wondered, looking around. The plants seemed to have multiplied since she moved them from the greenhouse, seemed to have grown up the walls and across the ceiling. It was a still life vanitas painting: the bright white of Reg's hospital bed, the way his skin strained skull-like across the bones of his face, his few possessions—a Bible, a watch, his reading glasses, a pipe, her grandmother's wedding ring—arranged by his side next to the bed. And everywhere, everywhere, the flowers she'd brought him, their scent masking the sour smell of death that seeped from his skin.

Esther leaned down to kiss her grandfather on the forehead one last time. "I love you," she whispered into his ear, and his lips trembled like he was trying to form words, but there was so very little left of him now, not enough even to say he loved her back. She pulled out her phone and found the emergency death slide-show Rosemary had been making since Reg's diagnosis; it was her pièce de résistance. It seemed a shame to save it for his funeral, where he would never see or hear it, so Esther climbed into bed next to him like she'd used to when she was a kid, turned up the volume, and hit play.

With Johnny Cash playing in the background, Reg's life passed before her. A chubby, smiling baby captured in black and white. A small boy in high socks pushing a wooden cart. A skinny teenager jumping off a cliff into the ocean. A wedding picture of him and a young Florence Solar, who was only nineteen at the time and looked like a hippie in her '70s bridal gown. A series of shots of him during the war, smiling among his platoon mates. Reg in his police uniform standing next to his Toyota Cressida. With each of his newborn sons. A newspaper clipping about him receiving a commendation for bravery for disarming a gunman. With his newborn daughter. Shots of him with his three children as they grew up. A picture of him gardening. On vacation. Eating. Cooking. Laughing. Dancing with his beloved wife. At the weddings of his children. Holding his newborn twin grandchildren. Then many, many pictures of him with his grandkids. Getting his hair and makeup done by little Esther, holding little Eugene's hand to cross the road, getting climbed on by all the cousins, reading to the twins, a glass of milk in his hand.

And then the disease. The red and blotchy skin. The thinning hair. The watery eyes. The gouged-out cheekbones. Pictures at Lilac Hill. Pictures in a wheelchair. Pictures of a thing that vaguely resembled but was no longer him.

The slideshow ended with Frank Sinatra's "I Did It My Way," which was cliché, but also appropriate. The final photograph, timed perfectly with the crescendo of the song, was a close-up profile shot of Reg in his greenhouse, surrounded by his orchids, unaware that the photographer (likely Florence Solar) was there. In it, he was bent over to closely inspect the bud of a flower.

Reginald Solar slipped away thirty-six seconds after the slide-show ended, a small smile on his face, a brightly blooming orchid held tightly in his palm.

ESTHER WAITED IN THE ROOM for the medical staff to declare Reginald dead, even though she already knew he was gone. As she stood by the window, she saw a man strolling across the parking lot, a short man in a dark coat and hat, a cane held in his gloved hands. She wasn't quite sure what it was about him that made her slip through the window and run to her car to follow him. The man was already pulling onto the road by the time she had the key in the ignition, but Esther didn't mind: She had a feeling she knew where he was going.

Ten minutes later, the cloaked man brought his car to a stop in the driveway in front of a quaint house with white window frames, a twisting garden path, and an American flag curling in the breeze. The house built by Reginald and Florence Solar. The house she'd robbed only an hour before.

The man got out of his vehicle. Esther followed suit.

"Excuse me!" she called after him, but he didn't hear her, or if he did, he didn't slow. "Wait up!"

She caught him at the front door, where he already had a set of keys out, ready to let himself in. Before he stepped inside, he turned, and she saw him clearly for the first time.

"Can I help you?" he said. He was young, not much older

than Esther, and spoke with a Southern accent. On his head was a black hat, the type that gangsters used to wear in the '20s, and his face was pocked with acne scars. Even when looking straight at him, Esther couldn't quite make out the color of his eyes or hair.

And there, in the buttonhole of his jacket, was a bright purple orchid.

"You were at Lilac Hill," she said. "You knew Reginald Solar. You knew my grandfather."

"Not really, I'm afraid. Not at all."

"Don't make me ask."

"Ask what?"

"Are you him?"

"Am I who?"

Esther didn't want to sound too crazy if she was wrong, so she said, "Horowitz. Are you Horowitz?"

The man smiled. "Please excuse my presence at Lilac Hill. I simply bought Reg's house when he moved out."

"You *live* here now?"

"Yes. I purchased it as an investment property, but when I walked through it for the first time, well . . . I fell in love."

"Then . . . why were you at the nursing home?"

"A storage company contacted me some months back. They were having trouble getting a hold of Mr. Solar's family and had this address listed as a backup contact. I collected the items from his unit so that they wouldn't be sold or destroyed or end up on *Storage Wars*, although I do love that show. I finally managed to find out where Reginald had moved, and just tonight delivered a message to Lilac Hill in the hopes that the staff would pass it on to his family. I didn't know if I'd ever be able to reach you, yet here you are. You can come in and have a look, if you'd like."

"How can you not be him?"

"Who, exactly, do you think I am?"

"Well . . . Death?"

The man gave her a bemused look. "Your grandfather must've been quite the storyteller, to have you believing he knew Death. Come inside."

Esther thought that was a very odd reply indeed; she went inside regardless. The house was strangely decorated, like when her Grandma June had moved into a brand new modern apartment at the age of seventy-eight but kept all of what Esther called her "old people stuff." Old people all just seemed to own the same things: a cabinet full of plates and glasses that no one was allowed to eat or drink from, a hideous floral couch, a rocking chair, an herb rack, heavy wooden furniture, dozens of knickknacks collected over many decades (now proudly displayed on every available household surface), and faded photographs in mismatched frames all over the walls.

Two packed suitcases (old-fashioned brown leather ones; *more* old people stuff) had been placed by the front door. "Are you going somewhere?" Esther asked, but the man ignored her.

"Milk?" he said from the kitchen.

"No, thank you. You, uh, still haven't answered my question."

The man appeared in the kitchen doorway. "The one about where I'm going or the one about if I'm Death incarnate?"

"The latter would be good."

"If I were Death, and your grandfather knew me, would it not comfort you to know that he had gone with a friend?" Esther didn't answer. The man smiled. "The boxes are through here."

All of the items from Reginald Solar's storage facility were now kept in the room Florence Solar had once used for sewing. The concentrated contents of a life. Esther sifted through some of the boxes, trying to decide what to take now and what to come and collect later. In the end all she removed was a portrait of Reginald in his police uniform from sometime in the late 1970s, when he was young and handsome and not yet haunted by ghosts.

On her way out, she found the Man Who Might Be Death sitting in the living room sipping his milk.

There were so many things she wanted to ask him to fix. Liberate her father from the basement. Leave her brother be. Give Hephzibah a voice. Let her mother have one big win and then release her from her obsession. Lift the curse. Lift the curse. Lift the curse.

As she was about to open her mouth to let all these requests gush out, Esther realized this:

- Reginald Solar had lived with his fear, but it hadn't killed him.
- Therefore, the curse was likely, as Eugene had insisted,

a fiction, and Death—if the man in front of her was indeed Death—had, in his own strange way, protected the Solar family rather than condemned them.

- Curses needed to be believed in to continue, and the only one who'd kept the curse thriving was Esther.

So instead of asking the man to lift the curse, she asked him: "If your family believed they were cursed to live and die in fear, what would you say to them to make it easier? To make them less afraid."

"I would say that everybody dies, whether they live their life in fear or not. And *that*—death—is not something to be afraid of."

"Thank you," Esther said. "We'll come by another day to collect his things."

As she turned to leave, she spotted it. There, on the wall above his head, was a small framed photograph. A Polaroid, now faded from the sun. A wedding. A woman in a pale pink sundress with a strand of pearls at her throat. A man in a heinous lavender tuxedo with white shoes and a ruffled shirt. And between them, a second man, a man with red hair and freckled skin, a man dressed in an officer's uniform. A man who looked very much like he could be Reginald Solar.

The Man Who Might Be Death caught her looking at it. "My wedding, to my beloved, may she rest in peace. Such a shame that the faces are no longer discernable; it was the only photograph we had of the event." And it was true; the faces *were* unclear, as was the name on the soldier's uniform. But Esther knew. She knew.

"Now, if you don't mind, I must be on my way. Good day, Miss Solar. I have a plane to catch."

"Where are you going?" she asked again.

The man put on his hat, picked up his bags, and smiled. "I hear the Mediterranean is nice at this time of year."

36

THE RED WOMAN

ESTHER TOOK the last orchid to Eugene, who was too drugged up to realize she was there, then slept in a cot by his bedside. When he woke at sunrise, she told him of Reginald's death, and they cried together for a little while, until Eugene slipped back into sleep.

The Solar house felt strange when she opened the front door. It was morning, still gloomy, but the candles were unlit and the lamps were dim. Drifting sunlight bled through the windows, but it was not enough to shift the shadows that congealed in every corner of the room. Esther opened the basement door and went down the stairs, but there was only darkness there too. No twinkling string lights. No Christmas carols played on repeat. A dozen pictures of her past self smiled out at her from the darkness and made her believe, again, that there was such a thing as ghosts.

Peter was in the hospital, in the early stages of stroke rehab. The house was unrooted without his weight to hold it down. It had lost its anchor. It felt as though if a stiff breeze blew through the trees, it might drift away into the sky like a dandelion.

In the kitchen, just as Rosemary had said, was a large black burn mark where Fred had supposedly burst into flames and become a spark. Esther was skeptical that a) this had occurred at all, and b) if Fred was *indeed* a goblin, that he'd supposedly given his life to save Eugene's. Maybe one of the rabbits had simply scared him to death and he'd spontaneously combusted in a fit of wild rooster rage. Still, she knelt at the scorched wood, which kind of did look rooster-shaped if she squinted, and gave thanks to the creature that her mother was convinced had kept them afloat for the past six years.

Esther went to her room and sat on her bed and contemplated what it meant that the curse wasn't real. That it wasn't a spell that made Eugene so sad, just depression. It wasn't magic that bound her father to the basement, just anxiety. It wasn't a jinx that drove her mother to the slots, just an obsession. For the first time, all the broken bits of her family and herself seemed fixable; curses couldn't be broken, but mental illnesses could be treated.

Esther stood and looked around her room, at the costumes Jonah said she used to hide from being seen. Is that what they were for? All these years she'd told herself she wore the costumes to hide from people, and from Death. Had she really been using them to hide from herself?

Tears of frustration and betrayal and pain burning in her

eyes, she started to tear down the cage of fear she'd built for herself, ripping apart strips of silk and shredding half-drawn patterns, until all she could do was collapse on the rug-strewn ground in a heap of color and fabric. There, sobbing on the floor, she noticed that the wood beneath the layers of paper and fabric was blue, which she was almost certain it hadn't been before she'd covered it with several Persian carpets years ago. Esther cleared away some of the mess she'd made; more and more blue appeared on the floor, some of it light, some of it dark, some almost white, some almost black, all in a circular pattern she recognized well because she saw hundreds of them every day.

Esther peeled back a carpet and pushed her bed to the side of the room. On the floor, right where her bed had stood moments ago, someone had painted a huge nazar, the blue, white, and black paint faded and peeling now. Scattered over the charm to ward off the evil eye were dozens of sage leaves; some fresh, some brittle, some almost dust now, each with a different wish on them, all written in her mother's handwriting.

> *Keep her safe.*
> *Give her courage.*
> *Let her escape this town.*
> *Don't let her become like me.*
> *Make her see how much I love her.*
> *Make her see how much I love her.*
> *Make her see how much I love her.*

Esther picked up a handful of them and held them to her chest before a sound from the hall made her breath catch. Her heart kicked up its tempo and her brain whispered *run, run, run* from the fear, but she didn't. *Let the monsters come,* she thought, her mother's wishes grasped tightly in her palm. *Let them try and take me now.*

She stepped out into the hall and noticed something she hadn't seen when she came in. Outside the bathroom door, Rosemary had laid out her jewelry in a long line on the wood: her tiger's-eye, her sapphires, her amber rings, the nazars that wrapped around her ankles. Her clothing—stitched with coins and stuffed with herbs for luck and prosperity—had been neatly folded and placed next to the trinkets. Another sound came from the bathroom. Sloshing water.

Esther pushed the door open. Rosemary was on all fours dressed only in her underwear, her knees and the soles of her feet stained red with blood. Her ribs were visible through her thin skin. A web of blue veins. The frightening mountain range of her spine. Wedged between her knees was a bucket of soapy water. The tiles were slick with bleach and blood and detergent. Esther always thought if you cut your wrists, your life just kind of leaked out of you quietly, poetically, pooling in delicate puddles at your sides. That was not the case. Though the skin might be broken, the heart still roared with life, pumping away at four miles per hour. There were arcs of blood on the walls. Spatters on the ceiling. Eugene had tried very hard to die in this small room, and his heart had tried very hard to keep him alive.

Esther exhaled at the horror of it and Rosemary noticed for the first time that she was there.

"Oh, no, Esther," she said, her thin body springing up. Blood on her hands, blood on her knees, the blood of the son she almost lost. Jesus. The poor woman. "I can do this," she said as she tried to push her daughter from the room. "You don't have to see this. I don't want you to see this."

Esther put her hand to her cheek. Wiped away a speck of red. "Pop's gone."

"Oh, honey." Rosemary tried to hug her with her elbows, careful to keep her bloody hands away from her clothes. "Oh, honey, I'm so sorry."

Esther put her head on her mother's shoulder and held her around her thin waist, hoping she could feel what she no longer had the words to express: *I love you, I love you, I love you.*

Was it so bad to hold onto something that was broken? All those years she'd judged Rosemary for staying with her father when she could've cut and run, but could she blame her? Rosemary left her first husband because he was a monster, but Peter was still good and kind and gentle, and perhaps that was worth staying for, even if the person was ruined.

As she watched her mother kneel again to wipe up her son's blood, Esther thought she finally understood the woman who'd raised her. Jonah had once told her that one day, everybody would realize that their parents were human beings, and that sometimes they were good people and sometimes they were not. What he failed to mention—what she was only coming to appreciate at that exact moment—was that most of the time people were neither good nor bad, not righteous or evil, they were just people.

And sometimes love, even if it was all they had to offer, was enough.

It had to be.

37

O BROTHER

HEPHZIBAH WAS at her house when Esther got home from Reg's funeral several days later, sprawled across her bed with Fleayoncé on her back and a laptop open in front of her. Familiar figures danced across the screen, chased by a horde of homicidal geese. Hephzibah giggled.

"What are you doing?" Esther whispered.

Heph turned and raised her eyebrows. "Watching you be a hilarious badass," she signed with a grin.

Esther slammed the laptop shut. "Don't ever watch them again. Jonah put them on the internet even when I specifically asked him not to. Do you know how messed up that is?"

"The videos are beautiful."

"That doesn't make it okay."

"I get that but . . . it's not like he was trying to hurt you. He was trying to help you. I think you should give him a chance to apologize. To explain himself," signed Heph. "It would be the bravest thing to do."

"What do you know about bravery?" Esther snapped. "You don't even have the guts to talk to your best friend. How do you think it makes me feel when you speak to almost everyone except me?"

Hephzibah stood slowly, her jaw set, and walked out of the room without another word. "Yeah, go," Esther said as she went.

Eugene appeared in the doorway less than a minute later. "*What* did you say to her?" he demanded.

"Something that I knew would hurt her." Eugene pursed his lips, flared his nostrils slightly. Causing Hephzibah pain was off-limits to everyone, even Esther. She changed the subject. "How are you feeling?"

"Like I'm *super* sick of telling everyone how I'm feeling."

"Sorry." Eugene sat down on the end of her bed, his head in his hands. Esther patted him on the back. "How weird was it seeing Dad outside today, right?" Despite the doctor's protests, Peter had insisted on attending his father's funeral. He'd worn Reginald's red knit cap and reading glasses, and Esther and Rosemary had taken turns pushing his wheelchair.

"It was nice," Eugene said. "I know I was supposed to be super sad all day because Pop's dead, but the whole thing just made me feel kind of . . . normal. For the first time in a long time."

"On that note, I think it'd be a good idea to try therapy again, but really *try* it this time, don't just go in there with the intention of scaring the shit out of people. It's like a broken bone, you know? You can't keep walking on it and expect it to heal."

"Is this the superstitious Esther Solar acknowledging the existence of mental illness and not just behaving like I'm cursed?"

"Shut up."

Eugene ran his hands through his hair. "I don't really want to talk to anyone."

"I don't really care. If you broke your leg and didn't want to go to the hospital, I'd take you anyway."

"I don't want people to know I'm crazy, you know?"

"Oh, honey. You slit your wrists with a veterinary scalpel. I think it might be a little late for that."

Eugene laughed. "No way. I can totally get away with the tortured artist thing. I only did it for my *craft*."

"Oh great, this only adds to your mysterious legend. The boy witch, in so much pain he couldn't face another day. The girls at school are going to fall for you at an unprecedented rate."

"Ugh. Just what I need. Adventures of the Boy Witch, Episode One, in which our hero survives a brutal attack by his own mind."

"You know what? I think it's actually a really good idea. You could write a web comic about a depressed superhero. I mean, who saves the superheroes when they're mentally ill?"

"That's . . . not a terrible idea."

"Well, I mean, I am practically famous on the internet, right? I could plug you on my channel."

"Wait, you're gonna keep going?"

"It was a joke."

"You know, if I *were* to write a web comic, a certain charming young artist would be a handy mentor for me to have around."

"You can be friends with him. But he betrayed me when he promised he wouldn't, and I can't forgive him."

"Esther."

"What?"

"I mean . . . it's not like he cheated on you, or killed your cat, or hit you, or had six kidnapped girls locked up in his basement."

"Well I haven't verified the last one."

"You didn't check for basement girls? Damn, you're gonna get a *rude* awakening one day. Always check the basement."

"Betrayal is betrayal, Eugene."

"Is it though? Remember when we were like seven, and we were at Pop and Gran's house, and Gran found that expensive plate she loved broken and hidden under the bed in the guest room?"

"Yeah, they blamed me for some reason, even though I had no idea how it got broken."

"I broke it. I ratted you out. I said I saw you do it."

"*You little shit.* I didn't get to go swimming that afternoon because of that."

"So there you go," he said, clapping his hands together. "Jonah and I have both committed a heinous betrayal against you."

"You're my brother. It's different."

"Why?"

"Because I love you."

"You love him, too."

"I want to talk about you, not him."

"You do though, don't you? You love him."

"Eugene."

"Okay, okay. Maybe not as much emotional development as I thought." Eugene stood, but before he left, he leaned down and kissed her forehead. "If I can work up the courage to walk in to a therapist and say—" He exhaled loudly, shook his head. "Shit this is hard. If I can say to a therapist, 'Hi, I'm Eugene and I need a cast for my very fractured mind because I frequently have suicidal thoughts,' then you can be brave enough to forgive him. Deal?"

"I'll think about it."

"Everyone we let into our lives has the power to hurt us. Sometimes they will and sometimes they won't, but that's not a reflection of us, or our strength. Loving someone who hurts you doesn't make you weak."

"Staying with someone who hurts you *does*, though."

"Jesus. Try telling that to a victim of domestic abuse. Try telling them that they're pussies for not running."

"This is different and you know it."

"I get it. You think Mom's weak, because she stayed all these years."

"Yes."

"You think she should've left Dad, like she left her first husband."

"Yes."

"Sometimes you're brave if you run. Sometimes you're brave if you stay. It's important to know the difference. Important for both of us, probably."

Esther had never thought of it like that before. "So you'll talk to someone?" she asked.

"On one condition."

"I can't let him back into my life. Not yet. I'm not ready."

"I'm not going to force you to make up with some dude if you don't want to. That'd be pretty shitty brotherly love. You're first, always."

"Then what's the condition?"

"You have to come with me."

"To therapy? Eugene, I'm totally—"

"Fine? Sane? Stable? Happy?" Eugene shook his head. "I know working your way through the list is helping you, and I think you're brave as hell for facing some of your fears. But I don't think your makeshift self-help is enough. If I need more, then you need more. Come with me."

Suddenly she got why Eugene didn't want to go to a therapist, even though she could see clearly from the outside that it would help him, that it was the best thing. The thought of sitting down in front of a total stranger and spilling her guts out on the table for a therapist to sift through like a medium scrying animal entrails for a message . . . made her skin crawl. She *liked* to keep all of her emotions locked inside where she could see them and catalogue them and control them and make sure they didn't spill out.

But she said okay because she wanted him to go. She *needed* him to go. Her life depended on his continued existence.

"I know you think love is dangerous. But I look at you and me, and I don't see that."

"Really? Because you have more power to destroy me than anyone else. I gave you that control by loving you and you went and tried to kill yourself. Why would I want to give anyone else the power to hurt me like that?"

"That's just the thing. It had nothing to do with you. So maybe love isn't the poison you think it is. Maybe people just make mistakes. Maybe they're even worthy of our forgiveness if they hurt us."

"Ugh. Sink the scalpel a little deeper next time, oh wise and annoying one."

"You can't say that to me, I'm emotionally fragile." Eugene grinned. "I'm gonna go find the cheapest therapist in town and hook us up with an appointment." He opened his laptop and sat it on the floor in front of her. It was open to the *Semi-Definitive List of Worst Nightmares* YouTube channel. "Now, time for you to do something you're *actually* afraid of."

38

THE GHOSTS OF ESTHER'S PAST

THE DAY after Reginald's funeral and subsequent ash scattering, Little Creek inexplicably began to dry up. Within a week all the water had sunk into underground reservoirs and the riverbed was as bone dry as it had always been before the murder of the Bowen sisters. The remains of the girls were located two weeks to the day after Reginald's death, not far from where he first found them, each with wild orchids bursting from their rib cages.

Esther felt strange living in a world in which Reginald Solar no longer existed. Death made perfect sense in the scientific (the redistribution of atoms, etc.) and philosophical sense (anything that lived forever would have no value, like the Reaper's most hated jellyfish), and Esther understood that it was natural and necessary, but trying to wrap her head around the undeniable fact that her grandfather no longer had a *body*, that the electrical signals that had sparked through his brain making him *him* no longer sparked . . . it made no sense. She was a smart and (mostly) rational human being, and still she couldn't make herself understand *how* it was possible that he was just . . . *gone*.

And then the thought that *she* herself would die . . . Well, that was another panic attack entirely.

So Esther started going to therapy with Eugene, as she said she would. They shared one-hour sessions, to save money; fifty minutes for him, because he needed it the most, and ten minutes for her at the end. The therapist, Dr. Claire Butcher, was nothing like what Esther had expected. For one thing, she didn't seem like a psychotic ax murderer, as her name might suggest. For another, Esther assumed it would only take one session with Eugene before she'd diagnose him as schizophrenic or chronically depressed and try and pump him full of tranquilizers and have him institutionalized. Instead, she mostly listened. Sometimes she gave Eugene coping strategies—breathing exercises, podcasts to listen to as it was getting dark, links to videos on meditation, the option of trying prescriptions if these approaches failed—but she was never forceful, or frustrated, or condescending. Together they came up with plans to wean him off light and—shockingly—Eugene had begun to try them. Each night, he peeled a strip of electrical tape off one switch. Each night, he lit one less candle than the night before. It might take years, but he was breaking through his own protective dam against fear, and he wasn't drowning. He was teaching himself to swim.

Esther told Dr. Butcher nothing of importance. "I'm just here because of Eugene," she said the first week, but Eugene wasn't going to let that slide. He told her everything Esther refused to:

about the curse, about Death, about Jonah, about the list, about their grandfather, even about how she compartmentalized her life into lists sometimes. It took him two weeks (well, technically only twenty minutes) to cover everything, and once he had, Dr. Butcher started working on tactics with Esther too, coaching her through her anxiety and grief and utter mortification that there was footage of her on the internet.

She also mentioned something about a "fear of commitment" and how Esther was attempting to "mitigate any future pain" by finding faults with the people she grew close to. By finding excuses to stay away from them, by avoiding intimacy and any deep emotional connections, by cutting off her feelings to preserve her emotional well-being, she insulated herself against pain but also against life.

Esther thought this was very reasonable behavior. Dr. Butcher did not happen to agree. To this end, she gave Esther three steps to control her anxiety and fear:

1. Externalize anxiety

The first thing to do was to imagine her anxiety as a thing apart from herself; the world's most hideous, unpleasant pet (apart from Fleayoncé). Esther saw hers as a black misshapen lump with teeth and hair growing randomly from its bulbous body. Its skin was slick tar and it had a mouth full of sharp toothpick teeth. It was also the size of a grapefruit and couldn't quite get its tiny bat wings to function properly, which meant it was always bumping angrily into walls. She named it Gertrude, and when it whispered to her that she was too fat or too ugly or people were judging her or she was going to die or she wasn't smart enough, or brave enough, or good enough, she flicked it off her shoulder and told it to go away.

2. Correct thinking mistakes

This one was a little harder. Whenever her brain told her that she was absolutely, 100 percent about to die in a tsunami, or that velociraptors were unquestionably outside her bedroom window, or that a cougar was definitely, without doubt, going to maul her in her sleep, these were thinking mistakes, because they were a) unlikely to happen, b) might not be catastrophic if they *did* happen, and c) even if they *did* happen and even if they *were* catastrophic, Esther might surprise herself and, like, kick the velociraptor's ass or something. It was hard, when the anxiety got ahold of her and started pumping adrenaline through her system at the perceived threat, to cycle through these steps, but the more she did it, the easier it got.

3. Exposure

The goal in facing fear, Dr. Butcher said, was actually facing it. Not waiting to not be afraid, but seeking out your fears and meeting them head-on. Esther knew this already, of course—she'd been doing exactly that for months. But then Dr. Butcher told her it might be a good idea to watch the YouTube videos. That if she didn't, the knowledge of their existence would continue to fester and grow black in her mind, and she wouldn't be able to move on from them.

ESTHER DIDN'T WATCH THE VIDEOS. She didn't talk to Jonah.

Several national newspapers covered the strange happenings of Little Creek and criticized Reginald Solar, recently deceased, as one of the failings of the justice system for the unsolved murder of the Bowen sisters. She cut the clips from the papers and included them in Reg's scrapbook, alongside all the old reports of the Harvestman and the one bizarre, misplaced article about the man who'd drowned in his bathtub.

Four weeks passed without a single fear being faced.

It was during this time period that Esther decided to re-frame Reginald Solar's portrait, the one she'd taken from the unnamed man who now lived in his old house, a man with a face she already couldn't remember. Tucked behind the glass and photograph she found a small, square condolences card, now warped and buckled by water damage. Inside was nothing but a name, with blue ink bleeding down the card. The writing was hard to make out now, but Esther was fairly certain it said *Arthur Whittle*. She searched the name on the internet, but couldn't find anything that seemed relevant.

Then came the fourth Sunday, post Jonah Smallwood. Esther hadn't looked at her list for a month, but she knew it so well by now that she didn't have to. The fear this week—29/50—was ghosts. She wondered what Jonah would've had planned for today. Wondering about Jonah was something she did often, despite how much it hurt.

Esther got home from work just before midnight. She'd taken

a job at the nearby 7-Eleven to help Rosemary out with Eugene's and Peter's medical bills, on the proviso that her mother went cold turkey on the slots. So far the arrangement seemed to be holding up. Rosemary's car was in the drive, as it had been every night since Peter exhumed himself from the basement. Esther didn't mind working every night, or falling behind on her schoolwork, or feeling like hot coals had been buried in her heels at the end of every shift: it was all worth it to have her family whole.

The house was quiet in the low light. It was a strange thing, to come home to dimness when all you could remember was light. The first thing she did was check on Eugene, as she did every night. Lamps still surrounded his funeral bed, as they had for years, but he had a mask over his eyes and appeared to be sleeping. At *nighttime*.

The second thing she did was head toward the kitchen to heat up her taquitos, which is when she found Fleayoncé sitting at the base of the staircase, staring intently at the second floor landing with her tail flicking.

"Fleayoncé, don't do that, you creep," she said. This was why pets and children were so eerie; they saw things they weren't supposed to. She picked the cat up and took her to the kitchen and set her on the bench, but Fleayoncé just slunk down (well, kind of slumped down) to the floor and went back to the foot of the stairs. Esther followed her and looked at the spot the cat was fixated on: the door to her childhood bedroom.

She scooped the cat up again. "Seriously," she said to it. "You need to stop." Fleayoncé just meowed, sounding more like a goat than a feline. Then the wood creaked upstairs and Fleayoncé hissed and twisted her way out of Esther's grasp.

Someone was up there.

Esther thought about calling the police, or maybe a priest, or maybe just burning the house down. But something called to her, like it had that afternoon on the cliff all those weeks ago. Something upstairs whispered *yes, yes, yes*.

Go forward, onward, into the unknown.

The thing with facing fear, she reminded herself, was that you actually had to *face* it.

The wood creaked again. It sounded like footsteps. Esther unlocked her phone, turned the camera around, and pressed record.

"Why do I feel like this is going to end up in a B grade, found footage horror movie?" she said to the camera. "Okay, so, something just moved upstairs. Which would be entirely normal in most houses, but no one has been upstairs in my house for about six years now, so, if I'm being entirely realistic here, it's probably a poltergeist. Let's go find out.

"I'm Esther Solar, and this is apparently '29/50: ghosts.'"

The discarded furniture on the staircase had been there for so long now that it had begun to grow together. She tried to yank a dining room chair out of the mound, only to find that tendrils of creeping vine held it firmly in place. There was no way to go but through. Luckily for her, she was now both a) a master spelunker, and b) fairly certain there were no troglofaunal flesh-eating humanoids inhabiting the staircase. (Surely they would've eaten her by now if there were.) So she found an opening in the haphazard stack between the shopping cart and a wardrobe, and began to climb. After a few minutes she was joined by Fleayoncé, who batted at her soles and darted through the rubble with surprising dexterity, scaring away rats or bats or critters that had taken residence in the scrap heap in the last half decade.

Finally she broke free on the dark landing and tried the light. It buzzed angrily, a bee woken from its slumber, then snapped on.

The world upstairs was preserved in a thin film of dust, a portrait of a past life frozen in time. Esther pushed open the door to her parents' bedroom, the one they'd shared before Peter disappeared from their lives. It was as it had been the day her father was swallowed by the basement: the bed was neatly made, the light switches were not taped permanently on, and her mother's jewelry—the pieces she'd worn for their beauty and not for their luck—were spilling from a metal box atop a chest of drawers. All their clothes—none of them with coins stitched into the lining or bulbs rotting in the pockets—still hung in the closet. The small bathroom was halfway through being painted: a drop sheet still covered the floor tiles and a tin of paint still sat in the corner, waiting to be opened. It had the feel of a place abandoned in a hurry, without time even to pack personal belongings or photographs. Which had indeed been the case.

Rosemary had woken them in the middle of the night, shaking and sweating and speaking of ghosts. She'd ushered Eugene and Esther downstairs, still dressed in their pajamas, and all three of them had worked together to block off the staircase. They'd slept on the floor inside a salt circle in the kitchen. It hadn't felt like it at the time, but it was beginning of the end.

Eugene's room was next. It was so cluttered with toys and books and posters that Esther's heart hurt. It was a kid's room. A normal kid's room. Sometimes it was hard to remember, but Eugene had been a normal boy only six years ago.

Esther's door was last. She opened it and walked inside and turned on a white lamp hung with crystals. Fleayoncé slalomed in and out of her feet. It was a little girl's room. Almost shockingly so. There were fairies on the duvet cover, a large dollhouse built by her grandfather, and a basket of toys, mostly Barbies and baby dolls, things that she'd already started to feel far too old to play with when her mother made her leave them. There were fur cushions on her bed and several posters of "Love Story"-era Taylor Swift on the walls and a scattering of clothing that was both so tiny and so pink it was hard to believe she'd ever worn them.

What made her breath catch, though, was the photograph on her bedside table, and the hand-drawn card that sat beneath it. Esther wiped the thick coat of dust from the frame. She was in the middle, freckled and pale with a firestorm of red hair atop her head. Hephzibah was to her left, as faded and ghostly at eight as she was now. And to her right was Jonah, smiling cheekily. They all had their arms around each other's shoulders.

The card was as she remembered it: two crudely drawn

pieces of fruit that could've been apples or grapes or perhaps even avocados. *We make the perfect pear,* said the writing beneath them.

Maybe Rosemary had been right. Maybe there were ghosts upstairs after all.

39

HOW TO RECOVER FROM THE HEINOUS BETRAYAL OF YOUR GOOD FRIEND/LOVE INTEREST IN FOUR SIMPLE STEPS

STEP ONE. Reconcile with your mute best friend.

Malka Hadid answered the door when Esther knocked on Monday morning before school. Her husband, Daniel, had once explained that his wife's name meant "queen" in Hebrew, and Esther had always thought it was appropriate. Malka was possessed of the kind of beauty that made her seem ethereal, like an elven queen out of a storybook. Her eyes were an impossible shade of amber and her hair fell in a tawny curtain to her chest. She was Hephzibah all over, only fuller and brighter, like the warmth and saturation had been turned up.

Malka crossed her arms and looked down at Esther expectantly. "Do you happen to know why my daughter hasn't spoken to anyone in four weeks?" she said in her Israeli accent, which was more like Israeli mixed with Arabic mixed with French, because Malka was fluent in four languages and conversational in another three.

"I might've had something to do with it," Esther confessed.

Malka sighed. "Come in. She's in her room."

If Esther's room was a cluttered museum, then Hephzibah's room was a mad scientist's laboratory. Her uncle was some famous physicist in Tel Aviv who—when he found out about Heph's love of science—started sending her monthly packages of Bunsen burners and telescopes and microscopes and fossils and peer-reviewed journal subscriptions and a large, somewhat creepy bust of Albert Einstein. Planets hung from the ceiling and one entire wall had been devoted to articles on and illustrations of Heph's favorite gen IV nuclear reactor, the Transatomic WAMSR (Waste-Annihilating Molten Salt Reactor), which Esther knew far more about than she needed to.

Hephzibah was sitting cross-legged on her bed, her arms folded and jaw set. It was the longest they'd gone without seeing each other since they were little kids, and the mere sight of her made Esther want to kick herself for being such a dick.

If a person could be home, she'd built her foundations in both Eugene and Heph.

"Hephzibah," Esther began, but Heph held up a hand to silence her.

"Stand around the corner," she signed.

"Please let me—" she tried again, but again Heph mimed for her to zip it.

"Go. Around. The. Corner," she signed again, each movement exaggerated.

"I'm trying to apologize here."

Hephzibah groaned and flopped back on her bed and signed to Esther without looking at her. "Shut up, you bitch. I'm trying to talk to you. Go around the fucking corner!" That's how Esther knew it was all going to be okay. Bitch was the first word they'd learned in ASL and they'd used it so frequently in middle school that it had almost become a pet name.

"Bitch," Esther signed back, smirking.

Heph looked up, a crack in her serious expression. "Bitch."

"Bitch."

The hint of a smile. "Bitch."

"I'm really sorry about what I said. I know better than anyone that you can't just turn off your fear because someone else wants you to. I was a—wait for it"—Esther switched to ASL again—"bitch."

Heph nodded. Licked her lips. Motioned with her head for Esther to leave the doorway and step into the hall.

Esther did as she asked, then heard bedsprings creak as Heph rose and walked across the floorboards toward the door. For a few minutes, all she could hear from the other side of the wall was Heph's breathing, until her hand appeared in the hall. Esther held it. Squeezed it.

"You were kind of right though," she said finally, quietly, from around the corner. Not signed. *Said. Out loud.*

"Is that . . . *is that your voice?* Oh my God, Hephzibah, no wonder you haven't been speaking all these years. That's terrible!"

"Bitch," said Heph with a giggle as Esther pulled her into the hall and gave her a brief yet crushing hug.

STEP TWO. Watch the goddamn videos already.

After reconciling with Hephzibah, Esther decided, finally, that it was time to take Dr. Butcher's advice and watch Jonah's channel.

After school, the two of them went back to Heph's house. Malka and Daniel Hadid were working on a story in their home office (a terrible slew of suicide bombers in Istanbul—Death had again been very busy), so they had the place to themselves. Heph got the projector working in the living room, and then Eugene showed up out of nowhere, saying he couldn't stand their mother hovering around him anymore, which was not something either of the Solar children ever expected to say.

They all sat down together on the (very nicely upholstered) couch in front of the screen, on which "1/50" was waiting to be played.

"Okay, do it," said Esther, but as soon as Heph moved the mouse, she changed her mind. "No, stop, wait a minute." Then she proceeded to pace around the room for ten minutes, waiting for the unconscious push that would lead her to watch it.

Everything you want is on the other side of fear, she reminded herself.

Esther knew it would be better once it was over. For the last month, like Dr. Butcher had said, the videos had been a splinter digging into her mind and ignoring them had only caused an infection that seemed to leak out into everything she did.

The push didn't come. There seemed to be a physical block

between Esther and the play button, a strong force field, the kind of fear she'd experienced only once before. Esther couldn't hit play, so she started to scroll down instead. Hephzibah immediately stopped her.

"Do you really want to read YouTube comments?" she signed. And then, as if suddenly remembering that she could speak, she said, "Do you really want to do that to yourself?"

"How bad are they?" Of course they would be bad. Of course the world would hate her, judge her, call her names.

"I don't know. I haven't even bothered looking."

Esther scrolled down and started to read the comments on "1/50: lobsters."

> I love this girl!
>
> This bitch got some balls on her for real
>
> God that was intense. I'm sweating. Fuck yeah, Esther!
>
> Why is anyone even scared of lobsters? Stupid
>
> It's called a phobia dickcheese
>
> Esther brave af
>
> Came here after watching the one with the geese. Was literally screaming at my screen OMFG
>
> I freaking *hate* lobsters. HATE them. You badass Esther.
>
> MORE MORE MORE MORE MORE yes please
>
> Ew they're so gross, they look like the facehugger things from Alien amirite

Not sure I'll know what to do with my life after 50/50

Why are these even popular, I don't get it?

SHUT YOUR MOUTH FOOL YOU DO NOT EVEN REALIZE

I had anxiety just watching this.

Cannot stand this shit. These videos are all so staged.

Can we dox this fucker?

I'm game.

But by far the most popular comment was this:

Hi Esther. I know I'm just a random stranger on the internet
and we'll never meet, but I wanted to thank you for this
channel, because it's changed my daughter's life. Before
Nightmares she had severe social anxiety and was badly
bullied at school. After she watched your videos, she
decided to try and make some of her own. So far she's
faced her fear of snakes, spiders and even public speaking
(she gave a presentation on your channel in class—up until
now I've had to write notes to excuse her from all class
presentations because she has panic attacks). I cried
when she told me she'd been able to stand up in front of
her class and speak about something she's so passionate
about. It wasn't something I thought she'd ever be able to
do. I know I speak for everyone here when I say thank you,
from the bottom of my heart, for your bravery; it means
more than you know.

A lot of people liked the channel. A lot of people had replied
and said similar things to the emotional mom. Their son, their
daughter, their brother, their sister, themselves; *A Semi-Definitive
List of Worst Nightmares* had spread bravery like a virus. It was

contagious and lots of people were catching it. There were new copycat videos popping up every day of people going head-to-head with fear, doing things they'd swore they would never, ever do—riding a rollercoaster, singing onstage, sticking their hand into a jar of cockroaches, surfing, skiing, bungee jumping, skydiving. Week after week, fear after fear, they went out into the world and became less afraid. They did something every day that scared them.

Now, again, it was Esther's turn, too.

"I'm ready," she said, and this time she didn't stop Hephzibah when she moved the cursor over the play button and clicked it.

It was uncomfortable, at first. Esther cringed at the way she looked onscreen and hated that people had seen her against her will, from all the angles she hated. Her face was speckled, and her hair was too long and too red, and she had the sensation that there were thousands of eyes on her, peeling away her skin. But—as with the first and only clip Jonah had showed her months ago—she soon saw a different version of herself. Esther the wolf. Esther the fear eater. Esther with the steely, determined eyes, the one who'd been so afraid in the early videos but now marched triumphantly in the direction of each and every fear, come what may.

Eugene and Hephzibah were in the videos too, as was Jonah. Esther had frequently snatched the GoPro and turned it on him. It was so strange: on film, Jonah Smallwood wasn't fearless. In real life, Esther was usually so distracted by her own anxiety that she failed to catch the small moments—a flicker of hesitation, a bitten lip, a deep breath—when Jonah, too, looked into the face of fear and wasn't sure, even if just for a moment, if he'd be brave enough to win the battle.

It wasn't these little windows into his fear that hurt her heart the most, though. Not the realization that he, too, had been afraid, that he'd packed away his anxieties and hidden them for her sake, because if he was scared she'd be terrified. What made her heart hurt the most was the way he filmed her. Esther had never imagined that love could be written in any other way except words, but the way Jonah had filmed her? The close-ups, the soft lighting, the way the camera followed her . . . it was like a caress in moving pictures. If she had to describe love to aliens without using words, she'd simply show them what he'd made for her and it would be enough for them to understand the beauty and the terror of it all.

By the time the sun went down and they'd watched all the way through to 25/50, Esther came to realize that her fear no longer belonged to her alone. It was shared by thousands—sometimes *tens of thousands*—of people, and she owed it to them and herself to see this through to the end.

STEP THREE. Build a new kind of dam against fear.

The comment from the woman about her daughter was the first that Esther printed and stuck to her bedroom wall to plaster over the torn up wallpaper.

Over the coming weeks and months, she'd print thousands more, each one a brick in the dam against fear. Each one a badge earned for bravery. Each one proof that facing her fears had made a difference, somewhere, somehow, to someone, in some small way.

Some mysteries might never be solved. Who killed the Black Dahlia? What happened to D. B. Cooper? Who was the Somerton Man?

A mystery that could be solved, though, was what it would feel like to conquer fifty fears. Esther could keep going. She could push on. She could find out.

But she didn't want to do it alone.

STEP FOUR. Send the *We make a perfect pear* card back to Jonah.

40

A SEMI-DEFINITIVE LIST
OF WORST NIGHTMARES

TWENTY WEEKS *later.*

Late summer again. Almost one year on now. Orchids grew wild around the town, blooming where they landed on the night Reginald Solar died. They shot up from people's front lawns, the cracks in footpaths, the roots of trees, hundreds and hundreds of them, all standing in defiance of death.

Little Creek, the penultimate resting place of the Bowen sisters, was still dry after Reginald's passing. A patch of purple orchids sprouted from the sand where his ashes were scattered after his funeral.

The blooms that were stolen from Reg's house had been brought back from the hospital to Esther's and now lined the front porch. The Man Who Might Be Death had never reported the robbery to the police. The Solar house looked very different— all but two of the eight oaks had been removed, and although a horseshoe was still nailed to the lintel, almost all of the nazars were gone.

There was movement in each room. Fleayoncé was cleaning her nether regions on Esther's bed. The Solar parents were in the bathroom where their son tried to take his life, Peter still in his wheelchair but looking healthier, Rosemary arching over him this way and that to trim the beard he no longer had the dexterity to manage, her engagement ring again on her finger. There were no candles in the hall. No lamps surrounding Eugene's bed.

The second floor, once blocked off with junk, was now clear after a cleanup orchestrated by Rosemary. Upstairs, Esther looked out the window, her hair cropped into a pixie cut. Her outfit was eclectic—white stockings with red sparkly Dorothy shoes, a green and white striped skirt that fell to her knees, a string of pearls around her neck, and a black shirt with a white collar, salvaged from her Wednesday Addams costume.

Hephzibah came up beside her and squeezed her arm.

"You ready for this?" signed Heph as she stared down at the front yard from an upstairs window. And then she spoke: "There are a *lot* of people."

Esther nodded. "I can't believe it's almost over."

Outside, a projector had been set up on a screen that'd been attached to the front of the house. The lawn was scattered with blankets and pillows. The two remaining trees were lit with string lights and paper lanterns. A sign on the footpath read: A SEMI-DEFINITIVE LIST OF WORST NIGHTMARES. And everywhere, there were people. People on the lawn. People on picnic blankets set up on the street. People in lawn chairs watching from neighboring yards.

It was supposed to be a small viewing party to watch "50/50," but the location had been leaked online, and people had traveled from all over the state—and some even from *other* states—to watch the final video live and meet its stars.

The patron saints of the anxious, depressed, and fearful.

Anxiety swelled inside Esther at the thought of several hundred sets of eyes on her, crawling all over her skin. Fifty weeks later, and the grapnel anchor still lodged in her lungs from time to time, but she'd gotten better at controlling it. She did some of the breathing exercises Dr. Butcher had taught her, then she went downstairs and opened the front door and stepped outside and was swallowed by shouts and applause and camera flashes.

"My name is Esther Solar," she said into the microphone that had been set up on the porch, "and I'm a fear eater." A cheer went up in the crowd. Esther smiled shakily. Each set of eyes made her skin wriggle and itch, but the experience wasn't as painful as it had once been. "Fifty weeks ago I would've had a panic attack at the thought of standing up here and talking to all of you. I would've had a panic attack at a lot of things actually, as you know. As you've seen. But here we are, at the end. I made it. We all made it.

"Thanks to Jonah, most of you know the story now about how my family was supposedly cursed to each suffer one great fear, and I know you've all been waiting for a long time to find out what mine is. So . . . here goes nothing. I'm going to turn the projector on."

The projector was set up on one of her grandparents' coffee tables, reclaimed from a pawn shop in the last couple of months now that a large chunk of Rosemary's salary wasn't going to the slots. As Esther turned on the projector and the image of her rowing a pale blue boat out into a glass-clear lake burned into the front of the house, she looked up. At the end of the street, on the corner, the Man Who Might Be Death leaned against a streetlight and watched her. Esther stopped and stared for a moment, worried that he was there for one of them, or even all of them. Maybe one of the eggs she'd used in her cupcakes was contaminated with salmonella. Maybe the projector was about to explode in an insane fireball that would swallow them skin and bone and teeth and all.

But no. Horowitz—for that is who she was convinced he was—saw her staring at him and smiled and dipped his hat, then lifted his hand in greeting. Esther waved back and watched him laughing softly as he turned to leave, though she knew he would return for her very shortly.

"Who's that?" said Jonah from behind her, looking down the street, where he saw—of course—no one of significance. Only a man. Jonah looped his arms around her waist and kissed her neck. He was wearing a ridiculous terracotta-colored suit with a patterned button up shirt (with little tacos all over it), a stripy tie, and a beret. Fleayoncé was slung around his neck like a drooling stole, and they stood on the lawn in the exact spot where he'd crashed his moped into tree roots after hitting the cat.

"No one," Esther said and then she smiled, and turned in his arms, and stood on her tiptoes to plant a kiss on his lips. It was a bittersweet caress—as all of their caresses had been for some time. Jonah had gotten a full ride scholarship to his number one film school, and would be leaving town at the end of summer to start studying. Each day made Esther both happier and sadder: Jonah was leaving, but that also meant he was escaping. The black hole could not keep him.

It couldn't keep her either.

What she hadn't told him—what she had told no one at all—was this: For three weeks now, a single purple orchid had appeared on her pillow every morning when she woke. Esther didn't know why, or when exactly he would come for her, but the Reaper had chosen his next apprentice. Esther Solar was now the Girl Who Would Be Death. Already she knew what her first act as a trainee Reaper would be: to stand at the end of Holland Smallwood's bed, scythe in hand, cloak drawn over her freckled face, and warn him that if he ever laid another hand on Jonah, or Remy, or anyone, that she would ensure his death was slow and painful.

"Are you ready to watch this?"

"Still can't believe you wouldn't let me help you film the very last video," he said as she pressed play.

Before the showing of "50/50," there were fifteen minutes of highlights from the past year. It hadn't been easy. Every week, Esther had wanted to stop, to walk away, to sink into her panic and let it consume her. It was easier to be afraid. Yet every week, she worked through the three steps Dr. Butcher gave her. Externalize your anxiety. Correct thinking mistakes. Expose yourself to fear.

Jonah had always brought her to the edge but he'd never pushed her over; Esther was the one who had to jump.

And jump she had. In the last six months, they had gone out

and faced spiders, snakes, cockroaches, and clowns. They'd given blood, gone to the dentist, and stepped off the edge of a bridge with elastic bands strapped around their ankles. They'd swum with sharks at the aquarium and leapt from planes and spent long, cold nights alone in the wilderness. People had watched them. People had loved them. People had joined the crusade against fear with challenges of their own: spend a night in a haunted house; be interviewed live on the radio; go to the beach in a bikini.

And then the very last video. "50/50." The one people had been waiting for. At first, a blank white screen, and then Esther came and sat down in frame.

"I know a lot of people have been taking bets about what my great fear might be: frogs, rollercoasters, serial killers. They're all scary things and I'm not going to go out of my way to bump into any of them, but the truth is, they don't scare me as much as this does," she said, motioning toward the camera.

"My greatest fear has already happened to me. It's been happening to me for fifty weeks. My fear is being seen, truly *seen*, for who I am. For a long time, I believed that I was a square peg in a world full of round holes, and that something inside me was fundamentally damaged somehow. I believed that I was not built to love or be loved, and I was afraid that if anyone saw me—like, really *saw me*—they would realize I was broken.

"Then my worst nightmare came along in the form of a boy. You know him. He started this channel and edited all but this video, which is why the others are a lot better than this one.

"Before I met him, I used to keep myself compartmentalized, like the *Titanic*—I was the unsinkable girl. I truly believed that compartmentalizing myself and making myself watertight would ensure I never sank. Obviously, it's a pretty crappy metaphor considering what happened with the actual *Titanic*. Because I *was* a ship and Jonah Smallwood was an iceberg and let the world pour into my lungs, I thought, after he hurt me, that I would sink to the bottom of the abyss and remain in darkness forever.

"Humans aren't ships. They have more compartments. The *Titanic* had sixteen. I have millions. The truth is, it wasn't when he betrayed me that tore open all my compartments. He'd already been doing it for a lot longer.

"For the concerned adults in the audience, I'm aware this sounds a lot like a sex metaphor, but it isn't." A chuckle from the audience. Screen Esther took a deep breath to readjust the grapnel anchor—smaller now, but still there—and continued. "I might never be the type of person who can say 'I love you' freely but, Jonah, I will say this: You opened my compartments one by one and let the world flood in. It took until fifty of fifty for me to realize that I wouldn't sink, because you'd slowly been teaching me how to swim.

"You didn't tear me apart. You found the only way to set me free."

Esther had been worried, when she'd filmed the video, that people wouldn't like it. It contained none of the adventure or humor or cinematography the channel had become known for.

But when the credits rolled, the crowd stood and applauded, maybe not because the ending had been a great one, but because the journey had been worth it regardless. Jonah squeezed her shoulder and then walked up the porch stairs with her and Heph and Eugene, and the four of them looked out at the empire that their bravery had created. Hundreds of people, each with fear buried in their hearts like splinters, each one a little bolder for having watched them for the past fifty weeks. The four of them held hands and took a bow, a solid minute passing before the crowd stopped clapping and cheering.

"So, uh, what you dressed as exactly?" Jonah asked Esther as the crowd began to disperse. "Normally I'm not so bad at guessing, but this one must be some obscure anime or something, 'cause I've got no idea."

"Oh, um. Everything was salvaged from some costume at some point, but this is all me." Esther twirled. "This—apparently— is my sense of fashion."

"Good Lord."

"I know, it's even worse than the costumes. I've gotten more stares today than I ever have before," Esther said with a laugh. "I have something for you. To celebrate the end of an era."

"Oh?"

"The best gift one can get: a solved mystery." Esther slipped her hand in her pocket and opened her fingers to reveal a small white condolences card on her palm. The one that Horowitz had given to her grandfather the day before Florence Solar died. Inside were two words written in running ink.

"I don't get it," Jonah said.

"Because that's only half the puzzle," Esther said. "Remember the scrapbook we found in the storage unit? Remember the last page, with the article that said some man had died under strange circumstances?" She handed the article to him, and Jonah looked from the card to the newspaper clipping they'd found in the locked box so many months ago. Written in small writing on the mailbox in the black-and-white photo was a single word: *Whittle*. "No way," said Jonah as it all started to come together. "It has to be a coincidence."

Esther shook her head. "It's not. You know it's not. Jack Horowitz couldn't save my grandmother, but he could give my grandfather something to console him. Something he'd wanted for a long time."

"The name of the Bowen Sisters' murderer." Esther nodded and smoothed out the newspaper clipping about a burglary gone wrong that left an elderly man drowned in his own bathtub. It was dated the day after her grandmother's death. Arthur Whittle, then 74. The end of a Cadillac Calais was just visible in the open garage. "You know if you believe this version of events, it means your grandfather killed someone."

Esther shook her head. "Maybe. If he did it, then he killed a man who murdered at least three children for certain, probably more. A man who was too old to stand trial or serve a prison sentence. But . . . I think he was there, but I don't think he did it . . ."

Esther told Jonah how she imagined the day went down.

It was raining, and a darkly cloaked figure—Reginald—stood in front of a run-down suburban house. In his hands he held a sympathy card, upon which was written a name. The ink had bled in the rain, little rivulets of blue snaking down the white paper, but the name was still visible: *Arthur Whittle*. Reginald looked from the card to the letters on the mailbox. *Whittle*, it read.

There was a flutter of movement in his peripheral vision, and then Jack Horowitz was at his side, also dressed in a black coat, also staring up at the house.

"I haven't decided yet if I'm going to kill him or turn him in," her grandfather said quietly.

"Then why am I here?"

Reginald slipped the card into his pocket and they walked up the drive together, where Death tried the side entrance to the garage; the door was unlocked. Reg looked back at the darkened street, where black trees whipped and seized in the wind, pelted by the rain. The windows of the houses across the street were dim, their curtains drawn. When he was satisfied that no one had seen him, he slipped inside. Horowitz was already looking around the garage, picking up and putting down junk with gloved hands, as enraptured by the mystery of this man as her grandfather himself. A car, concealed under a waterproof cover, sat in the shadows. Horowitz helped her grandfather peel back the fabric from the bumper. Underneath was a mint Cadillac Calais. The killer's car.

The men shared a look.

Death tried the door that leads into the house and found that it, too, was unlocked. Reginald wondered if locks simply fell open at his touch; no earthly lock could keep the Reaper at bay.

Inside the house, "Non, Je Ne Regrette Rien" by Edith Piaf played on repeat, loud enough that it masked her grandfather's footsteps. Horowitz's footsteps made no sound. Death nodded up the staircase. Reginald drew his service weapon, kept it at his side as he silently ascended the steps, Death a dark, protective presence at his back. There were photographs on the walls: Arthur Whittle on his wedding day, Arthur Whittle with his children, Arthur Whittle with his grandchildren. The upstairs room was smoky and dimly lit. Whittle sat in a black leather armchair, milky eyes fixed on the muted TV as he sucked on a cigarette. Reg breathed out, lowered his weapon. He couldn't do it. Killing a murderer left the same number of murderers on the planet, and brought no peace to the families of the missing children who would never find out what happened to them, would never have any closure.

It was Horowitz who, upon seeing Reginald falter, grabbed Whittle by a tuft of his remaining white hair and dragged him kicking and screaming to the bathroom. It was Horowitz, in the end, who turned on the faucet and held the old man under water until he stopped moving.

Reginald sat on the closed toilet lid and ran his hands through his hair as Death, breathing heavily, sat back against the tiled walls, his gloves and sleeves soaking.

"You said we'd only meet twice more," said Reginald as the Reaper reached over to turn off the faucet.

"There are some things not even Death can predict." Horowitz stood. Peeled off his gloves. "I'm so sorry about Florence, Reg. There was truly nothing I could do."

"The wake is on Friday, if you're so inclined."

Death nodded. Put his wet hand on her grandfather's shoulder. "I'll bring some milk."

"WELL I'LL BE DAMNED," said Jonah as he handed back the card. "The Harvestman has been dead for years?"

"No children have disappeared since Arthur Whittle drowned in his bathtub. It's good enough for me. It has to be."

As she looked at him, Esther thought about how this might be framed as a happy ending if their lives were like the movies. Maybe Jonah would say something smooth, and the music would swell, and they'd run to each other and make out under one of the oak trees while some indie song played in the background and the screen cut to credits.

But life was rarely full of clean and tidy resolutions. Good moments would inevitably, again, lead to bad moments, which would lead to more good moments, until there was nothing left but dust and stories. But that moment, right there, with him, that night—that was a damn good moment, and the good moments had to be remembered. And if all she could be, in the end, was dust and stories, she could think of far worse fates than to become dust and stories with a pickpocket, a skilled petty criminal, an underage drinker, a public nuisance, and the very best person she had ever met.

With Jonah there in front of her, she wondered if people really fell in love with others or if they fell in love with the best parts of themselves. Love was a mirror that made our bright bits shine like stars and dulled even the harshest ugliness. We loved to love because it made us beautiful. And maybe there was nothing wrong with that.

Maybe we deserved to be beautiful.

"Okay. Ready to find out the most interesting thing about you?" said Jonah as he tapped the covered canvas leaning against the side of the house. It sounded like he was rapping his knuckles against something solid, like glass. "Fifty weeks later, are you ready to see what I see?"

Esther exhaled and cracked her neck from side to side, like a boxer about to enter a ring. "Bring it on, Smallwood."

Jonah pulled back the sheet, a mischievous smirk on his face. For a moment, Esther was confused. There was no canvas, no paint. But then she got it, like he said she would, and she collapsed to the ground laughing, like he always did.

Because the portrait was her. *Exactly* her.

It had been all along.

RESOURCES

MENTAL HEALTH isn't as simple as a suicide-prevention number in the back of a book and an author you don't know telling you things will get better.

So I'm going to do a little more than that.

I'm going to tell you that I have friends and family who have suffered alone and in silence, people who only told me *years* after the fact that they were in incredible pain. That they had considered ending or even attempted to end their own lives.

It breaks my heart to think that people I love and couldn't imagine the world without—brave, smart, resilient people—didn't seek help. Didn't speak up. Drowned quietly, in full view of everyone who knew them, without ever asking to be saved.

I know their struggle, because there are times I've found it difficult to speak out, too.

To that end, I beseech you to read Adam Silvera's article "Happiness Isn't Just An Outside Thing"—you can find it on his Tumblr. It is frank, it is terrifying, and it changed my outlook on mental health forever. It is completely essential. Read it, read it, read it.

My hope is that this book becomes a conversation starter to speak openly and honestly about mental health issues with those around you. Ask your friends and family how they are. Tell them how you are. Don't be ashamed of seeking professional help. Be part of the movement to normalize talking about this stuff. Because it is normal.

Mental illness doesn't make you weak; it makes you human.

And, in case of an emergency, I implore you to contact the National Suicide Prevention Lifeline at 1-800-273-8255. There will be someone on the other end of the line who can help you see the value of your life, even when you're blind to it yourself.

Whether your problems are small or large (or even if you have none at all—you may be able to support somebody else), I will leave you with this mantra. I would like you to say it out loud, right now, until you take it to heart:

There is no shame in seeking help.

There is no shame in seeking help.

There is no shame in seeking help.

> "I'm not telling you it's going to be easy—I'm telling you it's going to be worth it."
>
> —Art Williams

NOTES

DURING THE WRITING OF THIS BOOK, I watched many online resources about dealing with anxiety and fear. None was more useful and inspiring than Dawn Huebner's "Rethinking anxiety: Learning to face fear" from TEDxAmoskeagMillyardWomen in 2015. Huebner's talk formed the basis of Esther's therapist's advice, and has also been invaluable to me personally (I can now sleep in the dark after watching horror movies).

For my depiction of Saigon during the Vietnam War, I looked to photographs and firsthand accounts, but I'm indebted to Sara Mansfield Taber's July 6, 2015, *Literary Hub* article, "My Saigon Summer, Before the Fall," for truly setting the scene in my imagination. Any inaccuracies are entirely my own.

Jonah's Shakespearean insults came from pangloss.com/seidel/Shaker/—an endlessly hilarious insult generator that I highly suggest we all start using on a daily basis. You mewling flap-mouthed flax-wenches.

WITH GREAT THANKS

THE WRITING of a sophomore book is a fretful experience, made no easier when the topic of said book is anxiety, panic attacks, and fear that bites to the bone. I am forever indebted to those who made it a little easier:

To Chelsea Sutherland, who inspired this book on a warm morning in Amsterdam when she point-blank refused to get on her damn Dutch bicycle. The story of Esther and her struggle with fear was born almost in its entirety as we (somewhat against your will) finally peddled back from Vondelpark in the summer sunshine. I am so grateful that you faced your fear that day. (Sorry again for making you cry.)

To my other sister, Shanaye Sutherland, who is one of the bravest people I know. Your strength, generosity, and warmth inspire me every day. I couldn't have written this book without you.

To my parents, Sophie and Phillip, but especially to my mother, who—like Rosemary—is a quiet fighter to the bitter end. Writing this book broke my heart on a daily basis when I thought about everything you have sacrificed (and continue to sacrifice) so willingly for your children. You are, the both of you, quite wonderful.

To my late grandfather, Reginald Kanowski, the namesake of Esther's grandfather. Even before I dreamed of being a writer, I wanted to immortalize the story of your life on paper. So much of you lives on in these pages.

Also to my grandmother, Diane Kanowski, who I erroneously stated would never read my first book because it was far too scandalous. I hereby retract that statement and apologize! Your continued support means the world to me.

To Kate Sullivan, who fraudulently signed me into class so many times that I should hire her to do book signings, and Rose-Helen Graham, for keeping me sane when we were living in the waking nightmare that was Sassoon Road. Most of all, thanks to both of you for your incredible enthusiasm.

To the Westpac Bicentennial Foundation, which supported me financially while I was studying abroad in Hong Kong and writing this manuscript at the same time. You made it far easier to juggle the two. Your faith in me and your support of young Australians has made such an impact.

To Tamsin Peters, my sister in every way except blood. One day I'll write you a book with dragons in it!

To my hometown cheer squad, who dangerously inflate my ego: Renee Martin, Cara Faagutu, Kirra Moke, Alysha Morgan, Sarah Francis, Jacqueline Payne, Sally Roebuck, and Danielle Green. You make me feel like a star on even the darkest days.

To Amie Kaufman, for words of wisdom that saved my sanity in a time of great need.

To Katherine Webber, always, for everything. You are brilliant and I love you. Look at us, we are *still* authors! #LAUWASA

Also to the rest of #TeamMaleficent: Samantha Shannon, Lisa Lueddecke Catterall, Leiana Leaututufu, and Claire Donnelly. I know you guys always have my back.

To my agent extraordinaire, Catherine Drayton, whose opinion matters to me more than most. Once I heard that you liked my strange little second book, I knew everything would be okay!

Also to the rest of the gang at InkWell Management, but particularly Richard Pine, for a warm welcome to New York, and Lyndsey Blessing, for being my foreign-rights goddess.

To the lovely Mary Pender at UTA, for your continued brilliance in handling film rights.

To my editor, Stacey Barney, who I *strongly* suspect has a little magic flowing in her veins. With the lightest touch, you helped this book to fully bloom. I can't thank you enough for your faith and your patience.

Also to the rest of the team at Putnam, especially Kate Meltzer, for much-needed words of encouragement, and Theresa Evangelista, for another stunning cover!

To the whole team at Bonnier Zaffre, but especially Emma Mathewson, who I want to be when I grow up, and to PR super-stars Carmen Jimenez and Tina Mories, for your warmth and kindness.

Again, to the whole team at Penguin Australia, but especially to Tina Gumnior, publicist extraordinaire, and Amy Thomas and Laura Harris, who both seem to say exactly what I need to hear, exactly when I need to hear it. How do you do that?!

Last (but certainly not least), to Martin Seneviratne, my partner in crime. Tea maker, deadline cheerleader, muesli connoisseur, all-around dreamboat. You make me feel brave every day; there's no fear I wouldn't dare to face with you by my side.

TURN THE PAGE TO READ
AN EXCERPT FROM KRYSTAL
SUTHERLAND'S DEBUT NOVEL

our chemical hearts

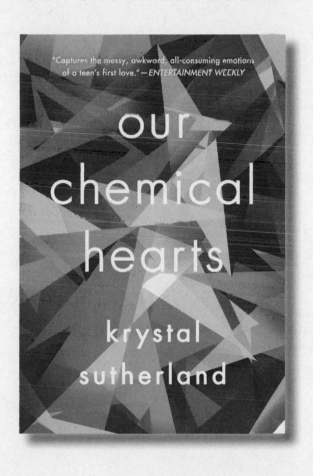

CHAPTER 1

I ALWAYS THOUGHT the moment you met the great love of your life would be more like the movies. Not exactly like the movies, obviously, with the slow-mo and the hair blowing in the breeze and the swelling instrumental soundtrack. But I at least thought there would be something, you know? A skipped beat of the heart. A tug at your soul where *something* inside you goes, "Holy shit. There she is. Finally, after all this time, there she is."

There was none of that when Grace Town walked into Mrs. Beady's afternoon drama class ten minutes late on the second Tuesday of senior year. Grace was the type of person who made an impression on any room she walked into, but not for the kind of reasons that generate instant and undying affection. She was of average height and average build and average attractiveness, all things that should've made it easy for her to assimilate into a new high school without any of the dramatic tropes that usually inhabit such storylines.

But three things about Grace immediately stood out, before her ordinariness could save her:

1. Grace was dressed head to toe in guys' clothing. Not the tomboy, skater-girl kind of look, either, but legitimate dudes' clothing that was way too big for her. Jeans that were meant to be skinny were held on her hips by a belt. Despite it being only mid-September, she wore a sweater and a checkered shirt and a knit cap, and a long leather necklace with an anchor on the end.
2. Grace looked unclean and unhealthy. I mean, I'd seen junkies that looked in better shape than she did that morning. (I hadn't really seen that many junkies, but I'd seen *The Wire* and *Breaking Bad*, which totally counts.) Her blond hair wasn't brushed and was badly cut, her skin was sallow, and I'm almost certain if I'd smelled her at any point during that day, she would've reeked.
3. If all this wasn't enough to really screw over her chances of fitting in at a new high school, Grace Town walked with a cane.

And that's how it happened. That's how I first saw her. There was no slow-mo, no breeze, no soundtrack, and definitely no skipped heartbeats. Grace hobbled in ten minutes late, silently, like she owned the place, like she'd been in our class for years, and maybe because she was new or because she was weird or because the teacher could see simply by looking at her that a small part of her soul was cracked, Mrs. Beady said nothing. Grace sat on a chair at the back of the black-walled drama room, her cane resting across her thighs, and said nothing to anybody for the entire class.

I looked at her twice more, but by the end of class I'd forgotten she was there, and she slipped out without anyone noticing.

So this is certainly not a story of love at first sight.

But it *is* a love story.

Well.

Kind of.

CHAPTER 2

THE FIRST WEEK of senior year, before Grace Town's sudden apparition, had passed by as uneventfully as high school possibly can. There'd been only three minor scandals thus far: a junior had been suspended for smoking in the girls' bathroom (if you're going to get suspended for something, at least make it something not cliché), an anonymous suspect had uploaded footage of an after-school fight in the parking lot to YouTube (the administration was freaking out over that one), and there were rumors going around that Chance Osenberg and Billy Costa had given each other an STD after having unprotected sex with the same girl (I wish I was making this up, dear readers).

My life had remained, as always, entirely scandal-free. I was seventeen years old, a weird, lanky kid, the type you might cast to play a young Keanu Reeves if you'd already spent the majority of your budget on bad CGI and craft service. I'd never so much as secondhand-smoked a cigarette, and no one, thank

God, had approached me about doing the no-pants dance sans a prophylactic. My dark hair skirted my shoulders, and I'd grown particularly fond of wearing my dad's sports coat from the eighties. You could say I looked something like a male Summer Glau crossed with Severus Snape. Subtract the hook nose, add in some dimples, and hey presto: the perfect recipe for one Henry Isaac Page.

I was, at the time, also uninterested in girls (or guys, in case you were wondering). My friends had been in and out of dramatic teenage relationships for close to five years now, but I had yet to even have a real crush. Sure, there'd been Abigail Turner in kindergarten (I'd kissed her on the cheek when she wasn't expecting it; our relationship rapidly declined after that), and I'd been obsessed with the idea of marrying Sophi Zhou for at least three years of elementary school, but after I hit puberty, it was like a switch inside me flipped, and instead of becoming a testosterone-driven sex monster like most of the guys at my school, I failed to find anyone I wanted in my life in that way.

I was happy to focus on school and getting the grades I needed to get into a semi-decent college, which is probably why I didn't think about Grace Town again for at least a couple of days. Maybe I never would've if it wasn't for the intervention of one Mr. Alistair Hink, English teacher.

What I know about Mr. Hink is still very much confined to what most high schoolers know about their teachers. He had bad dandruff, which wouldn't have been half as noticeable if he didn't insist on wearing black turtlenecks every day, the color of which clearly displayed the fine white dust on his shoulders like snow falling on asphalt. From what I could gather from his naked left hand, he was unmarried, which probably had a lot to do with the dandruff and the fact that he looked remarkably like Napoleon Dynamite's brother, Kip.

Hink was also fiercely passionate about the English language, so much so that on one occasion when my math class was let out five minutes late and thus ate into our English lesson, Hink called up the math teacher, Mr. Babcock, and gave him a lecture about how the arts were no less valuable than mathematics. A lot of students laughed at him under their breaths—they were mostly destined for careers in engineering or science or customer service, I suppose—but looking back, I can pinpoint that afternoon in our sweltering English classroom as the moment I fell in love with the idea of becoming a writer.

I'd always been decent at writing, at putting words together. Some people are born with an ear for music, some people are born with a talent for drawing, some people—people like me, I guess—have a built-in radar that tells them where a comma needs to go in a sentence. As far as superpowers go, grammatical intuition is fairly low on the awesomeness scale, but it did get me in with Mr. Hink, who also happened to be in charge of running and organizing the student newspaper I'd volunteered at since sophomore year in hopes of one day becoming editor.

It was about midway through Mrs. Beady's Thursday drama class in the second week of school when the phone rang and Beady answered it. "Henry, Grace. Mr. Hink would like to see you in his office after school," she said after chatting for a few minutes. (Beady and Hink had always been friendly. Two souls born in the wrong century, when the world liked to make fun of people who still thought art was the most extraordinary thing humanity ever had or ever would produce.)

I nodded and purposefully didn't look at Grace, even though I could see in my peripheral vision that she was staring at me from the back of the room.

When most teenagers get called to their teacher's office after school, they assume the worst, but like I said, I was tragically free of scandal. I knew (or hoped I knew) why Hink wanted to see me. Grace had been an inmate at Westland High for only two days, hardly long enough to have given another student trichomoniasis and/or handed out any after-school beatdowns (although she *did* carry a cane and look angry a lot).

Why Mr. Hink wanted to see Grace was—like much else about her—a mystery.

CHAPTER 3

GRACE WAS ALREADY waiting outside Hink's office when I got there. She was dressed in guys' clothing again today, different stuff this time, but she looked a lot cleaner and healthier. Her blond hair had been washed and brushed. It made a remarkable difference to her appearance, even if having clean hair made it fall in uneven chunks around her shoulders, like she'd cut it herself with a pair of rusted hedge trimmers.

I sat down next to her on the bench, entirely too aware of my body, so much so that I forgot how to sit casually and had to purposefully arrange my limbs. I couldn't get my posture right, so I kind of slumped forward into an awkward pose that made my neck ache, but I didn't want to move again because I could see her looking at me out of the corner of her eye.

Grace was sitting with her knees pressed up against her chest, her cane wedged between them. She was reading a book with tattered pages the color of coffee-stained teeth. I couldn't see the title, but I could see that it was full of poems. When she caught me looking over her shoulder, I expected her to close the book or angle it away from me, but instead she turned it ever so slightly toward me so that I could read too.

The poem Grace was reading, I assumed over and over again because the page was dog-eared and food-stained and in generally bad shape, was by a guy called Pablo Neruda, whom I'd never heard of before. It was called "I do not love you," which intrigued me, so I started to read, even though Hink had not yet succeeded in making me like poetry.

Two lines in particular had been highlighted.

> *I love you as certain dark things are to be loved,*
> *in secret, between the shadow and the soul.*

Hink stepped out of the office then, and Grace snapped the book shut before I could finish.

"Oh, good, I see you've met," said Hink when he saw us together. I stood up quickly, keen to unravel myself from the weird position I'd folded my body into. Grace shuffled to the edge of the bench and rose slowly, carefully distributing her weight between her cane and her good leg. I wondered for the first time how bad her injury was. How long had she been like this? Was she born with a bad leg or did some tragic accident befall her in childhood? "Well, come inside."

Hink's office was at the end of a hall that might've been considered modern and attractive sometime in the early

eighties. Pale pink walls, fluorescent lighting, painfully obvious fake plants, that weird linoleum that's supposed to look
like granite but is actually made up of hundreds of little bits of
plastic filled in with clear laminate. I followed Hink, my steps
slower than they normally would be, because I wanted Grace
to walk next to me. Not because I wanted her to, like, *walk next
to me*, you know, but I thought she might like it, that it might
be a nice thing to do, for her to be able to keep up with someone. But even when my pace felt maddeningly slow, she still
hung back, hobbling two steps behind me, until it felt like we
were in a race to see who could go the slowest. Hink was ten
steps in front of us by then, so I sped up and left her behind
and must've looked like a total weirdo.

When we reached Hink's office (small, bland, green-tinged;
so depressing it made me think he was probably part of a fight
club on the weekends), he ushered us inside and motioned for
us to sit in the two chairs in front of his desk. I frowned as we
sat down, wondering why Grace was here with me.

"You're both here, of course, because of your exceptional
writing abilities. When it came time to pick our senior editors
for the newspaper, I could think of no two better—"

"No," said Grace Town, cutting him off, and her voice was
such a shock to me that I only just realized it was the first time
I'd heard her speak. She had this strong, clear, deep voice, so
different from the broken and timid image she portrayed.

"I beg your pardon?" said Hink, clearly taken aback.

"No," Grace said again, as if this were explanation enough.

"I . . . I don't understand," said Hink, his gaze flicking to me with this pleading look in his eyes. I could practically hear his silent scream for help, but all I could do was shrug.

"I don't want to be an editor. Thank you, really, for thinking of me. But no." Grace collected her bag from the floor and stood.

"Miss Town. Grace. Martin came to me specifically before the start of the school year and asked me to look at your work from East River. You were going to take over as editor of their newspaper this year, I believe, if you hadn't transferred. Isn't that right?"

"I don't write anymore."

"That's a shame. Your work is beautiful. You have a natural gift for words."

"And you have a natural gift for clichés."

Hink was so shocked that his mouth popped open.

Grace softened a little. "Sorry. But they're just words. They don't mean anything."

Grace looked at me with this kind of disapproving expression I wasn't expecting and didn't understand, then slung her backpack over her shoulders and limped out. Hink and I sat there in silence, trying to process what'd just happened. It took me a good ten seconds to realize that I was angry, but once I had, I, too, collected my bag and stood quickly and made my way toward the door.

"Can we talk about this tomorrow?" I said to Hink, who must've guessed that I was going after her.

"Yes, yes, of course. Come and see me before class." Hink shooed me out and I jogged down the corridor, surprised to find that Grace wasn't there. When I opened the far door and stepped out of the building, she was already at the edge of the school grounds. She could move goddamn fast when she tried. I sprinted after her, and when I was within earshot, I shouted, "Hey!" She turned briefly, looked me up and down, glared, and then kept on walking.

"Hey," I said breathlessly when I finally caught up with her and fell in step beside her.

"What?" she said, still speed walking, the end of her cane clicking against the road with every step. A car behind us beeped. Grace pointed violently at her cane and then waved them around. I'd never seen a vehicle move in a way I'd describe as *sheepish* before.

"Well . . . ," I said, but I couldn't find the words to say what I wanted to say. I was a decent enough writer, but talking? With sounds? From my mouth? That was a bitch.

"Well what?"

"Well, I hadn't really planned this far into the conversation."

"You seem pissed."

"I am pissed."

"Why?"

"Because people work their asses off for years to get editor, and you waltz in at the beginning of senior year and have it offered to you on a platter and you turn it down?"

"Did you work your ass off?"

"Hell yeah. I've been buttering Hink up, pretending I'm a tortured teen writer who really relates to Holden Caulfield since I was, like, fifteen."

"Well, congratulations. I don't understand why you're angry. There's normally only one editor anyway, right? The fact that I said no doesn't impact you at all."

"But . . . I mean . . . Why would you say no?"

"Because I don't want to do it."

"But . . ."

"And without me there, you'll get to make all the creative decisions and have the newspaper exactly how you've probably been envisioning it for the last two years."

"Well . . . I guess . . . But . . ."

"So you see, this is really a win-win for you. You're welcome, by the way."

We walked on in silence for a couple of minutes longer, until my anger had entirely faded and I could no longer remember exactly why I'd chased after her in the first place.

"*Why* are you still following me, Henry Page?" she said, coming to a stop in the middle of the road, like she didn't give a shit that a car could come hurtling toward us at any second. And I realized that, although we'd never been introduced and never spoken before today, she knew my full name.

"You know who I am?" I said.

"Yes. And you know who I am, so let's not pretend we don't. Why are you still following me?"

"Because, *Grace Town*, I've walked too far from school now

and my bus has probably already left and I was looking for a smooth way to exit the conversation but I didn't find one, so I resigned myself to my fate."

"Which is?"

"To walk in this general direction until my parents report me missing and the police find me on the outskirts of town and drive me home."

Grace sighed. "Where do you live?"

"Right near the Highgate Cemetery."

"Fine. Come to my place. I'll drop you."

"Oh. Awesome. Thanks."

"As long as you promise not to push the whole editor thing."

"Fine. No pushing. You want to turn down an awesome opportunity, that's your decision."

"Good."

It was a humid afternoon in suburgatory, the clouds overhead as solid as cake frosting, the lawns and trees still that bright, golden green of late summer. We walked side by side on the hot asphalt. There were five more minutes of awkward silence where I searched and searched for a question to ask her. "Can I read the rest of that poem?" I said finally, because it seemed like the least worst of all my options. (Option one: So . . . are you, like, a cross-dresser or something? Not that there's anything wrong with that; I'm just curious. Option two: What's up with your leg, bro? Option three: You're definitely some kind of junkie, right? I mean, you're fresh out of rehab, yeah? Option four: Can I read the rest of that poem?)

"What poem?" she said.

"The Pablo whoever one. 'I do not love you.' Or whatever it was."

"Oh. Yeah." Grace stopped and handed me her cane and swung her backpack onto her front and fished out the threadbare book and pushed it into my hands. It fell open to Pablo Neruda, so I knew then for sure that it was something she read over and over again. It was the line about loving dark things that I kept coming back to.

I love you as certain dark things are to be loved,
in secret, between the shadow and the soul.

"It's beautiful," I said to Grace as I closed the book and handed it back to her, because it was.

"Do you think?" She looked at me with this look of genuine questioning on her face, her eyes narrowed slightly.

"You don't?"

"I think that's what people say when they read poems they don't understand. It's sad, I think. Not beautiful." I couldn't see how a perfectly nice love poem was sad, but then again, my significant other was my laptop, so I didn't say anything. "Here," Grace said as she opened the book again and tore out the page with the poem on it. I flinched as though I were in actual pain. "You should have it, if you like it. Pretty poetry is wasted on me."

I took the paper from her and folded it and slipped it into my pocket, half of me horrified that she'd injured a book, the other half of me elated that she'd so willingly given me something that clearly meant a lot to her. I liked people like that. People who could part with material possessions with little or no hesitation. Like Tyler Durden. "The things you own end up owning you" and all that.

Grace's house was exactly the type of place I expected her to live. The garden was overgrown, gone to seed, the lawn left to grow wild for some time. The curtains on the windows were drawn and the house itself, which was two stories tall and made of gray brick, seemed to be sagging as if depressed by the weight of the world. In the driveway there was a solitary car, a small white Hyundai with a Strokes decal on the back windshield.

"Stay here," she said. "I've got to get my car keys."